KARMA
WEARS
VERSACE

DETECTIVE AISHA SAWYER IN

KARMA WEARS VERSACE

ROD PALMER

BLACK WREN PRESS

Published in the United States by The Black Wren Press, LLC,
South Carolina.

This book is a work of fiction. Except in the case of historical fact, names, characters,
places, and incidents either are products of the author's imagination or are used
fictitiously. Any resemblance to actual persons, living or dead, events, or locales is
entirely coincidental.

The Library of Congress has cataloged as follows:
Palmer, Rod
Detective Aisha Sawyer in: Karma Wears Versace / by Rod Palmer
1, Sawyer, Aisha (Fictitious character) – Fiction. 2. Crime, Mystery – Atlanta – GA
Case# 1-7513239462

ISBN: 978-1-7339633-0-5

Cover design, illustration & interior formatting:
Mark Thomas / Coverness.com

As she has planted, so does she harvest;
such is the field of karma.

~ *Sri Guru Granth Sahib*

SO LITTLE TIME

Like a thief, Chosen peeped with cupped hands at her ex-landlord's door. The man was asleep on his couch, his Stetson hat tilted down over his face. Chosen had timed it perfectly; Ben's daily, whiskey-induced coma. She backed away from the glass and saw the overlay of her reflection, backed by a magnificent sunset; the sky, ill with pink and grey hues, and the sun, a neon red disc on the horizon.

Chosen plucked through the ball of keys in her hand until she found the right one. She glanced up again. Ben was gone; his couch imprint rising back to form.

Ben reappeared; his face framed by the glass square. Chosen gasped. Two pairs of eyes stretched wide, Ben's pair at the sight of Chosen and Chosen's at the sight of Ben. She backed away.

Ben came through the door pointing a revolver. Chosen was stricken with fear, her eyes teary under the shadow of her ballcap's brim. "Ben. No," Chosen pleaded. "Not like this."

Ben's eyes were as soulless as a shark's. "Like *how* then? I done tried the other way, Chosen. How long you think I'm 'on let you string me along? To beat all, last time you pulled that stunt – running off with my keys like-at… Fool me twice, shame on me."

Chosen pleaded, "I *told* you… that was an accident, but even if it wasn't, how're you gonna pull out a gun over something as petty as that bro – like – what the fuck?"

Ben deflated with irreverence. "It's not the keys; it's the time lost." He waved Chosen up the steps while he backed further into the house; the chrome pistol losing its gleam to the shadowy foyer.

Chosen acquiesced; fighting only tears.

Ben came around her and then closed the door behind them. He snatched the keys from Chosen and said, "Is this why you stole my keys? To come here trying to kill me like you did your lil' fiancé –"

"– Trap was my man," Chosen barked, while pointing into her chest. "He was my future husband. I mean, are you even thinking about what you're saying? Who in their right mind kills a fiancé, huh? Only a *husband's* death is worth something."

"I'll let the police be the judge of that – since you won't keep your word." Ben tapped his temple with the pistol barrel, pointing to his wit. "I'm sharper than you thought. Whatever you might try, consider me one step ahead." Ben motioned her to turn to the wall. He started patting her down.

Chosen had failed miserably, she thought – coming here

to secure her freedom, but achieving the opposite. She was a hostage, her nose to the wall like a punished child, cringing as her vagina was cupped from behind by a pervert with a sunken white face.

Chosen's eyes shut tight against the awful vision of a brutal rape and a shallow grave. This is what Chosen hates about beauty; the violence of it, man's need to own it. Not to mention the upkeep, being slave to a regiment of beauty products, the suffocation of body-shaping corsets, the surgeries, the credit card debt, all just to be an item on Atlanta's it-scene, but Chosen was determined to be more than just scenery, or groupie pickings for B-list celebrities. Chosen had awaited her professional athlete or rapper like awaiting heavenly wings, until the day the millionaire record executive eyeballed her from across the room and then called her over with the curl of his finger. That man was Kendall "Trap" Miller, the man Ben accused Chosen of murdering. Trap bought Chosen fine jewelry and designer threads, but never used his influence to springboard Chosen's modeling career so she could spread her wings and fly. No. Trap caged her with her financial dependence, and went as far as believing that his wealth was an entitlement to side-chicks. He was popping bottles up in VIP with a Mizz Bottoms on the day of Chosen's first miscarriage. Beauty had left Chosen lying discarded at the hospital. Later, it was intelligence and cunning that put Chosen in position to acquire Trap's multi-million-dollar legacy for herself. Chosen couldn't come this far (her millions awaiting the bank's procedural hold to clear in just a couple days) to let it all end here and now.

After cupping Chosen from behind, Ben ended the pat-down. Assuming he was safe, he flopped on his leather couch, holding his crotch while eyeing Chosen in sections.

Chosen spun around against the wall she was just sexually assaulted against, punching her open hand. "How do you supposedly know something, when there's nothing *to* know," she demanded, while both knew that her mere presence – this city dame out in back country Georgia, in the living room of a man with dirt-caked fingernails and antlers on his mantle – seemed like proof that Ben indeed had the leverage to blackmail her for sex.

Benjamin hadn't heard a word Chosen had said; he was lost in his examination of her body.

Chosen added, "Look, I'm about to come into some money..."

He smirked at her money offer; he had a much older, darker currency in mind. Ben is a man who had wired Chosen's apartment with the micro cams that he uses to track wild deer during hunting season. He'd sat hundreds of hours in the litter of beer cans, watching footage of Chosen dressing, undressing, and making love to a man whose ashes now sits in an urn.

Ben peered at Chosen and shuddered, undone by the reality of her: as if she'd stepped out of one of his grayscale videos with glowing retinas, into living color. Ben said, "I ain't fixin' to pretend. You *know* what I want." Ben heard, in his own voice, the coming-out of his inner-creep and he liked it.

Vomit climbed the back of Chosen's throat. Of all people, the man blackmailing her for sex was an alcoholic, long-bearded outdoorsman who would've been a wandering hobo had he not inherited well. Chosen sighed as she scanned the colorless, wooden living room imitating a forest cabin, her eyes stopping on Ben who had a hand stuck down the front of his pants. She asked, "How did you come to know whatever it is you *think* you know – by unlawful entry into my rental unit? Boy, the only person you'll get in trouble is yourself."

Ben warned. "Hold out all you want. But believe me, you do *not* want to see this thing play out."

Chosen smiled maternally at the adorable flaw in Ben's plot. She proposed, "For argument's sake, let's say your theory is true. How will you get 'what you want' if I'm in jail?"

He raised a knowing finger. "You'll post bond, no doubt. If you still don't give me what I want, I'll then be forced to tell police everything. For starters, my *cage* came inside before it went back out. And you were wearing gloves."

Chosen's smile was void of gladness, but animated with a wishing-away of this nuisance. "I have done absolutely nothing!"

"Then why are you even here?"

"Because I can't have *any* suspicion around me, right now – real nor imagined! I've got something *really* humongous going on right now." Chosen came over to the far end of the couch and sat like a pouting teen. "Just keep quiet for a few days, Ben, and I promise you, I will make it worth your while."

Ben inhaled the air, sweetened with her perfume; his exhale floated the request, "Lemme see them titties."

The idea of sex (if it came to that) felt like an ulcer in Chosen's gut. His liquored breath reminded her of the uncle that raped her when she was a child. "You wouldn't be doing this if you were sober. Is that *all* you do, is drink?"

"All I do is fantasize about you..." He rubbed Chosen's thigh and smiled as if he'd just shared a secret with a confidant.

Chosen's head shook. "At least give me some time to work up to it, Ben. For one: you're old. Two: you don't take care of yourself. Do me a solid and get you a haircut, put on something nice will ya?"

Ben looked away and said, "You say give you some time? Time is what I don't have… Gallbladder cancer. Weeks, months – if I'm lucky – I'll be in hospice on a morphine drip."

Chosen covered her mouth. "Sorry to hear." Silence lingered for a moment. Chosen offered, "Take it for what it's worth, Ben, but I think you should be out there making things right, getting right with God. If you *must* get you a piece of ass as your dying wish, go for someone you don't have to hold a gun to. Get you a high-class prostitute or something."

"A high-class prostitute ain't you. It has to be you. I'll take it, if you force my hand. What can they do to me? I *already* got a death sentence."

Defiantly, Chosen said, "Go 'head. Take it if you want it, but I have to warn you… My period is on," lied Chosen. She even offered to verify, her hand poised at her waistband. "And trust me, I bleed heavy. Uterine fibroids."

As expected, Ben's excitement dulled. He waived the offer and said, "A Detective Sawyer came 'round asking questions." Ben held up the detective's card as if it had the power of a big joker at a Spades table. "Sawyer told me, if something – anything – jogs my memory, to call her right away. So, if you leave here today without doing *something*? I'll be singing in Detective Sawyer's ear 'fore you can back out of my driveway." Ben stroked his big beard, smiling at an idea's lightbulb overhead. "That sweet *mouth* of yours idn't broke."

Chosen felt some relief that the gun was now out of the equation, but the thought of kneeling to the groin of a pale-skinned baboon was as sickening as the thought of having her brains blown out the back of her head. Chosen's nose wrinkled. "Boy, have you even washed your behind today? Don't *smell* like it." Chosen had to do something, though, to prevent him from calling the police and raising unwanted suspicion that might cause the insurance company to retract their payout. She shoved closer to Benjamin, sucked her teeth and said, "Move your behind over!"

Ben slunk down, sprite with anticipation. Chosen closed a gentle fist around her ex-landlord's penis and hammered away, like smashing grapes in his lap, all because he *knew something* – something that would appear to link Chosen with the two victims: her dead ex-fiancé, and the med-student who was just recently admitted to the E.R.

She let Benjamin fondle her breasts while she worked,

7

distractedly, thinking back to her own interview with Detective Sawyer where they talked more about hair and makeup than Trap's death. She remembered Sawyer claiming the investigation was merely exploratory, but leaving her business card with an ex-landlord, of all people, proved otherwise; it proved that Detective Sawyer wasn't just exploring, as she had said, Sawyer was reaching. Benjamin's deep moan brought Chosen back to the moment; his whiskey breath was nearly unbearable. As a distraction from the hairy, Neanderthal hands fondling her breasts, Chosen closed her eyes and focused on the sounds, the couch's rhythmic friction of leather, quickening as they approached the end, Ben's face blazing red with excitement while Chosen pounded away.

When it was done, Ben used the hem of his shirt to mop up his belly. He yawned and said, "Next time, I'm gettin' it all the way – and every which-away."

Chosen washed her hands in the bathroom while avoiding her own eyes in the mirror. When she returned to the living room, Ben was snoring.

Chosen's head shook. "Men are so weak," she said, as she studied the man who had threatened her life, the man whose hand between her legs resurfaced her childhood: the straight-jacket of fear, the touch loaded with taboo and sin, bearing the grown man's weight and his toxic breath, her own innocence leaving in one fell swoop, instead of the measured doses along the natural arc of maturation. Chosen was stewing at the sight of Ben on the couch, fast asleep and satisfied. Chosen was angry enough to snatch Ben's gun off of the couch arm, shoot his eyes out, and instantly close the final chapter of being under a man's thumb. A shooting death would, however, bring the suspicion Chosen sought to avoid. Instead, Chosen settled for turning the thermostat up to its full ninety degrees; it is summer. In Georgia.

Before Chosen got in her car, she stood in the yard and surveyed the countryside, seeing mossy willows twice as old as the oldest human alive. She felt the crickets chirping like the vibe of the universe moving through her. She studied the sunlit rim of the horizon as she contemplated her next problem: Detective Sawyer.

THE PROBLEM

Detective Aisha Sawyer gazed at pictures thumbtacked on corkboard, her head cocked slightly, eyes darting between images – from Kendall "Trap" Miller, Chosen's dead ex-fiancé, and then Meegan Appleton, the brown-haired med student on life support. Red yarn wove an intricate web, linking folks within the victims' circles: family, friends, colleagues, and lovers – people who could help hash out motives on either side. Sawyer stood watching, in her second-glance beauty, her cheeks curved like blown glass and her thick lips shining like a grill on a sports car. Her beauty doesn't shine for attention, but there's a glamour to her that shimmers forth like an illusion of light.

Sawyer rolled down the wrapper on her protein bar and took a bite. She was lost in her Zen, awaiting some divine hand to lay on her gut, to guide her through the misty unknowns, when she felt a presence as slight as a shadow stretching in from the doorway.

As expected, she heard Sgt. Jeffrey Gilliam's voice. "Get outta here, will ya?"

She didn't turn. She kept staring at her web. "You get out, Gil. This is my office –"

"– And you're spending too much time in it. Find yourself a nice little bistro and enjoy a real lunch – not some damn oat bar."

"I.I. captain." Sawyer said, while she kept on staring and chewing.

"You're at it again, I see."

Sawyer turned and shaded her eyes from the neon blaze of Gil's lime colored shirt. "God, Gil. Does that shirt come with a light switch?"

"Funny," Gil said, smugly. "You should try amateur night down at the comedy house." For a man with a torso like a large, bone-in ham, he still finds shirts that fits him perfectly, with collars pressed wafer thin. No matter the color – magenta, taupe, electric blue – they look masculine under that large, bearded chin of his. Gil added, "I don't know what this is you think you're doing –"

"– Working," Sawyer shot.

Gil's one hang up is that he sees everything as a challenge to his authority, even Sawyer's dedication to work through lunch is a middle finger at protocol.

"It's freaking rabies, Sawyer. This investigation is merely exploratory."

"Exploratory? I'll leave the cosmetics up to you and the captain. What *I* see is a murder with a biological agent. If it was just exploratory, you should've never let this case fall to me."

Through grit teeth, Gil grumbled, "It somehow got to you before I could stop it. And here you are, standing in front of a goddamn mural on the wall for the pageant case, when you've got other cases that require real detective work –"

"– *Move* my other cases then."

His laugh one-hopped. "Slow your roll, Sawyer. You were like this with that Marty Pringle case." A case where Sawyer's smoking-gun evidence was thrown out due to an illegal search, which got Marty's girlfriend pinned with his murder.

Sawyer's eyes burned, an enemy in her sights; her pointing hand curved inward to herself. "I was *also* like this with the Shelly Fowler case too, so don't get all selective on me, Gil." Shelly, who reported a home invasion that ended in the murder of the roommate that was seeing her boyfriend behind her back. Sawyer couldn't convince the department that Shelly was innocent until a string of subsequent home invasions mirrored the M.O. Shelly described.

Sawyer snatched her jacket off the back of the chair. "Follow me." She brushed past Gil and headed through the doorway.

Gil was soiled by the request. "I ain't following you," he fumed, expecting Sawyer to stop and explain herself, but she walked on. Gil then gave-in and hurried after her. "Where are we going?"

Sawyer looked back with her cell phone held away from her mouth. "Forensics."

Gil's head dipped, and he puffed; every stride in the footsteps of his subordinate, effacing him.

Darlene was at peace in front of a cadaver with its cavity opened like the hull of a wrecked ship, the face bloated and grey; a drowning victim. As always, the radio plays while she hums songs from the eighties, her peak years, the time of Cindy Lauper and Sinead O'Connor. A single, long, blue streak of hair falls down the left side of her short haircut like a war feather. It's not death that intrigues her; it's the narratives that death reveals. Behind the glass, Darlene looked up, eyes peeking out of her surgeon's mask with no specific look or sign, but Sawyer knew what that look meant, *be there in a minute.*

Gil was fretful, his eyes sleepy with impatience, tongue rolling in his cheek, the mind behind the mannerisms, stubborn in its judgment. Sawyer knew it would be tough to convince Gil of her theory because he is a man who only pretends to listen, in order to pass himself off as understanding.

Darlene came into the hallway, her wet hands surrendered. Gil jumped her with the question, "So, what do you two have to show me?"

Sawyer cut her eyes, knowing the question itself was void of curiosity.

Darlene smirked. "Well, hello to you *too*, Sergeant Gilliam."

"Oh, hi, Darl," Gil remembered.

Darlene led them to her office, explaining. "According to the post-mortem examination done at Piedmont, there were no signs of a bite mark. If there's no bite mark, there would have to be an open wound somewhere for the saliva of a diseased animal to infect. Kendall (Trap) Miller had no such wounds."

Sawyer added, "Kendall's pit bull even tested negative."

"Even if his dog was *positive*," Darlene countered. "This would still be a mystery to me, being that there's no site for the saliva to infect. These two victims catch rabies and suddenly everyone's running to get rabies shots like it's freaking H1N1. When Kendall arrived at Piedmont Hospital, they did not go into quarantine protocol did they? Why not? Because without the perfect conditions, the human to human transference rate is to the thousandth of a percent. In colloquial terms, we call it impossible."

Gil folded his arms. "So, what we're dealing with is a medical mystery, is what you're saying?"

Sawyer folded her arms tighter than Gil's folded arms and challenged, "Maybe a better question is, that if someone were to use rabies as a murder weapon, what would be the tell-tale signs?"

Darlene's pointer finger tapped her chin. "Make no mistake, rabies starts with a rabid animal. They would've had to find an infected animal, put the saliva in a syringe, maybe? Then, inject the victim within a day because rabies cannot live outside the body beyond twenty-four hours. In that case, maybe it isn't a bite we would've been looking for, but a needle prick. The problem with that, since rabies takes about thirty days to kill its host, a needle prick may have been healed, or become invisible to the naked eye. An examiner would not have found it unless they were purposely looking for it."

Gil sighed. "All this is assumption, of course. We don't want to assume," he said with his focus on Darlene, but the concern targeting Sawyer. Gil asked, "How long would it take to find *definitive proof* that Mr. Miller was injected with a needle?"

Darlene's face hung slack. "Why, never. He's been cremated; it's required by law when a body's infected with rabies. I'm aware this might sound terrible, but we need Ms. Appleton to die before we can gather more information unless, of course, you classify it as an *attempted* murder right now –"

"– And then her body becomes evidence, right?" The hope in his eyes was nothing more than bait. "Wrong! Don't pull that with me. We don't have enough to classify anything," Gil pouted. "Sawyer's putting you up to this isn't she?"

Sawyer leaned forward, her head swiveling to look in the eyes of the man standing next to her. "Now, *Gil…*"

"Don't 'now Gil' me. If we call it attempted murder, we'd have to name a suspect, and I am *not* about to name a freaking stripper in a homicide with a biological agent."

"Chosen is *not* a stripper," Sawyer shot.

"If you have to clarify to a jury that she's *not* one, what's the difference?"

Sawyer added, "Miss Appleton's family flew in today. They'll be pulling the plug on her tomorrow night. Her colleagues have a candle light vigil planned. This is *going* to happen." Sawyer slapped her palm with the back of her hand. "If we don't do something in about thirty-six hours. By law, the coroner can't hold the body for us, Meegan gets cremated and then what? We let a murderer off the hook?"

Gil looked over at Sawyer and asked, "So, we're banking on finding a thirty-day old needle prick? I'd rather wait on a rabid coyote to come out of the wilderness, reporting stolen saliva."

Sawyer sighed. "Two victims, no bite marks. So, you're saying that we, as born and bred detectives, are supposed to believe that a rare medical mystery struck twice in the same city just weeks apart?"

"She's right," Darlene agreed.

Gil rubbed his chin momentarily and then quit. "If we had a legit suspect, it'd be different… I'm sorry." He turned to go.

Sawyer looked to Darlene to stop him, but Darlene shrugged, meaning she'd already given her best shot.

Sawyer closed her eyes in advance regret. She sighed and said, "Actually, I *do* have a legit suspect. A doctor."

Gil pivoted. "Who?"

"Dr. Edward Cofield. He's been rumored to have had an affair with Meegan Appleton, and to beat all, Dr. Cofield hauls his butt down to Piedmont to get in on Kendall's post-mortem report. Maybe he *meant* to kill Meegan – silence her about the affair, maybe, but went down to Piedmont because he was concerned that maybe he's responsible for *two* murders instead of one. There's nothing exploratory about this, Gil. This is a murder investigation."

"You wait until *now* to tell me about the doctor and the affair? You could've saved me the trip down here."

Darlene frowned. "*Thee* Dr. Cofield?"

Sawyer replied, "There's only one Edward Cofield M.D. in Atlanta. Why?"

Darlene looked low, searching for the words. "You'll want to be careful. Dr. Cofield isn't just a doctor, the man's a medical authority; he sits on all kinds of medical boards. His research serves the entire medical community, here and abroad."

Sawyer found a grotesque lining in all the high praise. "Wouldn't want a double-homicide to impede progress, now, would we?"

Darlene's head raised a clip, her flared nostrils inhaling Sawyer's sarcasm to load her own. "If you're already assuming guilt, detective, that's precisely what I – along with the department that pays your salary – would ask you not to do. Dr. Cofield's name alone brings in millions a year in donorship to the Jordan Cancer Research Hospital. I wouldn't be so quick to name him as a suspect. What if it turns out that he's innocent? You would've needlessly damaged that name, costing, dearly, the hospital, the patients they serve, and the medical community, at large."

"We'll be discreet," Sgt. Gil said, and then looked at Sawyer. "*Won't* we?"

Sawyer nodded. "So, we *are* prioritizing this investigation, right?"

"I don't like this case… It doesn't offer the likelihood that we could find anything that'll fly in a court of law."

"True, this is a hard one," replied Sawyer. "But doesn't it

deserve more priority, in light of this information – not to mention the time constraints?"

"Thirty-six hours, Sawyer. You've got until Meegan's folks pull the plug; God bless them. A day and a half – and I want the damn dirty syringe. And just so you don't go all Rambo on this investigation, I'm putting you with a partner."

Sawyer's eyes maddened. "For what? Who?"

"Travis."

"No. Not happening, Gil," Sawyer said, as if that were that.

Gil's chest puffed out for the perceived challenge to his authority. "*Travis*, I said."

Sawyer's eyes stretched. "I told you never to pair us again."

"Because you saved the man's life once? That's all the more reason. Okay, tell me why not Travis, then."

"Because..." Sawyer stopped there because she didn't want to get Detective Travis reprimanded for something that happened a year ago.

Gil's head drooped forward, wide eyes waiting. "That's what I *thought*. Travis is your partner."

Sawyer pouted. "The man has the instincts of a clam."

"That's why I chose him. He'll keep you from getting all creative on us."

"So..." Sawyer cleared her throat for the setup. "With so little time and so much to cover, you *are* reassigning my other cases, right?"

Sergeant Gilliam towered over her and glared.

Sawyer smirked. "World renowned doctor, white girl victim..."

"One more word, Sawyer," Sgt. Gil threatened, which is his version of permission.

Sawyer brushed past him, smiling.

THE GREAT
DR. COFIELD

With only a day and a half before the plug is pulled on Meegan, there was no time to plan. Minutes after leaving forensics, Sawyer and her unwanted partner were scheduled for the Jordan Cancer Research Center to interview Dr. Coefield. Detective Jeremy Travis held the car door open for Sawyer, who rolled her eyes as she got in. Travis, in response, sighed and said, "Just being a gentleman."

Sawyer waited until Travis walked around the front of the car and got in the driver's seat, so she could look him in the face and say, "I've got a 'gentleman' at home. As long as you remember that, we won't have no problems."

As kind as Travis is, Sawyer learned that his kindness comes with an agenda, so every opened door is seen as an effort to open other doors that only her husband should enter.

They drove wordless for half the trip to the Dr. Cofield interview until Travis, while stopped at a red light, gave a side-eyed stare and asked, "You good?"

"Am I *good?*" Sawyer jerked away, as if the question had caught her across the face. She stared down the throat of the highway, devising a way to veer off the subject. "What kind of question is that," Sawyer said, while still facing forward, without so much as a glance back at Travis. "This is the most difficult case of all time. The murder's executed a month before the actual deaths? The event can only be narrowed down to a span of ten days. We can't even ask the question we ask with every murder case: *Where were you on the day of the murder.* It involves a world-renowned doctor who could afford the best legal team money can buy, so the investigation itself's gotta be flawless, so... Am I good, you ask? Sure... I'm good," Sawyer said, sarcastically.

Travis sighed. "Sawyer, don't act like you don't know what I'm asking."

Sawyer just gazed out the passenger window. Even as the man expressed concern, Sawyer felt his arrogance. They were investigating a double homicide and there Travis was, trying to make the afternoon about him. Sawyer answered, "I'm *good* as long we don't talk about it – how 'bout that?" Sawyer sees Travis as a man who has had it easy with so many women, he refuses to believe there is one who does not want him – at least in her imagination – if her life circumstance wouldn't permit in the flesh. His face looks cut from a mountainside. There's this carnal glare chiseled into his brow, and he is muscled like an athlete. These alluring qualities, though, Sawyer rejects. Pursuing a married woman makes him ugly in her eyes.

His grace goes away completely while in his role as a detective, where he comes off as a straight cornball, ergo, Travis then suggesting, "What if this was some mishaps at the veterinarian's office. Like, if Kendall Miller took his dog to the vet, right... And then maybe there was some kind of cross-contamination? I'm not so convinced this is a murder."

Sawyer, under a lazy-eyed gaze, replied, "What're you suggesting? We go inspect the veterinarian's office?" Sawyer huffed and shook her head. "We're not inspectors. We investigate murder; that's what we do."

"Yes, but shouldn't we rule out other possibilities?"

"Listen to how you sound..." Sawyer's lips twisted in disgust. "We rule out murder by *investigating* murder. And let DHEC, and whoever else, worry about inspections."

Travis replied, "What I'm not understanding, though, is how they were allowed to die in the first place? Couldn't they just get the rabies shot and be done with it?"

"That was *my* first thought, but it's not that simple. Their situation is different. They weren't bitten by a dog, so they had no way of knowing that they needed treatment, so the disease festered."

Travis's brows wrinkled. "I'm talking about when they came into the E.R. sick, why not give em the rabies shot then?"

Sawyer replied, "Because, by then, it's too late. Once the nervous system goes haywire, jaws lock, arms and legs refuse instruction, death is imminent; the shot can no longer help you."

Sawyer and Travis pulled up in the parking lot of the sandwich shop near the Jordan Cancer Research Center for a discreet meeting. Dr. Cofield sat at a window seat, the murder suspect staring out of the storefront glass, to the left of a painted cartoon sandwich with eyes, its brows suspended well above its sourdough head and a smile the width of its sandwich body.

Sawyer, on the walk into the building, gave one final instruction. "You're just a caddy, ok. I take all the shots, ya feel me?"

The doctor rose to his feet to greet them. Cofield was so cordial to the detectives, it was apparent that he didn't know he was a suspect, but thought maybe that the detectives called him to act as medical consultant, considering the biological nature of the supposed crime.

Sawyer looked the man up and down from arm's length, marveling at him. "Look at you, doc. I wasn't expecting this."

Dr. Cofield knew what she meant, but he asked just so he can hear it. "Didn't expect what?"

"A silver fox. Handsome... in shape..." True, no wrinkle lived in his sixty-year-old face, made even younger by contrast to the silver combover. Flattery, however, is a tactic Sawyer uses in casual interviews such as this; men tend to drop their guards when she appeals to their egos.

Dr. Cofield smiled proudly. "Got a forty-year old wife to keep up with."

Sawyer swatted his shoulder, saying, "She's about *my* age, actually. Your second, right?"

"Not by choice."

Sawyer was saddened. "Sorry, I… I didn't know."

There was a moment of silence. Next to Dr. Cofield, Travis sat bent forward, rubbing his hands underneath the table.

Cofield peeled the top off his sandwich. "Something isn't right about this case."

Sawyer asked, "Notice anything odd with Kendall Miller's post mortem report?"

He seemed stunned that the detective knew he'd been to Piedmont. "I believe the rabies was transferred from Mr. Miller to Meegan. It was transferred in such a way that the two had to be involved romantically – which doesn't surprise me."

Sawyer slanted a look Dr. Cofield's way and said, "Should it surprise anyone?"

"I'm not referring to race. I'm referring to Meegan's nature; she's a bit of a free spirit."

Sawyer asked, "You knew her on a personal level?"

"Anyone who knew Meegan, knew her on a personal level." His eyes slapped shut at his error. "There I go, referring to her in the past tense as if she's already…" His words washed away in a wave of sorrow, and his shoulders slumped.

Sawyer peered at the doctor's moment of tenderness. "I can see why she fell for you."

The realization that the detective knew of the affair made Cofield see the proverbial finger pointing at him. He straightened up, dabbed a tear with a handkerchief, asking, "You think *I* had something to do with this?"

"Tell me why *not* you, doc?"

He eyed his sandwich and gave up on it. "Aside from the fact that, who I am personally and spiritually renders me incapable of such an act, I'll also tell you how the *facts* exclude me as well." Dr. Cofield folded his hands in front of him. "Not long before Meegan fell ill, she called me, in tears. She was afraid."

"Of?"

"Of an abnormal pap. They did a biopsy to test for cervical cancer. The biopsy would've left a site on Meegan's cervix that's suitable for the rabies virus to enter her bloodstream. So, you have Mr. Miller's infected saliva, and Meegan's cut cervix, which suggests intimate contact – oral sex, to be precise. Since Meegan contracted the disease from Mr. Miller, a man I never knew existed, I believe that alone rules me out."

Sawyer glanced at Travis and back at Cofield, wondering if she were the only one who'd caught-on to what the man's explanation revealed. "Dr. Cofield," Sawyer said, in a chastising tone. "Now, earlier, I said I could see why Meegan fell for you. You, then, changed the subject. Later, I asked if you knew Meegan on a personal level, and you acted as if you two were nothing special, but when Meegan was faced with something as grave as a cancer scare, she called *you*."

"– Because I'm a cancer doctor, perhaps?"

"But not *her* doctor. It doesn't add up. If the facts rule you out, as you say, I'm left wondering why you would feel the need to be deceptive about the relationship between Miss Appleton and yourself."

Dr. Cofield shifted in his seat, his eyes on alert. "What do you mean deceptive? I wasn't being deceptive – I *wasn't*... Maybe the problem is the questions. Allow me to give it to you straight, ok?"

"Be my guest," said Sawyer.

"I oversee her training, so we talked often. Sometimes after hours – all work related. One afternoon, we kissed. I had actually believed, for a brief moment in time, that I was in love with her, but no. I was in love with her love of medicine."

Sawyer seemed intrigued. "In love with her love of medicine?"

"She was my protégé." Dr. Cofield's eyes stretched, his head shook, fighting his emotions. "The man that I am... my children will survive me in that respect, but they can't carry on my *work*, as neither chose a career in medicine. When your vision reaches beyond your time here on earth, you need a successor to take up the torch. Meegan was my medical heir, so to speak. She was ambitious, smart... *God* she was beautiful," his eyes stretched; a tear dropped. "She lived and breathed medicine."

Sawyer asked, "One kiss?"

"We kissed again when I broke it off, nothing sexual."

"I'll ask you again. So, you're saying, it never went any further than kissing? But before you answer, doc, keep in mind that if I find out that you're lying, our next interview will take place in the presence of your wife."

Cofield looked sternly out the sandwich shop window at the faded back of the cartoon sandwich logo and said, "There was a time when a fling with a med student barely raised a brow. Back in the eighties, my mentor, Bill Asher, had more than his share, but his work always stood apart from it. In the world we live in today… They find out about an affair and suddenly your work, your accomplishments, is somehow no longer what it has always been?"

Sawyer studied the man across the table from her. "I take it, that it's not your wife that you're worried about."

Dr. Cofield looked away and said, "To answer your question directly, it went no further than kissing."

After the interview, with Sawyer and Travis heading to the car, Travis was still coming to grips with what he had just witnessed. "You said you'd take all the shots... What shots did you take? You let him cruise through that interview."

Standing inside of their open car doors, peering at Travis over the car roof, Sawyer said, "Gil wanted us to question Dr. Cofield, so I did. But Dr. Cofield is not our killer." Sawyer then ducked into the passenger side.

Travis followed suit, shutting himself inside with a door slam, but sat stupefied with the keys in his hand.

Sawyer tried offering a better explanation, "The killer is Kendall Miller's ex-fiancé. Her name is Chosen."

"I was briefed earlier. Saw a few pictures of her –"

"– I bet you *did*."

Travis's eyes rolled. "What makes you think a woman like that, can pull off a crime like this?"

"Because I know."

Travis cleared his throat in preparation for his facetious one-liner. "Just like you *knew* about Marty Pringle?"

Sawyer's fist dropped on the console. "If I hear Marty's name *one* more time today!"

Stiff with shock at Sawyer's outburst, Travis said, "What makes you so sure then? I need something better than you 'just know.'"

Sawyer sucked her teeth and peered out the passenger window. She wasn't about to explain herself to Travis. For *what*, Sawyer thought. So, he could criticize or question her ability to see right through a suspect like she can see right through her daughters? Sawyer's gift, she believes, is akin to a mother's intuition; something a man wouldn't understand – especially Travis, a detective who believes only in his academy training and his criminal justice degree. Sawyer acquired her special gift through motherhood – through twice re-experiencing the womb but from the outside, spending the better part of a year in sync with the appetites, hormones, and temperament of the little fruit of life growing on a stem inside of her. By her second pregnancy, Sawyer not only honed her telepathy – so to speak – with the child inside of her, but also translated it to human beings living outside of her. Sawyer realized this nine years ago when she was eight months pregnant with Brianna. Sawyer was interviewing a sex offender who lived within a five-mile radius of where a missing girl's blood-stained shoe was found. Carl Voight seemed to have an airtight alibi, the questions were merely a formality, but Sawyer had gotten this feeling about the man that just wouldn't go away. There was a moment where Carl Voight had merely glanced toward the back yard, beyond the glass sliding door, and that simple glance made something harken inside of Sawyer. She couldn't shake the feeling that that simple, seemingly errant glance at the lawn, had a target. That feeling led to the unearthing of four bodies buried in the man's backyard. Sawyer had effectively fashioned a new crimefighting mojo from her maternal intuition. The trait that makes woman the more advanced gender, also makes Sawyer a more advanced homicide detective.

This is the memory Sawyer relived while a quarter mile of Peachtree street had passed under them. Although Travis remained quiet, focusing only on driving, Sawyer felt his energy turn disgruntled, his blown-off question creating a rift between them – a rift that could undermine the investigation. For the good of the investigation, Sawyer sighed and offered an explanation, one that Detective Travis could understand. "There's more to Chosen than meets the eye, Travis. When I interviewed her, she was rummaging through her purse, pulling out lip stick, hand sanitizer, various products... For each one, she knew the ingredients, the fillers, how it's manufactured. She said hand sanitizer has trace amounts of a chemical banned by the FDA for causing muscle failure in lab rats. She may *look* like a groupie chick, but there's brains behind the makeup."

"So, she read a few labels, big deal."

Sawyer was shaking her head. "The amount of that chemical is in such trace amounts, that it's not even required to be on the label. She's had some training in chemistry I'm sure, but what puzzles me, is that she has no record of degrees or even college enrollment… Nothing."

Travis grimaced. "*Because* she's nothing more than a groupie chick who Googled every product in her purse."

It didn't matter what Travis thought, Sawyer decided. *She* was leading the investigation, and she had only a day and a half to prove Travis and Gil wrong. She looked out the passenger window, watching the city float by, wondering why Chosen would flaunt her acumen in chemistry and risk aiding an investigation against her. The feeling that harkened inside of Sawyer while she was interviewing Chosen is that, like most perps, she hopes to get away with the crime, but pulling off an unprecedented homicide is an achievement that Chosen may want some level of credit for.

QUEEN B

C hosen strode into Hustle Hard Entertainment like she owned it because, as of nine o'clock that morning, she officially did. She'd had a meeting with lawyers to purchase the majority share of the company bequeathed to Trap's mother, Evangelist Lottie Miller, who leapt at the chance to rid herself of her stake in this abomination of an industry, as if it were a stake in a timeshare located in the infernos of Hell. By the end of the meeting, Lottie showed little interest in the millions she had just acquired. She kept asking, "So, it's done? I have no more ties to this wretched company? Are you sure? I'm just asking…"

Just hours after the documents were signed, Chosen's red bottoms hit the concrete steps of the bulky 8th street office building. It was after lunch for the rest of the business world, but just the start of the workday at Hustle Hard Entertainment. Men were at the studio still with heavy hearts for the loss of

Trap, their leader. Chosen twirled her out-of-season mink scarf as she sashayed past the gum-popping receptionist and went down the hallway, passing by a room with the door open where, inside, goons played PlayStation.

In the studio, the rest of the entourage sat around like dead men propped up in chairs, their heads bopping to the beat in a cloud of smoke, each one on-call for grunt-work, from street corner marketing, to mix-tape distribution, to running errands, security detail, and in the event of police stopping their vehicle, to claim full responsibility of any narcotics or guns in the car, sheltering Jamil "J Money" Baxter and Drew "Flikka" Simpson, the minority shareholders heading the recording session with the new protegee, mumble-rapper, Young Boss.

J Money was seated at the sound controls licking a blunt, looking down, his eyelids shiny. Flikka focused on Young Boss, lip syncing the bars. They didn't notice Chosen until she entered the booth. They greeted her like an old friend, but Chosen slipped through them, hit the sound button to speak to the rapper behind the sound proof glass, "Ay, lil nigga! Can't nobody understand what your ig'nant ass is sayin' bruh!"

J Money edged Chosen away from the controls. "Whoa! Whoa!"

Flikka grabbed her from behind. "Girl, you done bumped yo head, or what?"

Behind the sound proof glass, Young Boss was stupefied in front of the hanging microphone, the lazy beat still thumping.

Chosen shook loose. "*Get* off me Flick, lest you want your

head buss. Besides, that's no way to treat your new boss." Chosen handed them the signed document copies, taunting, "Read em and weep, fuckas!"

J Money and Flikka leaned forward, two mouths dropped open, four eyes reading, and ready for weeping.

Chosen continued, "As of today, no more weed in the studio. This is a place of *business*, people," she clapped, like a motivational coach. "And if you are not on the company payroll? You ain't gotta go home but you got to get the hell up outta here!" The young men in the studio came alive, berating in protest, trading insults with Chosen. J Money and Flikka stood bewildered in the midst of the mayhem, astounded that they couldn't wake from the nightmare of this Instagram chick barely worth her weight in silicon, fronting the money that they were scrambling to raise, and purchasing Trap's majority share of their company.

J Money caved forward, his head shaking. Flikka sighed and gripped the back of his neck. Never could they fathom the hijacking of their empire, which has footprints in the game since their makeshift studio in Jamil's folk's basement, since Atlanta's hip hop gold rush around the startups of UGK, Goodie Mob and Outkast. Now they were seeing their story turning into yet another tragic example of rap pioneers falling victim to mismanagement; their company sure to be ran into the ground by an Instagram chick.

J Money yelled and waived his hands to silence the back and forth argument between Chosen and the entourage. He then asked Chosen, "Where'd you get the money?!"

Chosen yelled back, "None of your damn business J!"

"I'm gonna ask you again. Where'd your broke ass get the money?"

Chosen spread two fingers. "You two should be ashamed that you *didn't* have the money – J: with your five baby mommas – and how about you, *Flik*? How many millions went up your nose? Ugly ass! I wasn't about to stand by and watch you two shit-heads squander Trap's legacy."

J Money lunged, but Flikka held him back. From behind Flikka's arm bar, J Money berated, "Who the fuck is *you* to be talking about Trap's legacy... Trap's *legacy!*"

"I was damn near Trap's wife."

J Money scanned the room as if surveying a congregation. "Hoe bought her *own* damn engagement ring and went around telling everybody she and Trap were engaged. Lyin' bitch!"

Chosen made praying hands and sighed to reset the discussion. "Call me all kinds of bitches and hoes if you want, but what you *won't* do, is utter one more bitch or hoe in Hustle Hard Entertainment's lyrics." Her mandate drew outrage and even laughter, but Chosen insisted with one pledged hand raised. "I made a promise to Miss Lottie that, if nothing else, our music *will* respect our mothers, our sisters, our daughters, *our women* – who are also a big consumer of our product, I might add!"

J Money squeezed his head between his hands and laughed like a maniac. "You have *got* to be kidding me! Even if this sale is legit – which I seriously doubt – you're just a shareholder; you vote on *executive* decisions. That's it. But as far as daily operations? Uh-uh… I ain't finna be bossed around by no simple ass bitch!"

"*Simple* bitch, you say?" Chosen chuckled into her fist. "I'm the majority shareholder of this company; therefore, it's *queen* bitch to you, J."

Flikka, who had went out of sight momentarily, returned with his phone raised, their lawyer on the other end. Flikka held the phone up and yelled, "Fuck everything this broad is sayin' bro, this sale isn't even legit because we were never notified!"

Chosen raised a finger. "But you *were* notified by certified mail. It was signed for. So, you might wanna check with your lazy ass secretary at the front desk."

At length, she argued back and forth with J Money, Flikka and the lawyer on speakerphone, who said they had a five business day period to run a trace on the funds used in the purchase of Trap's share in the company, and that if the funds were obtained illegally, or has any kind of lien or silent partnership as conditions to the sale, or comes with any unforeseen elements that may put the company in a legal quagmire, J Money and Flikka could contest the sale in court, or even have the sale revoked outright, in order to safeguard their investments.

Chosen seemed to be losing the argument against the three men, two in person, one on speakerphone, backed by the studio entourage, an audience biased against her.

Chosen's phone buzzed in her purse – a call she *had* to take, she claimed. She then exited, dancing backwards holding up two pink-fingernailed middle fingers. "See ya in the boardroom, bitches!"

Once outside, Chosen picked her phone out of her purse, and returned Detective Aisha Sawyer's call, and agreed to an interview.

*

Chosen went to the precinct with no fear. She checked her lipstick in the rearview mirror, left the mink, and tucked her sunshades' handle in the neck of her dress. She waited in the small interrogation room, distractedly, like a simple dental checkup.

Sawyer walked in holding a folder; Detective Travis, begrudgingly, in tow. A criminal profiler watched from behind the one-way glass, studying behavioral keys, which would be more telling than any information Sawyer might get out of Chosen.

Sawyer set down a manila folder that she would never open – a folder that Chosen never once glanced at. Sawyer asked, "When Kendall Miller died, the family asked that you not attend the wake, nor the funeral; why was that?" The question was irrelevant; Chosen's nuances, while hearing the fact of her ex-fiancé's death, meant everything to the criminal profiler observing from behind the glass.

"Kendall and I," she sighed. "Although we had a wonderful

relationship, that relationship ended badly. His mother, Evangelist Lottie Miller, actually wanted me there, but because certain folk spoke out against my presence, Miss Lottie requested that I stay back to avoid a scene."

"And how did you feel about that?"

Very businesslike, Chosen asked, "Forgive me, Detective Sawyer, but is this an interrogation, or is this Inyanla Vanzant's Fix My Life?"

"This is *not* a joke, Chosen."

"That's precisely the point I'm trying to make to *you*, Detective Sawyer."

Sawyer's finger tapped the table. "I know for a fact that Trap used to put his hands on you. Even *after* the break-up, he attacked you at the club, so leaving him wasn't enough. The moment Trap died, you became safer. Look, I'm gonna be straight with you. If you take *that* angle, that you feared for your life, a lawyer could build a legit defense around it. A jury might buy it if they feel like you're a good person. Problem is, good people cave-in and confess under the pressure from their good conscience. But the longer you delay this, a jury would doubt that you even *have* a conscience."

Chosen seemed to had crumble inside the moment she'd heard about that night at the club. Her face seemed hot with emotion. She was consumed by the reliving of the attack. It happened after she and Trap broke up. Chosen was at Savoy, the nightclub where one of Hustle Hard Entertainment's artists was performing. That night, Chosen could hardly breathe, in her tight corset. She was still raw from the second miscarriage, but walked with her head high and chest out, her glittered cleavage ballooning at the top of her strapless, sequin dress. Chosen, the thirty-year-old who had been intimate with only five men lifetime, was batting eyelashes at every man in sight.

Trap, demon possessed by jealousy, hypnotized by the pulsing strobe lights and the throbbing bass, left the VIP section, and shouldered through the crowd with a bottle of champagne in hand. He grabbed Chosen's arm, his jaw rippling from an angry teeth grind. *Can we talk for a minute?*

Talk was the second thing Trap wanted to do. He first led her to a back room, pulled her inside by her hair and slung her. He pinned Chosen to the floor with his foot on the center of her back and then doused her with champagne. *Since you out here acting so thirsty!* By the time security heard Chosen's screams and managed to bust in, they found Chosen up on her feet and *Trap* was the one bent over, bugged out in pain, as he frantically tried to wipe the pepper spray out of his eyes. So, it was after their relationship had ended that the violence became public, and if Chosen, the woman he abused, had attended the funeral, her presence would've exposed the preacher's eulogy as a grand lie.

Chosen came out of that memory, the wave of that evening receding from her, her focus returning to the interrogation room, the detective's small face, squinched with determination. Chosen sat up righteous. "You asked if I needed Trap dead, right? Well, while we're asking ridiculous questions, let me ask *you* one: who does your raggly nails, your eight-year-old daughter?"

The word daughter dropped on Sawyer like an anvil. She leaned forward, hands splayed on the table. "Wait a minute. How do you know I have an eight-year-old daughter?" Sawyer was half out of her seat, her face a steam engine. "Are you threatening my family?!"

Travis leaned toward Sawyer, ready to yank her back if needed.

"Daaang, girl." Chosen's eyes popped open and rolled dizzily. "Sheesh! It was just a lucky guess."

Travis's head shook slowly, his eyes intense as he assured, "It was a lucky guess, Sawyer; that's all, ok?"

Chosen aimed a lazy pointer finger at Travis and said, "What you *need* to do, bruh, is give her some dick and maybe she won't be so wound up all the time."

Sawyer bit down and took a deep breath. "I know, for a fact, that on the night when Trap put his hands on you at the club, while being hauled out by security, he threatened to kill you. I *also* know – after interviewing multiple people – that you replied verbatim: 'Nigga, you *already* dead –'"

"– Dead *to me!*"

"Coincidentally, a month after your threat, Trap was dead to everyone! *That* strikes me as very suspicious."

Chosen feinted a threatening backhand, "How 'bout I *strike* that suspicion right back out yo ass, then?" She watched the detectives deflate in exasperation, and only then did Chosen give a serious answer. "Look, chick, my threat was just as empty as Trap's. As you probably already notice, somebody say some shit to me, I gotta say something back, even better. He threatened me, so I had to threaten back with a lil mo' sauce."

Sawyer's head was shaking in denial. "You lost your cool. You just had to let Trap know that you had the upper hand. How was he 'already' dead?"

"Look, miss… the nigga died of rabies, alright? You know I ain't did shit that got nothing to do with no damn rabies; I'm a fucking *lady*. But I'm also a lady who understands how a woman like *you* would pursue the downfall of a woman like *me*. I get it. You're invisible when a woman like me enters the room, and plus you punch a clock ev-ery, fricking day, but got bargain brand clothes in your closet." Chosen pulled the pair of shades that hung on the neck of her dress. "Look at this right here: this is Versace. How many of your payroll checks would it take to get a pair of these, huh? How 'bout this Yves Saint Laurent dress? Trick *please!* Funny thing is, we can trade outfits, bitch, and you *still* couldn't fuck wit' me!" On the word still, Chosen's pointer finger snatched back and into a slack, upright fist.

All during Chosen's rant, Sawyer tapped an impatient foot and checked her watch. "Are you done? Because I haven't even started on you. What kind of fool would think that I'd be jealous of a woman like you – a woman who is the opposite of what I want my girls to become. I have a happy home, a loving husband. There is no envy here." Sawyer drew back with a smile as tight as a nun's, adding, "In fact, I pity you. I weep for the little girl that went through, what had to be, a love-depraved childhood to produce the pride-less heifer that you are today." Sawyer stood up straight looking over her nose. Chosen studied the back of her hand as if to ignore Sawyer, who continued, "Sure, men will give you material things, but will he give you his forever? Or will he go sniffing after the next Mizz Bottoms that comes along? You get only what you are *given*, so your glass ceiling is only as high as the man you toot your ass up to."

Chosen looked left and right, oblivious as to who this detective might've been referring to. "There ain't nothing no man won't give me. If I want his forever, it's mines," Chosen replied with her neck swerving and an underhand fist popping open for emphasis. "Hell, these ears ain't eem *heard* the word no, in a good sem years."

Travis had seen enough. He jumped Sawyer's reply with hands raised to silence her. "Sawyer, no. This ain't no damn Jerry Springer show. Heck's wrong with you. Let's step out and take five. *Now!*"

As Sawyer closed the door behind them, she heard Chosen giggling. Out in the hallway, Sawyer pointed a finger in Travis's chest. "You see, this is exactly why I didn't want you with me on this case in the first place –"

"– Because I won't let you play the dozens with the suspect? Maybe you *are* jealous, like she says."

Sawyer carried a sigh on a rainbow arc. "Oh, my *good*ness! You just don't know it, Travis, but you damn near got karate chopped in the throat just now for talking reckless. I am not jealous. I'm *unorthodox*."

"But it's not working."

"It is, too, working. Just like Dr. Cofield this morning... I don't interview from a freaking clipboard, alright. I batted a few lashes at Dr. Cofield, and before you know it, he was not only admitting to having a relationship with Ms. Appleton, but also to having physical contact with her a month before she went into the E.R., which puts him within the timeframe of suspicion." Sawyer watched her explanation beat Travis's counterpoint before he could issue it, and then Sawyer added, "Just watch me work. You just might learn something."

Travis extended an arm, welcoming the way to the door, but then Gil called from down the hallway; he was hurrying toward them. "Travis. Sawyer. You're done with this interview. Let her go."

"Do *what?*" Sawyer didn't look at Gil directly, her eyes fell to his bright shirt. Sawyer pleaded, "I'm just about to get what I need."

Gil's lips thinned against his teeth. "I saw you in there. I was behind the glass. This chick is not the killer – *if* there is a killer –"

"But Gil –"

"– You can't tell me this broad slid down off her stripper pole and A: suddenly possessed the know-how to harvest a biological agent, or B: use it without infecting her *self* in the process."

Travis chimed in, "That's what I've been saying this whole time."

Without looking, Sawyer posted a dismissing hand in front of Travis's face and warned, "Travis… That's not the way partners do each other, bro. And pardon *you*, Gil, how many times do I have to tell you that she was never a stripper. She was a bartender at a club."

"Now you're just splitting hairs," said Gil. "She is not capable, so it doesn't matter *what* the profiler says."

Sawyer, floored by some startling revelation, stared Gil in the face, covered her mouth with a hand and said, "So, the profiler must've seen something." Sawyer took off, leaving the men where they stood.

A ROUGH NIGHT

isha was quiet at the dinner table. She laughed, of course, when Brianna told the story about her belching in class during a spelling test. Aisha spotted the seventeen-year-old, Star, texting under the dinner table but let it ride. It was the husband, Darius Sawyer's glare that made Star shrink in her chair and apologize.

Everyone at the table, except Aisha, had a day to talk about. She was slightly more human than an android, but behind her stock responses, worked a background cache of computing and processes that Darius, her husband of twenty years, identified as signs of a complex criminal case that would reduce his loving wife, his best friend, his bae, to a mere houseguest until she finds a break in the case. She'd hardly touched her store-bought rotisserie chicken. Aisha is this family's pulse. That's never more apparent than when she's checked out because of her obsession with a tough case.

Darius, stuck with greasing Brianna's scalp later in the evening, sensed his youngest daughter wanting mommy's help instead, but being that she's now a board-certified big girl, she didn't whine.

Aisha was neck deep in one of her magical baths with lavender candles burning, her head resting against the back of the tub, peaceful in her Zen, her thoughts seeking a deeper understanding of the facts of the case. Aisha didn't know her hubby had entered the master bath until he cleared his throat, and then she saw him, the dead-ringer for 90's rapper Method Man. He wore a wise but loving smile. "Hey," he said.

"Hey," said Aisha. "You want in?"

He glanced around the low-lit bathroom, candle flame flickering on the tiles, but then realizing that the atmosphere was put together without him in mind. "Nah. You go ahead."

Aisha eyed him sideways but said nothing.

Darius mirrored her side look and said, "What?"

"Tell me what you think about this: why would someone have a near twelve-year gap in their life? No residence, no property? No college enrollment?"

Darius replied, "Look no further than your slack ass brother in law, Day-Day. Livin' with moms... Hiding from child support, until it caught up to him."

"Hiding," Aisha muttered. She wondered what Chosen could be hiding from.

"By the way, the girls are in for tonight," her husband said.

"Aw, Bree, too?"

"Didn't even have to bribe her."

Aisha knew the meaning of his announcement; the opportunity for alone-time. She assured, "I'll be out in a sec, hon." After the bath, Aisha went to the office to continue her research until she heard her husband finish in the shower.

Aisha found Darius on the couch, watching the news. She sat across his lap and kissed his lips – a little extra affection for doing it all in her absence. His hand reached through the split in her robe, caressing her lotioned thighs while they talked. Darius asked, "Still no break in the case, huh?"

Aisha feigned exasperation, "I don't even want to talk about it."

He smiled. "Yes, you do."

Aisha smiled back. "No, I don't. Wanna know what I *do* want to talk about, though?"

"What?"

A gentle hand turned his distracted face from the news to face her. "How I appreciate you. Thanks for taking care of dinner, for taking care of the girls. Thank you for all that you do, my rock star."

He flicked his pointer finger off the tip of her nose. "No, *you* do a lot, babe."

"But you," Aisha insisted. "You're better than you have to be. I should never take that for granted." She kissed him again and drew back slowly, and there it was: that sudden hush of inevitability. Darius counted the blessing that some long, overdue lovemaking was about to go down. He pulled the string on Aisha's robe, like opening a gift. Half the cape fell open and the sight of her reminded him what a privilege it is to be loved by this woman. What her body lacks in curves, it makes up for in its pristine appearance, its creamy essence, lean and unblemished except for the darkening of her belly, the emblem of having bore two children in honor of their longstanding love.

Darius is always thrilled how, after so many years, Aisha's body still eagerly wakes up for him, her nipples were hard as buttons after just a few kisses, and she was grinding in his lap with her mouth hung ajar. He pressed his palm on her belly and Aisha lay back on the couch. She asked, "D, what if one of the girls come waltzing out here?"

Darius, hovering from above, his shoulders rippling to support his body weight, replied, "May God help us all."

They giggled briefly. Darius pecked a trail from her earlobe to her collarbone. Aisha's eyes reduced to devious slits. Her head turned to the side, where she saw something that made her stop everything. "Wait. Stop babe."

Darius stopped, eyes wide in the night, an ear turned to the hallway, listening for footsteps. Darius was set to bolt to the far end of the couch and play casual, but no; the hallway was silent.

Sawyer shoved upward, elbows back to support her, as if sex was off. She gazed at the eleven o'clock news, disputing the nasally news anchor's report. "Isolated incident my ass," Sawyer shot.

Darius resumed kissing Aisha's neck. "It's alright, babe."

Aisha swerved away. "How is it alright? Everyone's willing

to just chalk these deaths up to the universe, have their candle light vigils, and call it a day. Maybe if they would call it the murder that it is, maybe someone would know to step forward with information that can crack this thing."

Darius searched for the TV remote. "This must be the case you're working on. Don't let it come between us, right now, babe." He kissed Aisha's lips but her spark was gone.

"I'm sorry, my love. It's not so much the case; it's the whole damn department. If it were one of the *guys* who had this really deep-seated hunch – say, Detective Blakely or a Callahan? They get behind these men, no question. When it comes to *me*, there's gotta be a litmus test."

Darius shook his miserable head and sighed. "I know all about it, babe. What else is new, like…?"

Aisha turned grim. "Since when does something have to be *new* to qualify as upsetting?"

Darius detected an attitude, so he switched strategy and went with flattery. "Look babe, you're the best damn detective in that department. *You* know that. *They* know it." Darius, relieved to see a half-smile, then mirrored it, as he continued, "It's not your ideas they disagree with, babe. It's your intensity. When you're really wound up, sometimes you come off like a wild woman." Darius chuckled; his wife didn't.

Her half-smile died in her cheek. "*Really*," Aisha glared. "I open up to you, and you take the opportunity to *critique* me?"

Darius took one last look at that shower glistened frame, the curly triangle patch of hair at the fork of her body, before the bathrobe flapped closed.

Aisha knows her man. Even with that kind, still face, she saw under-currents of humiliation. The man doesn't take rejection well. He'd hold it against her all week, avenging the insult with an affront of disinterest and one-off responses, denying there's anything wrong. As much as Aisha wished she were made differently, she couldn't meet him physically if he couldn't meet her emotionally; her body had turned as cold as clay.

*

On Darius's morning run, he found himself listening beyond the pat of his trotting feet and beyond the hiss of air pressed through his lungs. Beyond the blood coursing behind his eardrum; he listened to last night's argument playing out in his mind. He heard himself pleading for his wife to free her mind of that case for a day – tomorrow evening, to be exact – and they could drop the girls off at their grandmother's, so husband and wife can spend quality time. Darius surmises that putting himself last everyday anoints him the right to be first, to be catered to, upon request.

Although Aisha would never decline quality time, she declined the schedule. Sorrowfully, she had replied, *Gil gave me only a day and a half to come up with something. Tomorrow night I must attend the candlelight vigil.* To her husband's sigh of surrender, she had pleaded, *We're hoping, there we could find something – observe who attends, who doesn't attend, or maybe find someone at the memorial who's overcome with guilt and willing to talk to us*, she had said, with TV light flickering on the left side of her face. No matter the stakes, all Darius heard was that, again, work was winning and he was losing.

While coming hot around the first bend of the asphalt lap around the park, Darius thought about last night's error; he regretted letting pride hold back what he was really trying to say to his wife: *Baby I need you.* A man has his own way of crying out for help, which is rarely received as the distress signal that it really is. Being a man, with an ego, he asks from above – not from below, so it often sounds like a threat. Instead of *Baby I need you*, Darius said to his wife, *When you feel like you can no longer operate under the rule of compromise, you invite the devil into our marriage.*

No sooner than Darius relived the memory, while hitting the straightaway beside the first set of park benches, elbows pumping, he saw the devil herself with her red lipstick smile and lingering eyes, tickling a wave as she jogged past him.

Chosen outpaced Detective Sawyer's husband to give him a rear view. She wore the minimum: spandex camel-toe shorts and a mere sports bra to show off her cartoonish curves. Chosen knows how to entice – in more ways than one. She knew that taunting him with a wave would be taken as a competition.

Darius, being the only remaining regular, jogging this path for the last five years, this territory is his, as sure as if he'd scent-marked the shrubs; he refused to let a newbie show him up. Darius picked up the pace, slowly gaining, cursing himself with each accidental glance at her make-believe figure. Darius drew even. They jogged shoulder to rowing shoulder, the shadowy overpass of branches streaming over them like a film projector. Chosen picked up the pace, her pony tail bouncing, sweat beading on her upper lip.

They shot out into a clearing, neck and neck, the morning sun bright on their faces. A solo bird dove overhead. The quick winged shadow striking across the ground in front of them, seemed to signal go. Chosen bolted, head back, hands knifing, pink sneaker soles flipping back. Darius then accelerated, his stride churning like a spinning wheel under his body. While passing the mystery woman, he taunted her, his brows wrinkled in the attitude of *oh, what did you* think *was gon' happen...* By the time Darius broke off the sprint and plopped on the second set of park benches, he was bent forward and heaving for air. Chosen walked toward him, her stout thighs shining like a thoroughbred strutting off the race track.

She sat next to him. Each fought to catch their breath. Chosen managed to say, "I... let you... win."

Darius swallowed hard, as if choking down a hard-boiled egg. "Or rather... you refused... to fight... the inevitable." He sat upright, arms spread along the bench, his head lay back in suffering. "The name's Darius... What's yours?"

Chosen was still panting but recovered enough to give a sentence in one breath. "What's so important in a name, that it's the first question people ask? You can call me whatever word comes to mind when you look at me."

Knowing that *gold digger* might get him slapped, Darius said nothing. Withholding her name made Darius think she was either rude or crazy. He himself was just as crazy for engaging in a footrace with this stranger, Darius thought, as he watched the nameless woman cross her legs and smooth baby-hair behind her ear. Darius asked, "Does *are you new to the neighborhood* qualify as a worthy second question?"

"Because you see me running here, I must live here, huh," she said, as she rolled the band down her ponytail and shook her hair loose. "I was driving by one morning, about this time, and I felt an immediate attraction to this path. You know... running is like sex, you can't keep to the same old, worn path. Gotta find an exciting, new path."

Darius's reply stymied. If "path" was code for *mate*, he had just heard an invitation for sex, and any response that came to mind would've sounded like an RSVP. He just nodded matter-of-factly, but more solid in his assessment that he was conversing with a gold digger; Atlanta's full of them. This one, however, had mistaken him for a wealthy mark.

"What do you do," she asked.
Figures, Darius thought. "Network Engineer. Verizon. Pays the bills, I guess," he said, and then waited for the curvy centerfold beauty to mumble excuses to leave and go digging elsewhere.

Her face dimmed at his response. "I asked what you *do*; not your occupation."

Next, Darius figured he'd better sprinkle his marital status in his response. "Well, I… I spend time with my family… My wife and I, we –"

"– Darius, the *you* is singular, my fleet-footed friend," she sung, in a shaming tune. "What do *you* do?"

His head tossed back slightly. "Ah, *now* I know what you're getting at. I do music. Jazz. I'm a Herbie Hancock baby, but the day I first heard Sweetback? That changed everything. So, yeah… I do music," Darius said proudly, but then he paused, wondering if she had recognized who he was, which is rare nowadays. "I ain't even gon' lie, though, it's been a *minute*, since I've done music real heavy."

She squinted. "Look at you… Do you notice how you come alive when you talk about music?" The nameless woman just gazed, as if her smile held a secret.

Darius, hastening a response to beat awkwardness to the punch, asked, "So, what is it that *you* do?"

Chosen was pretending to be so in awe of Darius, she acted like she didn't hear his question. She extended her arms, with thumbs and forefingers making inverted Ls, framing a window into the past as Chosen narrated, "I'm picturing a stage with blue lighting, a scruffy white boy jammin' the sax, a drummer with his face hiding behind a curtain of dreads, and you on the keyboards with a brim tipped down over your eyes …"

Darius remembered fondly. "Fountain Blue. Played there on many a night. Crazy… I drive by the lot where that place used to be… It's now a Chipotle." Looking beyond, into outer space, Darius was delighted. "Wow... So, you're a fan. I guess that makes about a dozen of you, all total."

"Don't do that, Darius – or should I say Sip," Chosen said. "I did my research. Your jazz band, The Elect, was hot for a *minute*. And didn't you do some producing for Jaded, and Gold Standard – remember them?"

"Well, I'll be," he said. "A fan..." But then he stopped nodding, stopped smiling. On second thought, a fan following him in the park struck a chord of concern. "That's not the reason... you...? Are you following me?"

"Boy please. Your band broke up twenty years ago –"

"– Sixteen... Officially."

"Look who's counting," Chosen pointed out. "Sixteen years ago, I was in the eighth grade, sir. But here I am now, chairman of the board for an industry leading record label. I find clips of your old group, The Elect, on someone's YouTube channel and I like your sound so much, that I felt like you and I should talk business. I've got an artist with a voice as smooth as Anita Baker, but as strong as Aretha in her heyday. My producers won't know what to do with her. They'll choke her power."

Darius's head was shaking. "If her voice is like *that*? It's a producer's biggest challenge... A producer's instinct is to make the song *his*, but with a voice like that, he's got to swallow his pride and give all the glory to the singer," Darius said. "Even the song writing has to cater to her. A powerful voice with weak words sounds like nothing more beautiful noise. Ya go with fewer words, gives her room to finesse. Let lyrics put purpose to the outbursts and the contemplative spaces, giving the listener a moment to absorb her impact. Melody? Melody is merely her firmament."

Chosen gazed in awe at his expertise, which is clouds above her current producers who, to her knowledge, can't even read sheet music. Her pointer finger pecked Darius in his chest. "*That's* what I'm talking about. That's the type of stuff I'm *not* hearing from *my* producers."

Nothing about this felt real to Darius; the suddenness of it all, the foot race, the lottery chance of landing a recording deal while on a morning jog in the park. Darius wondered if he was dreaming, still in bed twitching in his sleep, but it all seemed so real, the sun warm on his face and his heart drumming in his chest. The nameless beauty was too unreal even for his dreams to conjure up. Aisha would kill him for attempting to work with a woman with the curves of a vase who also stalked him in the park, now sixteen years after music nearly ruined his young marriage. For most musicians, the industry doesn't open its doors to them once. This time around, Darius wondered if the first step through that door would be a bottomless drop.

MOTIVES

S awyer's thirty-six hours was waning. Ten hours before the vigil, Sawyer was behind a desk, lost in brainstorming. The phone rang. Daphne, the secretary that had patched the call through, ran behind it. She stopped, panting at the doorway pointing at the blinking desk phone. "Sawyer, you *have* to take that call!"

Sawyer swiveled around in her chair and answered. Ironically, the call came from a man who had done everything to avoid Sawyer. "Mr. Baxter?" It was J Money, speaking in codes as if the phone line was tapped. *I need to talk to you in person*, he demanded. What he had to report must've been big, Sawyer thought. She asked, "How fast can you get here?" J Money refused to meet at the precinct because he didn't want to *look like no snitch*.

Sawyer came alone. Travis worked the Dr. Cofield side of the double homicide, per Gil. The castle-like exterior to J

Money's six-million-dollar mansion was impressive enough, but it still couldn't prepare her for the interior, with its arched entryways, a decorative chandelier like a celestial peacock descending from the vaulted ceiling and then there was all the hidden decadence, like the gold embossed crown molding and the emerald stones set in the brass curtain ties. Even sunlight comes in humbled and blessed.

Sawyer followed J to the living room and sat on a velvet chair that was so fine, she massaged the material through her fingers.

J Money then said, in all seriousness, that Chosen had purchased the lion's share of his multimillion dollar company. Sawyer shoved up to the edge of her seat, tinged with confusion. "Come again? Not long ago, she could barely afford *rent*."

J Money rubbed his forehead, still coming to grips. "Yesterday, that hoe came in my office twirling a mink scarf, talkin' 'bout she *my* boss? Ain't no way. Ain't no fuckin' way, dawg."

"How does someone buy your company and it be a surprise to you?"

J Money dipped, helpless and embarrassed. "Because of a first cousin secretary that I should've fired long before this shit went down."

"How'd Chosen get the money?"

"A'ight, check this out: I had my lawyer try to find any reason under the law to contest the sale, and I'm tellin' you right now, that this nigga is a fuckin' genius."

"Your lawyer, or Chosen?"

"My *lawyer*... The fuck?" J Money twitched and frowned. "Anyway... Sho-nuff, my lawyer found an angle: suspected laundering and abating. Think about it: this is millions we're talking about. Knowing Chosen's scheming ass, it's *gotta* be ill gotten gains, so my lawyer reported it. Okay, Chosen was talking *all* that shit around lunch time yesterday. It wadn't eem three hours good before my lawyer had a faxed document watermarked by the Office of the Secretary of Treasury. That document was forwarded to the bank who – come to find out – had red-flagged Chosen's bank account."

"For what?"

"The bitch had a deposit clear for eighteen mil," J Money barked.

Sawyer's fists landed on her hips. "Eighteen million!" Sawyer then gazed into an abyss of confusion, mumbling to spirits. "Was it the lottery? A lawsuit? Inheritance?"

J Money's head wagged no on all counts. "The depositing institution was a First Marin Bank out of Carlsbad, California, and get this: the account where the money came from belongs to a life insurance company. Nobody but Trap. He must've had a life insurance policy with Chosen as the beneficiary."

Sawyer raised tight fists in front of her face. "I *knew* there was something! I am not crazy!" She savored the vision of saying *I-told-you-so* to Travis and Gil. "The name of the insurance company?"

"Global Life."

"But wait," Sawyer paused. "Why would Trap have Chosen

on his insurance policy? It's not like they were married; they were only engaged."

"Not even engaged. Man… one day Trap said some shit about marriage just to get out the doghouse. Chosen turned around and bought herself a ring with *his* credit card, telling everybody they was engaged; they wadn't never engaged."

"She bought her own ring? If that ain't thirsty…" Sawyer's head shook and then stopped. "If they were not truly engaged, then this life insurance policy is even more confusing."

"Here's what I gather." J swallowed hard and tugged his nose. "A'ight, so… Trap made Chosen quit her job because he thought work stress made her miscarry the first child. So, here's Chosen, carrying this man's baby – her lottery ticket in her womb – knowing she got em for eighteen years, but Chosen was thinking like: what if something happened to Trap? Dead man can't pay child support. Trap's mother gets everything until the child become of age, right… Chosen was constantly bitchin' about all of that to Trap." J's eyes rolled while his handmade mouth nagged in his ear. "Ask me how I know… Because Trap always came to me with his women issues."

"Wait, wait." Sawyer had folded her arms. Her eyes, shut in deep thought then popped open with her question, "Chosen was asking him for an insurance policy? Talk about bold."

"Actually no – come to think of it. The insurance policy is what Chosen *settled* for. She first demanded a house: paid for, cash," J. Money clapped his final three syllables.

Sawyer raised a hand to put J on pause. "Chosen *knew* the

house was never going to happen; that was a negotiation tactic. Put the initial bid out of reach and then haggle them down to what you wanted in the first place."

"She almost didn't get *that*. I told Trap don't do it. In fact, Trap *told* me that he didn't do it. Guess he did after all… I guess he figured the insurance policy would cost him less than a house, and if they broke up, he could easily call up and cancel the policy. I guess he put it off for too long."

"Why didn't you and your partner buy Trap's share of the company?"

"Believe me, we was trying. This house we're standing in right now, I put it up for sale. Chosen beat us to the punch."

Sawyer's head shook in disgrace. "All that money you bring in, and you have to put your house up for sale?"

"You see the Wraith outside, ma? Nigga got some very expensive vices."

In disgust, Sawyer looked away, her eyes wandering up the wall where, high up, there is a circular window with a swirling bronze design as intricate as a coat of arms, the window large enough to receive the nose of a passenger plane. "Mr. Baxter," Sawyer sighed. "No one is going to believe that Chosen pulled off this type of murder alone. She had to have gotten some help, so I've gotta ask you, who else knew about this insurance policy besides you?"

J Money seemed to have smelled something foul. "Wait. I know you ain't trying to –"

"– We're going to follow the trail of evidence, so you tell me everything now, because anything you withhold only makes you look guilty when it comes out."

"*Follow* the trail," J. Money encouraged. "That's what I *want* you to do. Let's not forget, *I* called *you*."

"*After* dodging me. Maybe you called me only after she double-crossed you."

J Money nearly lost it. "Trap was my nigga! Fuck I look like plottin' to kill Trap? I will kill *for* that nigga if anything. As a matter of fact," J Money looked up at the ceiling, speaking well beyond it. "Bro, if I find out for sure this bitch had something to do with your death, bro?"

Sawyer raised a hand. "Control that anger, J. Do you see what you just did to yourself?"

J paced away, the hand gripped over his eyes, wiped down.

Sawyer followed J with her eyes. "If something happens to Chosen, you just made yourself suspect number one. Don't jump to conclusions. The insurance policy, the death, may all be one big coincidence. If we had the evidence, we'd charge Chosen, but we don't."

"I don't give a fuck!" J Money trembled with rage.

There was a moment of silence, Sawyer waiting until her interviewee looked at her directly. "If Chosen had help, who would it be? Maybe someone she started seeing right after she and Trap broke up. Maybe a friend or family member of hers?"

"What family? Far as I know, she don't got no family. It's like one day the earth just burped her up."

Sawyer asked, "Do you know anyone close to her – doctor,

or biologist type – one who could turn a disease into a murder weapon? Because no one believes that Chosen could."

J Money drew back. "Why – the fuck – not?"

"You think she *can?*"

J Money plopped down on the chair, mumbling. "I can't believe I'm 'bout to do this shit… Talkin' to the police…" He took a deep breath and began. "A'ight, one of our artists was involved in a shooting. He got one of his mans-and-them to get rid of the gun, but the dude kept it. It was a gold Desert Eagle, worth about ten thousand dollars. That gun had a *body* on it and *this* dumb fuck went behind our back, tryna sell it on the street for just two bands!" J Money was animated, his head rocking in the cove of his shrugged shoulders as he barked out the details. He kissed two fingers and raised them up. "On *everything*, me and Trap was 'bout to roll up on buddy, and leave his ass stinkin' in the woods somewhere, ya feel me? But Chosen didn't want her man catchin' a case. She said, 'Wifey got this.'" J Money paused to mime his initial reaction, a slow head-turn with his brow puzzled. He then snapped out of it and returned to storytelling. "So, Chosen paid lil mans a visit, offered him a blunt – you know – a lil peace offering. Little did buddy know, Chosen had cured that weed in some kind of chemical. Word has it, Chosen left his apartment, and waited in the parking lot with one of our homies for like, a half hour. By then, the lil nigga was out like a light. Next –"

"– Wait." Sawyer's hand motioned like opening the curtain on the story. "What do you mean, 'out like a light'?"

"That weed. Chosen had something in it that knocked buddy out cold, like dead. Chosen and the homey went in and took that apartment apart, piece by piece, until they fount the gun – all along, steppin' over this nigga, movin' him from place to place… ya mans was *still* sleep. Underestimate Chosen if you want to. That hoe knows some shit."

"Nice story J, but you left out the names. If I don't have names, I don't have witnesses to what Chosen is capable of. You should know how this works."

J Money patted his chest as a way to refer to himself. "Aw naw, you got me messed up. J Money's got *no* idea how snitchin' works."

Sawyer's hands dropped and her shoulders slackened. "Right, you don't snitch, but you just gave me enough information to take behind the wall, find someone who knows the same people you know, and they'll gladly give me the names in exchange for a reduced sentence. So, do me a solid, will ya. Save me the leg-work and give me the name of either the guy who helped Chosen, or the name of the guy Chosen drugged."

J Money's head shook.

Sawyer pressed, "How about the guy she drugged? You didn't like him anyhow. And if *he's* willing to give a statement to what Chosen is capable of – since *you're* not willing – it could make her a named suspect in Mr. Miller's death. The insurance company will then contest the payout, which could undo the sale that put her at the helm of your company. So, quit dickin' around, J and give me the guy's name!"

"I can give you his name, but I doubt he'll even speak on it. Some things, a man will take to his grave." J Money suddenly started giggling with his fist to his mouth.

"Let *me* worry about that. I can be very persuasive." Sawyer studied J Money who, again, got a case of the giggles that his shaking head couldn't shake out. Sawyer asked, "What's so funny?"

J Money paused as if he considered sharing, but then waved off the thing he determined was too wild, too zany for ears.

"If it's important to this case, tell me what it is," Sawyer demanded.

J Money laughed anew, clutching his belly. "Nah, see... I'm about to tell you just how *gutta* Chosen is. Alright," J Money gathered himself with a deep breath. "Ok, Chosen knew dude would wake up and find the gun missing, and would blame her since she was the last person at his crib, so while he was knocked out, Chosen kinda staged things so he'd wake up thinking that a second visitor came in after her and *that* was who stole the gun. Here's what Chosen did: while dude was out cold, Chosen kissed lipstick all over his lips and face. And get this: she sodomized ya mans with a dildo and had the homie who was helping her beat-off on buddy's butt cheeks –"

"– Oh, God! She did what? Why not simply stage a robbery?"

"Maybe she thought dude would've suspected her of staging a robbery – I don't know. Chosen wanted to damage him, to shame him to where he'd never mention that night, or the stolen gun ever again. The lipstick says woman; the raw booty says man. Put 'em together and whatchya got?" J Money tried to suppress an impish giggle.

Sawyer's stomach turned in disgust, not only for what Chosen did, but also for J Money finding such humor in it. "So, Chosen's a rapist too. I get it. Just give me the guy's name."

J Money ran a knuckle under his eye to wipe a tear. "*What guy's name?* You talkin' bout the guy who woke up to a raw booty hole, cheeks dumped on, and a handwritten note, saying *I'm so glad I came to the wrong apartment, and that you let me in.*" J Money, sniffling, explained. "If th ey st aged a ro bbery buddy could go around seeking hood justice, maybe through process of elimination find out it was Chosen all along, but there ain't no hood justice for a dude asking around about the tranny that robbed him."

"Do *not* use that slur in my presence, J," Sawyer yelled, "The name!"

"Ok, damn, ma. His name's Amare Clark. Street name's Sosa."

"Sosa?"

"Like Sammy Sosa. He used to play minor league baseball and he had a reputation for always *S*moking *O*n *S*omething *A*wesome." J Money shrugged.

*

At midday, just hours after the footrace at the park, they were together again. Darius found himself at a hotel room door, a presidential suite, by the looks of it. Chosen was standing before him in a soft, white bathrobe, like she was draped in a cloud. The man's words were as hollow as an echo. "Everything in me, tells me I shouldn't be here."

Chosen turned and left the doorway, toweling her hair. "If you weren't *supposed* to be here, you wouldn't be."

"Fate? Is that *really* your angle? The only reason I'm here is, you threatened that if I didn't rush over here, that the deal was off the table. Got me leaving work early and stuff."

She stopped in the middle of the room and turned. "Regardless, you're here."

"*Here* just so happens to be in a hotel room with a…" He stopped short of saying beautiful woman. "I'm a married man," Darius said, as the door closed behind him.

Chosen walked over, hooked his arm and ushered Darius to the couch. She sat next to him. As she crossed her legs, her whole right thigh slipped through the split of her robe. "And you'll *still* be a married man after we talk business. I apologize that we had to meet at a hotel, but the renovations on my new home isn't done yet. The reason I needed you here right now, is because my partners called a meeting that'll start a couple hours from now. Before I walk into this meeting, I need proof that I have your commitment to the project."

"I still haven't discussed this with my wife."

"What is there to discuss? This will be extra income for you and your family – a handsome income, at that. I'm not asking you to slang dope, bro; it's just music."

"Music is not – and never will be – 'just music' when it comes to my wife and me."

"Is that why you gave it all up? For her? But are you ever whole without it?"

"I didn't give up nothing. I still play – at home. I taught my daughters to play. I'm involved with the music ministry at church, and–"

"–And *still*, you are dead inside. I've seen what you're capable of. If you let music have its way with you, everything else would be secondary, but you act like you're afraid of it."

"Keepin' it one-hunnet, music never caused us no problems. It was the hopscotching from city to city while she was pregnant with Star… the drinking… my world swirling around in a cloud of smoke… the women… not that I've ever done anything with *any* of them; they were just always hanging around, in the way."

Chosen eyed him, catlike. "You never cheated on your wife?"

"Never. But early in our marriage, *she* wasn't so sure."

"Well, I'm just asking for studio time. I'm not asking you to travel or perform, so what's your excuse? Most of the work, you can do from home. All I'm asking is Saturday afternoons in the studio. As I said, I'm doing what *has* to be done. No one's making authentic R and B anymore. Every other music genre gets to sing about love, while we're making music about spending racks, and getting high of molly and Percocet. My label is the only label willing to do something about it."

"Don't let *me* stop you."

"So many of our major record labels focus on Trap Music.

Why? Because you can't find an industry more dominated by young men with criminal records. Who else would you expect to put the humanity and emotion back into black music besides the only female chairman of an industry-leading label? I'm creating a whole new division in my company to make this happen. R and B needs to be raised from the dead and its savior is sittin' up here, telling me he's too busy doing carpenter shit?"

"Savior?" Darius fixed his eyes on Chosen; it would take more than flattery to con him. "Lemme try walking on water – see how that works out."

Chosen pulled a zip lock bag out of the pocket of her robe and dangled it. In the bag was a rolled blunt. "Do you smoke?"

Darius sighed. "In a past life."

"What you need to do is relax, bruh. You're tense." Chosen aimed the blunt like a feeding spoon. She came forward as he leaned away, but then Darius stopped; thinking if he leaned any further, she's liable to climb on top of him. Chosen pressed the blunt between his lips. Darius's eyes widened and crossed as if he were watching a butterfly land on the tip of his nose. Chosen took a lighter and lit the blunt with one hand, while the other hand massaged the back of his neck. She watched him take a long pull and hold it in. He tried to pass it back to Chosen, but she craned back with one hand up to God, begging pardon. "Forgive him Father for he know not what he do," she said to God. Next, she said to Darius, "Weed makes me horny. A few pulls off that, and I'm liable to rape you, boo-boo."

The married man cancelled the topic of discussion with a

sickly look-away. Nearly twenty years into his sobriety, there Darius was, smoking, the blunt between the pinch of his thumb and index, knowing it could trigger his drinking. He let Chosen do most of the talking. She talked about music, her plans, how she admired his sound. All along, Darius's focus strayed. He couldn't look at anything without being consumed by it. Staring at the floor, the beige carpet, he was an ant immersed in the dunes of wool. He looked over, sleepily. "Do I look high?"

He noticed that he was getting heavy and stiff, his body solidifying like concrete. He was becoming a monument, like Abe Lincoln locked in his chair for eternity. Darius's eyes, alone, were imbued with life. He peered left and right; What's-her-name had disappeared. He had no idea how much time had passed – if centuries had elapsed, and then his eyes, too, began to fail him, its wetness thickening like tar.

*

Sawyer knew Sosa would run. On the way to his home, she researched the name in the database and learned that he had a bench warrant out, on a simple possession charge. After banging on the front door, announcing *Atlanta P.D.*, she snuck along the side of the house, just a car's width between the mustard awnings and the chain linked fence bordering the adjacent yard. She went along the crop row of grass between tire-worn tracks. She stalked past a ten-speed bicycle leaning on a rusted grill. She ducked below the side windows, her firearm down by her side. For a moment she was distracted,

69

studying the ground where there lay the detached arm of a baby doll embedded in the dirt. In that moment, Sosa, just ten feet away, had eased past the house's edge and into view; he was at the fence, bracing to leap. They startled each other, snapping to attention in a heart's thump. "I only wanna talk," Sawyer said.

"Is that right…" The young man is stalky, yellow, freckled, his brow maddened by the bright sun.

Sawyer holstered her weapon. "Sosa. Hear me out, okay?" He backed away, an open hand grazing the top of the fence. Sawyer came forward hesitantly, speaking softly, like trying to win the friendship of a stray; any sudden movement breaks trust. "You're not in any trouble. Promise. I only wanna talk. No harm in that."

"While you' steady telling me you *wanna* talk, you could've done said what it is."

"Someone did something really bad to you. And I'm looking to prosecute them."

"Somebody do me dirt, *I* handle the shit."

"How about when you don't even know who did it? When you wake up and all there is, is an anonymous note."

His head dipped, his face wincing as if he were in pain. "Naw. You don't know nothing. I ain't *told* nobody nothing."

"What do you remember about that night, Sosa?"

His eyes closed and his head shook. "I think I let this broad in my house. Turns out, she must've been a dude. What do *you* know about that night? You should be answering the questions and *me* seeking justice."

"Maybe you dreamed letting someone in your apartment. That never happened." Sawyer's head cocked curiously. "You didn't black out from a high. You were *rendered* unconscious. There was no consent." Sosa's knees buckled. He held onto the fence, balancing against it. Sawyer approached. The neighbor's dog twitched out of its sleep and came out of the shade of the shed's shadow. Sosa, so lost in his grief, didn't seem to hear the barking, coming in shots of three. Sawyer added, "We can put this person away for a very long time."

He straightened upright holding his thumb to his chest. "I'll save y'all the trouble. Tell me who 'this person' is."

"You don't need to know that right now. Just tell me you'll come down to the station."

Tears sparkled in his eyes. His cheeks tensed, grief imitating a smile. "I got a warrant."

"Give me by tomorrow morning so I can get a deal in place for you. If I don't see you down at the station first thing tomorrow morning, I'll have to *act* on those warrants. Show up and that simple possession charge goes poof into thin air."

Sosa's head shook in rejection. "Come to you for what, so y'all can make me take the stand and relive the shit I've been trying to forget for over a year now?"

His concerns, Sawyer observed, is no different from male to female victim; the fear of shame, the crucible of being dissected and reliving his victimhood in front of a jury of strangers. "Standing up to it. Facing it. It's how you take away the power it has over you."

They stopped talking. The dog kept barking. Sosa's eyes narrowed, his mind time-traveling his past. "So, the last person I saw that night was Chosen. But I remember her leaving. Plus, she couldn't have dropped nothin' on me because I poured my *own* drinks."

"There was something in the *weed*. Propofol, I'm guessing."

"I would know if my shit was laced."

"Chosen is very good at what she does."

"Y'all sure y'all ain't got this wrong? There was something else that Chosen, as a woman, *couldn't* do." The thought of it nearly made him wither where he stood.

"She had help. A man –"

"– Who! Tell me who!" His fist punched his open hand. "That's the mother fucker I need to see!" A tear escaped down his cheek and then another, faster than he could wipe.

"You were penetrated, but not by *any* man. She used something artificial. The semen you found, was from manual stimulation. They came for that Desert Eagle. They did what they did so you wouldn't pursue the theft of the gun because of the shame of the rape that came along with it. Your shame is their only protection, Sosa." Sawyer noticed a shift in Sosa's weeping, coinciding with the realignment of facts. Somehow knowing that he wasn't copulated by a man, gave him some relief, but he was still a rape victim. Sawyer embraced him. "Look, we don't have to mention the rape if you don't want to. We only need a statement on how she drugged you, which implicates her in a homicide we're investigating." The man's chin rested on Sawyer's shoulder. She rubbed circles on his back. "Tell me you're coming down to the station tomorrow morning, Mr. Clarke." His crying head trembled yes.

A woman, late twenties came out, showing concern, but also with a shimmer of jealousy towards the woman embracing her man. She asked, "What's going on out here?"

Sawyer backed away from the embrace. "Talk to her. It's too big to hold inside. It'll split you at the seams."

THE VIGIL

Of one thing, Sawyer was sure: her husband was being petty. He ignored his phone all day to avenge his rejection the night before. Sawyer, parked on the curb outside the candlelight vigil, chastised Darius's voicemail. "D," she sighed. "I'm not doing this with you, ok. This is petty. Call me when you get this message," she demanded, but not without the obligatory, "Love you."

She teased her bang in the rearview mirror and re-touched her lipstick. She was running late. She speed-walked in six-inch heels toward the assembly. The crowd was hushed, but piping with emotion. Program speakers sat in a row behind a platform with a microphone stand. The lone, broken voice of a colleague and friend spoke of the wisdom of loss and of the guilt of living on; the sound system vaulting her message up through the treetops, descending over the crowd like a net. Sawyer wandered along the enlarged photographs of

Miss Appleton atop ski slopes and hiking; she was a woman of adventure. Other photos showed her nested in family and friends with an ever-present smile, arms spread in a bit of showmanship. She was full of life; all the more sobering to see flower arrangements en lieu of her death, just hours after her parents made the heart-wrenching decision to pull the plug. The evening was somber, yet blessed. Maybe the wind swirled a certain way, or maybe it was a young lady Sawyer overheard in passing say, *She's here, right now. I can feel her among us.*

From the rear, Sawyer spotted Travis chatting with a swirly-haired blonde, a starving artist type in a cloth dress and panama hat. As Sawyer passed through murmurs, she noticed the woman's bashful shine as she smoothed a ribbon of hair behind her ear. Apparently, Detective Travis wasn't discussing the case as he should have; he was flirting.

If Sawyer was not upset with her husband, she would've never approached Travis from behind to hug his waist and pull his arm around her shoulder like a cozy shawl, even sizing up the woman in mach contempt. "Hi, I'm Aisha, and who might you be?"

In shock, the young lady eyed her suitor, her cheeks rosy with embarrassment. "Why... pleased to meet you Aisha. And *I* am... Just Leaving, actually." She backed away, hands up and determined to stay clean of their mess.

Travis tried to clean it up. "No, you don't understand. This is my *partner*" – precisely what the woman suspected. She faded back into the crowd of mourners.

Travis's head lay back, agonizing the loss. "What do you think you're doing?"

"Keeping you on task," Sawyer answered, as she threw his arm off of her and faced him. She noticed Travis's shirt, unbuttoned four from the top, exposing his chest, the straight canyon cut down twin plateaus of muscle. Sawyer began buttoning his shirt. "We've got much more important business to attend than you sniffing behind skirts."

Travis noticed that Sawyer was not in her work slacks and flats. Until that blessed night, Detective Travis had never seen his partner so polished. She was taller in heels, vibrant in full makeup, her face – *goodness*, Travis thought – was finished like a jewel. Her strapless cream blouse and amber skirt hugged her body like no work-kakis ever could. His eyes followed the glisten of her trophy legs all the way down to the feminine curve of her instep standing in high heels. Travis bit his bottom lip, in awe-struck appraisal. "Damn Sawyer."

Sawyer rolled her eyes.

Travis raised hands, pleading his case. "Just complimenting. That's all."

"Is *that* what you call a compliment?"

Travis smiled wryly. "Let me try again. You look damn beautiful, Sawyer."

She honored his correction with a nod. "Thank you. You're looking rather dapper yourself, young man," she ribbed.

Another speaker approached the microphone; the assembly shuffled to face front. Travis and Sawyer followed suit, focusing ahead, trying not to look like cops. "Where've you been all day," Travis whispered, from the crook of his mouth.

Sawyer, an even better ventriloquist, replied, "Solving this damn case, is where I've been."

"How are you solving the case while I was elsewhere doing the same thing."

With a competitor's glare Sawyer countered, "You don't have *half* of what I got."

Travis raised a brow. "Wanna bet?"

"Chosen had a life insurance policy on Mr. Kendall Miller to the tune of twenty million dollars."

Travis snapped. "Twenty *million* –" The couple in front of them looked back, aggravated half-faces rotated over their shoulders. Travis blushed and apologized. He then whispered to Sawyer. "Come to think of it, though, a twenty-million-dollar policy is par for a guy of Mr. Miller's wealth, so don't get caught up on the amount."

"I'm caught up on how she used the money to buy his company," Sawyer winked, as if, on that note, she'd killed the debate.

"Congratulations, Sawyer. You got *motive*. I've got a witness who says she walked in on Meegan and Cofield when the man threatened to kill Meegan. That's *intent*."

"Touché, Mr. Travis, but check this out: you say Chosen isn't capable of the crime? Well, I found out she possesses the know-how to put people under general anesthesia."

Travis leaned in. "But do you have a *witness?*"

"I'll gladly introduce you to Amare Clarke tomorrow morning when he comes in to give his statement." Sawyer then shaped her hand into an L against her forehead and mouthed the word *Loser*.

Travis's hand wiggled at his throat. "Who me? Pssht," he dismissed. "You' *right* to wear that L on your forehead like that. Gil mentioned your witness but he said it wasn't enough."

"That's why we're here."

"I'm not done tellin' you how I –" A crowd hush cut Travis's explanation. The speaker buckled with grief. While T ravis waited to say his piece, he eyed Sawyer's profile, pondering the year since he convinced himself that he wasn't in love with her. Seeing Sawyer standing there unaware, candlelight glowing like morning on her face, roused his feelings again. He tried to talk himself out of it. She's not going anywhere; she's married, he thought. Her heart is an impenetrable vault. He sighed, thinking he'd do better not to torture himself with wondering how to break the lock, nor daydream about the lifetime of riches that lie therein.

Travis and Sawyer were not alone. Chosen was there. She stood at the outskirts of the vigil, outfitted like a jogger. She didn't expect to see the two detectives there, standing shoulder to shoulder, certainly not acting how they were acting – the whispering back and forth, Sawyer's earlier buttoning of Travis's shirt, and Sawyer's short skirt, looking fit for a date. Chosen smirked as she recalled the advice she gave the sexy male detective during interrogation. Considering how chummy they seemed, Chosen thought maybe the brother took the advice to heart.

Luckily, Chosen had spotted them before she got deep into the crowd. She was slowly retreating backwards, eyeing her exit, slipping through a group of dog walkers onlooking while their park was held hostage for a day; candlelight dashing shadows across the grass like ink. Chosen noticed how Sawyer was sensing something, how she checked back over each shoulder.

Travis sensed Sawyer's paranoia. He asked, "You good?"

"Don't look now... Chosen is here."

"You trippin', Sawyer. If all that booty was on deck, I would've spotted it by now."

"Just a second ago, she was standing at six o'clock, twenty yards off."

"And now?"

"I've lost track of her." Sawyer scanned around inconspicuously. She gave a head signal for Travis to follow her as she began walking.

Travis went along with a sigh. "You see her?"

"If we go this way, I might."

Travis, hoping to take the wind out of his partner's sail, said, "Did I mention that Cofield knew Kendall Miller?"

They were walking side by side on a carpet of grass. Sawyer's head turned ninety degrees. "If Cofield knew Miller, then he lied to us."

"Cofield *despised* him, actually. Miller was the reason why

Meegan broke up with him. Turns out Meegan and Mr. Trap were talking about marriage."

Sawyer nudged Travis with an elbow. "See the espresso shop across the street? Chosen just went in."

The two detectives marched double time, Travis doubting the endeavor. "What are we supposed to do? We don't have the right to apprehend her."

"I just want to talk to her," Sawyer said, as they entered the all-night espresso shop. From the entrance, they scanned the place. Sawyer's hand pointed from under her chin. "Restroom."

They covered the ladies' restroom door, each on a side, backs to the wall, smiling to calm the patrons who seemed to sense danger. As quick as a revolving door, Sawyer went in the ladies' room and came out. "There's one in the stall. Not Chosen. Maybe not even human by the smell of it," Sawyer said, with a wrinkled nose.

As the door swung closed, Travis caught the foul breeze and then choked like a cat on a hairball. They hurried down the cramped hallway en route to the exit. Travis stopped Sawyer with a tug on the elbow. "What's the rush? How about a cup of coffee?"

Sawyer went blank at his impudence. "We've got a job to do, remember?"

"Wasn't *my* idea to come here. But I figure, since we *are* here…" He handed the clerk his debit card and ordered caramel lattes. "You'll love it. Promise."

Sawyer ended up staying, against her better judgement. She

and Travis sat at a high table, huddled over frothy cups. Sawyer asked, "Your witness, who is she?"

"Chelsea Dwyer. Med student like Meegan. She was Meegan's friend; her go-to."

"Well that's just dandy, but what does she know?"

"Chelsea knows, that before Trap came into the picture, that sweet, adventurous angel who all those candles are lit for, was juggling like five dudes." Travis's hand splashed open five fingers.

"And who the hell are *you* to judge," Sawyer said, kidding but not kidding. "What's good for the goose is good for the gander."

Travis sipped. "About ole Cofield… Bruh was ticked when he learned that he wasn't Meegan's one and only. Cofield straight flipped when he found out that one of Meegan's fuck-boys was a *brotha*, and that the brotha was winning, even though he degrades women in his music."

Sawyer's cup stopped short of her mouth. "Think Meegan was in love with Trap or his millions?"

"All I know is that Trap was in love with *her*. He proposed after only a few dates."

"That's the same man who had Chosen out here stressed out, miscarrying babies and buying her own engagement ring," Sawyer's head shook sorrowfully. "If only plastic surgeons could implant class and a moral compass, Chosen would've been *chosen* by now." Sawyer took a careful sip of the hot drink. They went quiet for a spell, and then Sawyer was ready to pick up and go. "We'd better get back. Let's take these with us."

"Sawyer." Travis trapped her hand to the table with his.

"What's up?"

"There's no need. We already beat the clock. Gil's already made the decision to name Cofield as a suspect, so forensics'll get to examine Meegan's body."

Sawyer flopped back and exhaled in defeat, her thumb flicking the side of her cup. She wished it was Chosen who would be charged for the murders.

"By the way," Travis called. "That ghost we chased in here tonight? I'll keep it between just us, alright?"

Sawyer looked him up and down like he was short. "My judgement is not clouded by this case, Travis – if that's what you're implying. I *saw* her."

"Where she at, then?"

"If you really wanna do me a favor, Detective Travis, pretend I'm one of the guys and spin it as a simple miscalculation. Don't make it out to be some sort of meltdown because I'm a woman." Sawyer was done with the conversation; she'd said her piece.

Travis's hands slid back to the edge of the table as he sat up straight. "Don't do that, Sawyer. I'm not that guy."

Her brow flattened in judgement. "Maybe you're not that guy, until Gil's around. Yesterday, when we were interrogating Chosen, I noticed that when Gil showed up, your allegiance changed; partners don't do that, ok. I know you got aspirations bro, but chase them in your own skin, that way you don't have to switch up in front of the bosses."

"That had nothing to do with Gil, but everything to do with that bootleg interrogation." Travis then sighed in surrender. "What do you want me to do? How could I make it up to you?"

Sawyer shot him an unforgiving look. "We don't even roll like that, Travis."

"Look, Sawyer, as bad as I want to be right. I've gotta admit that what you found on Chosen today sounds really compelling. We had – what – a day and a half to break this thing and you nailed it; Gil just happens to be biased towards the information I found on Cofield. Look, if you want Chosen as the focus of this investigation, I'll back you. You and me, we'll go to Gil first thing in the morning when your witness shows up."

She sighed. "But really, after everything you've found out on Dr. Cofield, I'm not so sure anymore. Thanks for the offer, though. You can be a real sweetheart when you wanna be."

Travis tried not to show, in his face, that he'd just learned something: it's not the open doors, nor the compliments about her looks; it's valuing her ideas, taking a position beside her on her stances, is what softens her. Travis asked, "My question is, how'd you know Chosen was even worth going after, in a case like this?"

"Be*cause*…"

"Ain't no *because*… You were right that there was more to Chosen than meets the eye. How is that?"

"The same way I know that Dr. Cofield is innocent. Because

Dr. Cofield doesn't have the blood of a killer running through his veins; Chosen does."

"I wish I had that instinct that you have," Travis said.

"Don't call it instinct. It implies that there's no intelligence behind it when there is. I call it metaphysical intelligence," Sawyer checked Travis's reaction to the name she'd just coined on the fly.

A dare in his eye, Travis said, "Well, I guess I have the metaphysical intelligence of a clam, then?"

Sawyer remembered her words and realized that Sgt. Gil had snitched, and Sawyer was embarrassed for it. "I only told Gil that because I didn't want a partner – *any* partner."

Travis used silence to toy with her.

Scrambling for exoneration, Sawyer added, "No, really. I didn't mean it."

Travis cancelled the victim role. "As if there's no truth to it… Not many can see the hearts of men." He smiled slyly. "You're special. I mean it."

Sawyer suspected that Travis was fat-mouthing her, so she withheld any response.

Travis said, "I'm curious though. How do you *just know*? What's the feeling? Is it like staring evil in the face?"

Sawyer pointed her considerations out the storefront, gazing at the distant vigil; the candlelight's halo over the mourners. "Evil is a real thing, but that's not what I see. I see the thing that licenses evil-doing; like narcissism on fleek."

"Narcissism?"

"A narcissism so inflamed, it perverts right and wrong into self-fulfilling prophecy. And just like people have nervous tics, and temper tics, there's a tic for that level of narcissism. I don't know it until I see it, but I know I saw it in Chosen." The two fell silent for a spell. Sawyer asked, "Your witness... You sure she'll blow the whistle on such a big-wig like Cofield? I mean, this is her career, ya know? Med student, aspiring surgeon, outing someone as big as *thee* Dr. Cofield; this is going to follow her. Are you sure she won't back out, for fear of retaliation from Cofield loyalists, or being blackballed in some way?"

"That was my question to her, off top. She says she *has* to do it. It's for her conscience, her healing."

"Cofield is the one who needs healing – threatening folks, cheating on the wife he claims to love."

Travis spied left and right. "Maybe he *does* love her. Just not love as *you* know it."

"Any love that makes concessions for infidelity ain't love. It's only a holding-on of something far less than love – the fear of being alone, maybe. But I'm sure you have a different theory to offer." Sawyer's eyes thinned, daring him.

Travis blushed. "Before you go-in on me, just listen for a sec, ok?"

"Oh, I'm listenin' sucka," she said, ala Sanford and Son's Ester Anderson.

Calmly, Travis added, "Love is in the mind, right... and the mind is this huge galaxy of experiences, fears, trials, familial connections, all bouncing off of one another." Travis's hands imitated a solar system around his head. This is the man who had a therapist con him out of the love he has for the woman who now sits before him. All his re-thinking reverted the moment he saw Sawyer in the glow of the vigil's candlelight, facing him, buttoning his shirt up to the neck. Now, the only definition of love that he abides is one that would make concessions for them. "The mind is too mixed up and random to think we can hold up the one ideal example of love and tell the other seven billion people in the world that, if you're not doing it this way, you're not doing it. No wonder half of all marriages end in divorce in this country. If we try thinking of love, instead, in the terms that it's rooted in, for any given person's psyche, we'll realize that many of the things we consider – within the realm of love – to be inappropriate, or to be relationship problems, aren't really problems at all."

Sawyer's cup stopped half raised. "Who'd you steal that line from?"

"From my own self-work."

Sawyer shrunk Travis with a glare. "Wherever you got it from, I doubt that its intended purpose was to try to excuse cheating."

Travis felt her chill and shook it off. "Not ex*cus*ing. Under*stand*ing."

Sawyer pounded the table. "Some things don't need to be understood!" Sawyer shrunk from her outburst, feeling embarrassed and ambushed by her emotions, a plucked chord reverberating at her core.

A bewildered Travis asked, "Are we still talking about

Cofield and Meegan?" He watched Sawyer go murky, as if she were sinking in a lake of despair; Travis knew that Sawyer was hurting. "Sawyer. Talk to me... Sawyer." He reached for her hand and Sawyer seized up, evading his touch, her fists tightened in front of her face. Travis saw tears. He got out of his chair. "Yo, yo," he uttered softly. "What happened?"

Sawyer gathered herself with an inhale through her nose and exhaled through the o of her lips. She said, "My husband's cheating."

"No way. He should know what he has – or maybe he wonders what he *doesn't* have. But it ain't nothing out there – not like you."

"He goes running every morning. Comes back drenched in sweat. Usually he beats me home before I take the girls to school. This time, he didn't. So, before I came into work. I swung by the house again and he was just getting back, but he wasn't sweating at all; he was dry as a bone. Today he wasn't answering his phone. I call his job and they say he left early..."

Travis's heart felt as large as a football in his chest. "There's got to be something I can do. I'm here for you."

"It's alright, I'm ok," Sawyer sniffled.

"No, Sawyer. You're not ok." He wrapped a consoling arm around her, his chin resting in the plush of her hair. Sawyer gave; she leaned into his embrace. Travis listened. He held off all outside sound, the latte machines buzzing in the background, the espresso shop's table chatter. He honed his ears to Sawyers heart, and then distinctly heard the impenetrable vault's lock slip.

POOR DARIUS

Upon waking from his marijuana-induced sleep, Darius found a handwritten note on the table. It read: *You were sleeping so soundly, I didn't want to wake you, Chosen.* Darius wondered what *Chosen* meant. He guessed that What's-her-name was referring to him, in short, as R&B's chosen one, or that she'd chosen him professionally (or romantically?). No. The thought seemed wacky that a woman of What's-her-name's caliber, who could pick any man by simply pointing, would settle on a married father of two in his mid-forties. The note trembled in Darius's hand as an airplane roared overhead. Darius was groggy, his back stiff as a coat rack. It was nighttime.

He popped to his feet, thinking he was in trouble. His phone read nine o'clock; still within the realm of using work as an excuse. He found six missed calls, all from Aisha. He cursed himself once, and then again. He had a kink in his neck and his mind was foggy. Memories surfaced in jumbled scenes. He remembered Chosen in a bathrobe, talking at length about music. He remembered the blunt between his lips, smoke curling. He pinched his shirt out from his body and sniffed.

Before that day, the last time he smoked weed, they were called spliffs, so the time lapse, Darius surmised, explained his extreme reaction, slipping into dead sleep for hours on end.

On the way out, he passed by a wall mirror, but went back to it. What he thought to be a bruise on his cheek was a smear of red lipstick. He wiped and wiped, ensuring every trace was gone. He reminded himself of his age, his marital status, versus What's-her-name's beauty and wealth and wrote the cheek-kiss off as innocent.

Darius moved quickly. He couldn't return Aisha's call until he figured out how to explain himself, so he hurried to his truck and peeled out of the parking garage, speeding homeward.

There was some traffic congestion around Central Park. He saw the congregation at the park's amphitheater and remembered that the woman he was preparing to lie to, was somewhere in that crowd, doing her job while worried sick about him. Still his mind searched for a lie but then his eyes landed on one.

Instead of *at* the candlelight vigil, his wife was across the street at the espresso shop, embraced with a man and wearing the skirt Darius often begs her to wear for him. Their twenty years had come to this. His heart broke and spilled the sands of time into his bloodstream, giving his anger a creepy, tingly texture. He grew lightheaded. All manner of intelligence leapt out of him and left behind a savage with only a three-word vocabulary: Aw *hell* no! He snatched the steering wheel and rode up the sidewalk, the truck bouncing as if by hydraulics, the air freshener bungying from the rearview mirror.

Patrons saw the headlights' blinding glare growing to consume them like afterlife. They scurried and braced for the torpedo blast and the spray of glass and brick, but there was no blast – only patron's screams and the rummage of chairs and tables as they'd dove for cover. The shadow of a man walked across the headlight glare. Darius slung the shop door open, eyes crossed with anger. "What the fuck, Aisha!"

Sawyer scrambled towards him, crazed and fretful, heart pounding like a marching band. "What is it, baby? Tell me the girls are okay!" A mother's first instinct.

Her husband's upper lip lifted in disgust, his eyes menacing. "This is what you call work?"

Sawyer held her head with both hands to make her spinning world stop. "Wait a minute, D. What are you asking me! You come rolling up on this place like a damn monster truck on some suspicion type shit, when I couldn't reach you all day?! Where the hell *were* you?"

His hand slung underhanded as if he'd tossed a bowling ball. "Why are you dressed like that!"

"Why do you *think*? Huh? I'm under cover!" Aisha's hand ran back through her hair as she looked around, taking it in, the headlights beaming inside, the customers and employees creeping out of hiding. She was incensed. "You must be out of your damn *mind!* Twenty years and you don't know me any better than this? Are you *kidding* me, right now?"

Travis came forward like a man hoping to cut in on a dance. "Look, maybe I can help clear things up."

Sawyer shot, "How about you don't!"

Travis continued anyway. "Bruh, we came in here after a suspect – what we *thought* was a suspect. I invited her to stay for a cup of coffee. That's it!"

Darius flinched as if he was liable to jump Travis but he had a second thought. Darius asked, "Say, bruh. What's your name?"

"No," Aisha yelled. "You don't need to be worried about him. Who you need to be worried about, right now, is me. *Where* have you been all day!"

Ignoring his wife, Darius repeated the question. "Your name, bro – that's all I'm askin'."

Sawyer warned Travis. "This doesn't concern you. This is *my* marriage!"

Travis peered around Sawyer and at the husband. "Naw, Sawyer. He done come in here, scaring folks half to death, when all we were doing was talking about *him*."

Darius peered angry eyes at his wife. His voice pitched high. "You' *confidin'* in this nigga?"

Sawyer turned and pushed Travis. "I told you this doesn't concern you. Get out!"

Darius was hit with an epiphany. "You wanted quality time after all – just not with me."

Aisha screamed, "Stop blowing this up D; this is nothing!" Aisha heard herself and hated how calling it nothing made it sound like something. Her husband's head shook in disappointment and in righteousness. Aisha flared, her pointer finger stiff as a blade. "D! I swear to God..."

That pointed finger, suddenly, was the only thing in the world that mattered to Darius. "Get your hand out my face!"

Travis stepped forward like Sawyer's bodyguard. "Or what!"

"Hold up!" Sawyer raised holy hands and spun around to Travis. "Didn't I tell you to get the steppin? Boy, is you dumb? Is you slow?"

Travis went back a step, explaining. "I was just trying to –"

"– No! *Try* to get your monkey ass outta my sight." Her eyes thinned. "You think just because I shared something personal with you tonight that something's changed? I'm just as repulsed by you today, as I was yesterday!" Her hands went to her hips, and a foot stamped to scold. "*Why* are you still standing here?"

Travis squinted to dull the glare from the truck lights, his mumbling lips debating with his ears over what he'd just heard, but then with an evil grin on his lips, Travis said, "Get it right, Sawyer. My name ain't Boy. My name is Detective Jeremy Travis."

Sawyer's head dropped.

"*Travis*," Darius blasted, his head yessing like a wood pecker in conformation. "That's what I *thought!*" He grew sick at the sight of his wife, saying, "I hope it was worth it."

Sawyer inhaled to yell at him, but thought better of it. "D," she exhaled. "You'd better listen to me, right now…"

Before closing the door behind him, Travis looked back. "You two love birds take care now."

Darius hurried to his truck. Aisha darted after him and got in the passenger side. While waiting on the clear of traffic, Darius began his rant. As usual, Darius used the argument as a platform to unload everything that's been bothering him since forever – even threatening to get into music again. Sawyer, awaiting her turn to let him have it, sighed and turned to the passenger window, her eyes steering inside the espresso bar just as they began pulling into traffic. She drew a bead on a woman in hooded sweats coming out of the bathroom hallway and into the service area. It was Chosen. All that time, Chosen must've been hiding in the *men's* restroom, which they never checked. Chosen pulled the hood back. A curl of hair teased at the corner of her mouth, her glare itself was a declaration of war. Sawyer, while hearing her husband's unfettered anger, and his litany of gripes, Sawyer stared Chosen down like an archenemy in her sidemirror shrinking in the distance as the vehicle drove away.

TO HAVE AND
TO HOLD

Before the day Ben held Chosen at gunpoint, she had stolen his spare set of keys to enter Ben's home and sabotage the exchanger on his furnace. As planned, she had showed up the following day hoping to catch Ben in his daily coma, and seize the opportunity to turn on the thermostat to leak carbon monoxide through the inside vents. Since Ben hadn't contacted her about getting what he wanted, in "every which-away," Chosen figured that that night, Ben stayed asleep while the carbon monoxide replaced the oxygen in his bloodstream, and then died of affixation. Oddly, there was no report of Ben's death.

Ben's silence – with still no report of his death, was odd enough for Chosen to take a road trip and see for herself.

The idea seemed risky, revisiting the scene of your own crime, but the countryside is low risk because it is secluded, with no surveillance cameras everywhere to capture and timestamp your coming and going. The countryside relies on eye witness, and Ben lives in a rural area where the homes are set back a quarter mile off the main road and neighbors live at the blurry perimeter of human sight.

With a gloved hand, she unlocked the front door. There Ben sat just like she left him, the thermostat still blowing, the house hot as an oven. The dead man wasn't reported missing because no one missed him; he was a loner. Even though Chosen had pinched the bottom of her hoody up over her mouth and nose, still the stench of human rot made her woozy. Benjamin sat with his knees spread, flies swarming him. For weeks his heart had stopped pumping against the pull of gravity, so his bodily fluids settled at the kink of his sitting body; a rancid slime pooled under him. Chosen snuck over to retrieve the gun and got an up-close view of brain fluid oozed at the orifices of his face, jelled to the consistency of pudding at his nostrils, ears and eyes, where wriggling spaghetti of maggots nested. Chosen gave a one-word eulogy, "Pig!"

That night Chosen lay in bed, staring at the hotel ceiling, contemplating the right moment to reveal the sexy selfies that she took with Sawyer's husband while he was unconscious on the hotel couch. Chosen sighed, regretting the pain it would inflict, but Detective Sawyer needed to be stopped, or at least distracted from this case by forcing her to focus on something more important than justice, like her marriage.

The news was absent of any report of an investigation. Chosen guessed that Detective Sawyer's persistence was a personal vendetta, like many jealous women who view Chosen's body as an unfair lifehack, as if Chosen, one day, arose from a surgeon's table imbued with mutant powers, to manipulate blindness in men, to where all they could see is her. They blame Chosen for simply walking into a room, instead of blaming their men for looking.

They feed into the stereotype that a woman with a body like Chosen no longer has to grow personally and spiritually as a woman, because life gets handed to them by rich men. Naturally, Chosen is never surprised by hatred coming from women who are complete strangers. Chosen has learned to be slow to anger, and slow to perceive shades of social rejection from women, but Detective Sawyer's was obvious, by how insulting the detective was during the interrogation.

If anyone should be jealous it would be herself, Chosen thought, while contemplating the good thing Sawyer has: a man who gave up *his* dreams for *her*, instead of the other way around. Darius couldn't get anywhere as a jazz performer, since jazz had already declined to the status of just a novelty, but as a producer with two chart-topping hits (one with Jaded and another with Gold Standard), he had the foundation for a career that could've won him national notoriety, mansions, and a revolving harem of exquisite women. Darius sacrificed it all for a regular chick, the type who'd have to pay to get into a night club. Darius is a good man, Chosen thought; the kind of man she could go for.

Now that the money issue is settled for life, her suitor doesn't have to be wealthy anymore – just kind, loyal, adventurous, mature, and attractive; all of the qualities she'd found in the man she was using to distract Sawyer from her case.

Chosen wished Darius could've participated in the intimacy they shared on the couch. For now, she could only relive the memory by viewing the selfies she took. Chosen reached over to the nightstand and retrieved her phone, and indulged in the images.

She scrolled through the selfies of herself and Darius to decide which pics would make the cut to be revealed to his wife, Detective Sawyer. Chosen teased, "Would it be this one?" Her chin tucked in appraisal at the image of her straddling Darius while he was unconscious. She marveled at the pixel clarity of her thigh tattoo. "Now that's *fire* right there," she said, because her wrist, in the foreground, blocks Darius's sleeping eyes, so in the still capture, he appears to be to be involved in it, even delighting in it. Chosen favored another pic, with Darius's face ears-deep in her bosom, or maybe the other one taken from above while facing her sleeping prince, her red lipstick transposed to his lips, Darius's head lying snug against the couch arm, sleeping soundly as if satisfied from lovemaking.

Before now, Chosen couldn't imagine ever coming for a woman's husband. She's too fearful of karma, but the way

Sawyer insulted her in the interrogation room, made Chosen believe that she needed to *be* Sawyer's karma.

*

Aisha screamed at her husband. "What the hell were you *thinking!*" That was the one question Sawyer couldn't seem to get a straight answer to. The girls were at Aisha's mother's, so she had all night to break him.

Darius replied, "I made an executive decision about my *own* happiness, babe."

Aisha slung her head to clear a bang out of her eye. "So, while you were ignoring my calls, were you busy taking your happiness into your own hands?"

"You act like *I* was the one hugged up, sippin' lattes." Darius, opening the refrigerator, gave a dis glare over his shoulder. "Like, where do you get off questioning *me?*"

"Negro *what,*" Aisha jerked so hard with that outburst, her bang fell again. "You been gone all day. I called your job and heard it from them – not from you – that you took off early? And don't *think* I didn't notice that dry ass shirt when you came back from your morning run." She watched her husband unscrew the cap of an apple juice. "You're holding back because you think I can't handle the truth. Give me the truth; it's what I need."

His brows went uneven. The truth: it's the daily concern of his detective wife; she's built a career around matters of truth. "You kiddin' right? How does twenty years with no infidelity issues earn this level of suspicion?"

Aisha pushed him, like a soft patty cake to the chest. "Should've been twenty-*one* years with no issues, so *damn* the years. I'm worried about today. Where were you *today?*"

Something pinched and twisted inside of Darius, turning him devilish. "I'm getting back in the studio." Not altogether a lie. "I'm a musician. Music is in my veins just like catching bad guys is in yours."

"You promised."

"I promised when I was like twenty-four years old, babe," he frowned. "But how are you asking all the questions when you were the one who got caught with the man who forcibly kissed you on the mouth last year?"

"I saved his life."

Darius's eyes rolled. "C'mon, now... Kissing you *in the moment* is understandable, but a week after the fact? Damnit that's premeditation. You should know that, *detective.*"

Aisha's brows reached; she had one better. "But did you have to ask, though? I came straight home and showed you my swollen knuckles from punching him in the face."

"Yet a year later, he gives you his shoulder to cry on?"

"It's what any decent person does for someone who's hurting."

"I ain't even trippin' off that, babe. I'm talkin' about when we were arguing. Why was buddy trying to step in, like he's that dude? What is it about yall's relationship that makes him think he can step to me?"

Aisha's hand, rubbing her brow, snatched down.

"Relationship! *You* don't even believe your own bullshit! You're just trying to switch the focus on me when we both know that the real reason you weren't answering your phone, and the reason you're now crawling back to music is all because I rejected you last night. Let's just call it what it is, D."

On that note, Darius was done. He was being cornered in the argument anyway, like she does with criminals much savvier than her church-going husband. Darius turned and walked, straight-backed, toward the living room.

Aisha was hot on his heels, arms spread in dramatic fashion. "Oh God, every time when you know I'm right, you start playing the victim. Think I haven't seen this before? Look, I'm not saying you actually *did* anything, but you're my husband and I know you. I know when you've done something you're not proud of."

He stopped in a flare up of emotion, but his mouth couldn't make words. He then continued speed-walking through the living room and towards the bedroom, a frantic mute.

Aisha followed. "It's better to tell me because if you don't, the thing I'll *decide* to hold against you is probably worse than the truth."

Darius thought about confessing. He could admit that he conducted business in a hotel room with a sexy woman in a bathrobe, but that nothing happened, although he did wake up with lipstick on his face. Worst case scenario, Aisha would believe something *did* happen, and then charge Darius with the murder of their marriage, sentencing him to life without the possibility of a happily ever after with the love of his life. Best case scenario, Aisha would believe him, word for word, that nothing happened, but still charge him with the reckless endangerment of their marriage, for going alone to a woman's hotel room, and then entering even after she answered the door in a bathrobe. Darius had no idea what that penalty would be. He found himself in envy of a criminal's privilege to know the penalty their pleas would render, but for himself, he could only guess. Trust took years to rebuild, and again Darius would find himself back at square one, with a hammer and a blueprint of Rome.

Sawyer took his silence for surrender; she massaged his hand. "Talk to me baby."

He sat down on the edge of the bed, lowered his head, frowning, weighing the risk and the cost of the truth. His only safety (aside from lying) was in a deeper truth, more telling than the events or his whereabouts. "All this is my fault."

"I'm not saying that anything's your fault, bae."

"No, it *is* my fault." He hugged himself and his face clenched.

Aisha could hear her husband's ego, his pride, breaking like an iced lake, popping with cracks zigzagging across its surface.

He continued, "We're doing *all* this carrying on because I was too proud to say three words to you." He bit his bottom lip to hide its trembling. A tear drop made an earthquake in their bedroom. Either he was disarming his wife's wrath, or he was hurt to the point that he couldn't hold it in – this being the man who waited four years after his father's death to shed the first tear; the hurt could be coming from anywhere, past wounds reopened, even. Darius is the only person alive whose tears could remove the planet from beneath her feet and leave her suspended helplessly in orbit. She knelt before him, searching for his eyes which he hid behind his hands, spread like an open book.

Aisha transplanted his hands from his face to hers. She palmed his chest. "What's going on in there, my love?"

His lips tightened and his head shook. "You can't go missing in my life whenever you get a difficult case, babe. My needs keep on needing, and it causes me to get distracted."

Aisha braced herself. He must be withholding something awful, she thought. The tears – the talk of distractions. It didn't matter that he'd somehow made her to blame for his actions; she only needed to hear him say what he'd done. Aisha gazed with sincerity. "I'm sorry. I'm sorry," Aisha said, her hand stroking back over his head. "What happened? You can tell me baby."

He sighed and looked up to the ceiling for help, for strength. "I need you, baby."

Aisha twitched. "What?"

"I need you."

She couldn't remember her husband ever saying those words. The man who acts like he doesn't even need sleep – needs her. She felt engorged with sorrow for him. Swift tears raced down her cheeks, as she stood and looked fondly from above, her two hands cradling his face, tears like glass in his eyes, shimmering in lamplight. "You know I love you, D." She kissed his forehead.

He nosed up for her lips. His kiss, the tender give in his lips, conveyed that *need* was sexual; he was humbled and begging for a lifeline.

For Aisha, banishing angst from their marriage bed to mend him, felt like maturation, felt holy. She sat on his lap and their kiss turned into a cosmic ride, unwilling to transition into the next thing, until Aisha pulled away and looked her husband in the eyes. Never more certain, she said, "Do what you want with me." Beyond those words, conversation was forbidden; in these matters, the flesh is wiser than the mind.

He was starving for her. He sucked her bottom lip and licked her throat with his whole tongue. Aisha's head pressed back in the pillow, studying his intensity. She bit her lip in suspense of the crazy lovemaking sure to ensue. Her fingers raked the sheets from the anticipation alone.

They braced for the douse of pleasure. They exhaled, open-mouthed, as bodies came together, a motion that begged repeating again and again for forever, their lips fastened throughout the ebb and flow, pleasure rising like tide, threatening to drown them both. Aisha's mouth flung open wide, panting airily, and leaking the feeblest moan. She felt the coming together of that flow, that throttle, that depth – and that orgasmic, radiating hot-spot that only her husband has ever known, but it's stationed right at the brink of pain. Fearing one overzealous thrust punching into her stomach, she clutched her belly to stave off disaster, but this man knows her, knows her by decades, knows her by fractions of an inch.

CAN I GET
A WITNESS?

Travis saw a call coming in from Sawyer. He frowned at the device, remembering her insult from the night before. He answered, half expecting to hear an apology.

Sawyer was frantic. She'd slept late, groaning as she recalled. "My car! I left it at the park!"

Travis was still salty from the altercation the night before. "Why are you telling *me*. I'm not your boss."

"I need a favor." She begged Travis to keep an eye out for Amare "Sosa" Clarke, because no one else knew he was showing up, since Gil showed no interest in the witness.

Travis listened while Sawyer described Sosa's height, build, the freckles. Travis never said no, outright. He was all impersonal grunts and yups. He even pulled the phone from his ear and gave it a ridiculous look when Sawyer reminded him that they were supposed to go down to Gil's office together and try to make the case for Chosen being the focus of the investigation. *Remember? Remember?* Travis hit the End button, *remembering*, also, when Sawyer had called him repulsive.

He gestured throwing the phone against the wall – it's how he felt, it's valid – but he kept his hand closed so the phone didn't fling out. He controlled the action, as he learned in therapy. The force of the throw that never happened had turned Travis around and suddenly, he was face to face with Gil, who looked on, baffled by Travis's pirouette. "Is you *on* somethin', man," Gil asked, but quickly waved off any chance to reply. Gil continued, "Y'all's witness, Chelsea Dwyer, just called. She's on the way."

"*Yall's* witness?" Travis chuckled into his fist.

"What's that supposed to mean," asked Gil.

Travis looked away in deep thought, his conscience eating at him. "I know Sawyer's your girl and everything, Gil, and I, for one, owe the woman my life, so this is especially hard for me, but there comes a point –"

"– *Say* it. Hell, I ain't got all day," Gil said while tapping his watch.

"Sawyer's been MIA."

Gil's arms folded and he raised on tiptoe. "Really…"

"Everything we got on Cofield, *I* got – while Sawyer was off chasing behind the stripper chick."

"She called me yesterday about some witness. I had to tell her again, that we weren't going down that road." Gil's jaw rippled from grinding teeth.

"Well, she ain't listenin' sarge. Not only has she been distracted on this case, but she's also losin' it, big dawg. Last night at the vigil, she led us off the damn scene on a wild goose chase, talkin' bout she saw Chosen. We ran up in this coffee shop, man… Sawyer busted in the bathroom – no Chosen. Ya girl's so far gone, right now, she's seein' ghosts."

Gil rubbed his chin, thinking about the Pringle case. "Seeing ghosts, huh? Wouldn't be the first time."

"It's getting to a point where I can't hide her mistakes no more. She knows I'll do anything she ask, off the strength of her saving my life, but I feel like it's getting manipulative, now. But *you* should know what I mean, right Gil?"

Gil squinted. "No, Travis, I *don't* know what you mean."

"I'm saying that ever since she got that Medal of Bravery, you let her do anything she want 'round here."

Gil's brows jumped. "Now, *that's* the sound of bullshit right there. Everybody know *I* don't play. As a matter of fact," Gil rubbed his chin. "As of this moment, you're the head of this investigation from here on out. Sawyer has a problem with it, you tell her to take it up with me."

"I won't let you down, sir," said Travis, as they shook hands.

Gil said, "So, here's the plan on Cofield. We don't know what the medical examiner will find on Meegan's body, so prepare for a character case. If Cofield had one affair, he's had twenty. Find the Me-Toos."

Travis glanced out of the station's glass front and saw the walking description of Sawyer's witness. Travis thumbed back over his shoulder. "Hate to cut and run, Gil, but based on what you just said, I gotta prepare a different set of questions for Chelsea."

Amare had just come in. Travis, slowed from a trot, offering a hand shake. "Amare?"

He looked up, dazed. "Yeah."

"Come holler at me for a second, my brotha." Travis turned him by the shoulders, redirecting him back outside. "Walk wit' me," Travis said as he glanced around conspicuously. Once he'd guided Sosa to a safe distance, Travis said, "Don't fall for it, bro. You 'bout to get hemmed up."

"How'm I 'bout to get hemmed up when I already talked to the lady detective?"

"Sawyer."

"Yuh. This something I got to do – for *me*."

"Thing is, Sawyer's telling you that that possession charge'll get dropped when, one: she don't call them shots, and two: she ain't never cleared it with those who do. That's why I'm out here talkin' to ya now... She made it sound like a sure thing, but she got you walkin' into a maybe, bruh."

Amare peered down the rows of parked cars, eyeing his exit. "Alright, so... Yeah..." He shook Travis's hand, extending the handshake to the length of his exit speech. "I can't fuck wit no maybes, mane. Good lookin-out my brotha," Amare said, as he began strutting away.

Travis pulled out a pack of cigarettes and stared at it again. He bought it on the way to work that morning, figuring the day would be too heavy, facing Sawyer after the previous night's rejection and now this new twist: sabotaging her potential witness, Sawyer's only hope to add legitimacy to her hunch about Chosen.

*

When Sawyer finally arrived at work, Gil pulled her in his office. Travis was out back, staring at the cigarette pack, contemplating how lighting up again would restart the slow-drip of minutes off the end of his life. He remembered the day he nearly lost his life all in an instant, had it not been for Sawyer.

Following up on a no-show for an interview, he and Sawyer went to the witness's home. Travis didn't wear a vest because it hides his chest muscles, and because they never suspected that the reason the witness no-showed was that her estranged husband showed up on a death wish and was holding her hostage.

Chilling screams came from inside. A single round fired. The screams ceased. Sawyer approached the house with her firearm held out stiff as a board, telling Travis, who had no vest. "Stay! Don't be crazy." Sawyer spied the windows looking for a shot, but almost caught one herself. A shot blew inches past her head; dirt splashed behind her. Sawyer couldn't return fire into the home without being sure the victim was down.

Seconds later, a full-cab pickup barreled out of the garage and banged into their unmarked car. Travis, who was squatting behind the car door, using it as a shield, was thrown nearly ten yards back, twisting midair, his gun sliding out of reach when he hit the ground. He was getting up slowly. He was disoriented, a nasty skid on his hand. The perp threw the truck in gear again, ignoring Sawyer, who was yelling for him to freeze. Sawyer noticed that a disoriented Travis was in the truck's path. Sawyer dashed. While running across the yard with everything she had, she still aimed for a shot, her elbows locked, one eye closed. The homicidal husband hit the gas again in an attempt to run Travis over. Sawyer, in the nick of time, popped the fatal headshot while tackling Travis out of the path of the truck which bucked down the driveway, squealed across the street and crashed into a parked car. Travis remembered coming to his senses while on the ground, Sawyer over him, with the sun and clouds providing a heavenly background. A woozy Travis said, *You're my angel.*

When one saves the life of another, a bond is made. Travis had witnessed this bond across lines of race, color and creed, thick as blood between men, but Sawyer is a woman – a woman Travis had always held in high esteem. She never bat an eye for a man other than her husband, as far as Travis could tell. She opts-out of after-work functions just to spend even more time with the man who she already shares a bed with. Travis, coming from a childhood where even a mother's love wasn't a given, he couldn't help picturing how it would be, nested in a love so sure and replenishable, while never having to worry about her sizing him up against the field.

Travis was raised by his grandmother. His mother was

a heroin addict who was always away, either in the streets, in rehab or jailed on short stints, so Travis was always either dealing with her absence or her reappearance. A child's world, so void of reality and understanding, allowed Travis to imagine that his mother lived far off in an enchanted place and that only her love for him compelled her return, even to this much lesser world of such gloom and gravity.

When Travis matured enough to know the reality, that his mother was right there in the neighborhood, prostituting and shooting-up in abandoned houses, he then hated his mother out of regret for once loving her, but when she died with a heroine needle standing in her wrist, her death made Travis love her out of regret for once hating her; this was Travis's discovery in therapy, the therapy he committed himself to, after trapping Sawyer's face to his, lips on lips.

The relationship with his mother put love in a vacuum of regret. His love, though valid in his heart, is dysfunctional in life, so his two children, a boy and girl, come from different mothers who've both went on to marry men who were more stable emotionally.

After getting little work done in the office, due to the anxiety of having to face Sawyer again, Travis was out back, leaning against the building with his cigarettes. He couldn't shake the previous night's coffee shop incident, where Sawyer treated him like he was nothing. 'Repulsed' by him, Travis shuddered. The comment was small, but the damage cataclysmic. Shards of his broken heart were floating in his chest like satellite debris.

His hands shook as he tapped a cigarette out of the pack. He wondered how he could face Sawyer now after betraying her, a betrayal that lead to Gil placing him at the head of the investigation.

Travis pinched the cigarette between his lips and raised a lighter behind a cupped hand. Having the instincts of a clam, he didn't sense Sawyer approaching his blind side.

Sawyer shoved him. "Bitch!"

"Girl!" He flicked the cigarette, eyes wide in a day-mare of the reflex that nearly happened.

"I thought you and me were supposed to be going to Gill this morning about Chosen."

Travis regrouped and again, backed into the side of the building, one leg up. "That *was* the plan, but your witness got cold feet."

"What conversation *did* you have with Gil then? Because he's accusing me of slacking on the case, telling me that I'm losing it? That I'm chasing ghosts?" Sawyer aimed a finger-gun. "That had to be you!"

Travis came off the wall, staring Sawyer down. "You think I went running to Gil? No, he came to me. When I told him you were running late, he spazzed on me like the shit's my fault – you know how he gets." Travis morphed into an imitation Gil, chest puffed, brows muscular with anger. "Where's Sawyer, what's she been up to, why the heck this, why the hell that – *Don't* give me that I-don't-know crap, Travis…" Travis morphed back to himself. "I tried to lie to him, but he pulled it outta me."

Sawyer looked ill. "So, you're mister innocent. I guess you had nothing to do with Gil appointing you as the head of this investigation, either?"

Travis turned hostile. "Hold up... Why are you even around me? Don't I repulse you?"

"*Now* you do. I'll be a damned fool to ever trust you again."

Travis watched her march away. He sensed that Sawyer was looking for a private place to weep. Back against the wall, a cigarette between his lips as he looked long and hard, realizing that if he had the power to bring forth Sawyer's tears, he's more dear to her than he thought. No; Travis tried to dismiss his thoughts. His thoughts – when it came to Sawyer – could not be trusted. He was 'doing it' again – making something out of nothing, he thought, but in a second flicker of thought, he bent the question. *Am* I? He took a pull from the cigarette and blew through his nose.

Travis spread Sawyer's words out before him like witchdoctor bones, picking them apart, looking for signs. When he reminded Sawyer of her being repulsed by him, her *Now I am*, meant that she was not truly repulsed by him as she said the night before; she'd spoken out of anger, Travis determined. How'd he ever believe the insult in the first place, he wondered, when earlier that night she put her arm around his waist and buttoned his shirt. Sawyer's exit line, 'I'll be a damn fool to ever trust you again,' also held a jewel; that *again* meant everything; it means she had already grown to trust him – trusted him enough to confide a marital secret and then cry in his arms. Travis had turned on Sawyer only because he thought Sawyer had turned on him in the espresso shop, but he was wrong. She was only putting on a show for her husband. Travis had mistakenly took everything she'd said to heart, so the hurt had stood up inside of him like a wall. He thought betraying her would demolish that wall of hurt, but it did not destroy it; it only effaced it with ugly graffiti. Travis pulled from the cigarette while listening to its crackle of ash. The blown smoke gave a visual of the bit of spirit that left his body. Travis was now dealing with the regret of betraying the woman who had saved his life.

THE CONTRACT

Darius needed answers – answers to take back to his wife who couldn't understand how he said he left work early pursuing a contract with a record label but didn't even know which record label, nor the record executive's name, nor the office location. Without those simple details, his excuse for his leaving work early that day, and being missing all day, sounded like pure make-believe. Darius also had his *own* question about the lipstick on his face.

He called the contact listed as Whats-her-name. She picked up with, "Hey, I was just fixin' to call you. Can you get away from work for a few minutes?"

Through the phone, she sounded busy, like she was outside walking. Darius replied, "I can't be taking off work like that."

"Come during your lunch then. I want you to meet the first artist you'll be working with."

"Before I agree to meet, I got a couple questions, first."

"I'll answer your questions when you get here. When I give you your advance."

"Advance?"

"Meet me at this address: 1232 Clairmont, okay?"

The office address answered one question, and a check in hand will answer all the other questions.

Darius went during his lunch hour. He assumed it was Clairmont *drive*, the commercial district, but the street numbers kept counting down past the Department of Veterans Affairs Medical Center, clearing block sixteen hundred, into Clairmont *avenue*, the residential district. Darius's head rotated as he past the VA building but he noticed, in the backdrop, the building for the Center for Disease Control and Prevention, which made him think about the mysterious rabies incident on the news, the one his wife declared was no accident. Urban legend has it that in the CDCs basement, behind retinal scan access, there are refrigerated vaults containing all known transmittable diseases, like affluenza and Hepatitis, flesh-eaters like MRSA, ancient diseases like leprosy and continent killers like the Black Plague. A cancer doctor, like the one involved in Aisha's case, could reasonably have a relationship with someone who houses the disease he's made a career treating – someone who has access to many other life-threatening diseases, namely, rabies.

1232 Clairmont avenue was no recording studio, nor office building. It looked like off-campus housing for Emory College, a two-story townhome with two mailboxes marked Upper and Lower. The Mercedes G-Wagon parked outside, he figured, belonged to What's-her-name. Darius was poised to knock when the curtain opened, revealing a young lady about twenty with an almond face, her hair cut lower than his. She opened the door and stepped back. Chosen got up from the couch, smoothing her dress. "This is the producer I was telling you about."

The slim young lady with jeans tight around her bony hips, scowled as if the man before her had fallen far short of her expectations, for someone wearing the title of producer. She asked, "Your producer works at Verizon?"

Chosen giggled. "For now."

"I'm Darius," he said, as he entered the cramped apartment, which smelled like Ramen noodles and book pages.

"Trinece," she said.

Chosen came over and hugged Darius tight like he was the afternoon's prize. She half-turned out of that hug, and said, "It don't matter where he's working or what he's wearing. This man can churn out hits in a clown suit. All I need from you, Trinece, is to show this brotha what you're workin' with." Chosen pulled Darius over to a worn, toothpaste blue couch and said to her protégé, "Let's get it, Trinece. This man is on his lunch break."

The young lady squared her shoulders, ready to blow, but stopped. "Should I do something slow or up-tempo?"

Chosen replied, "Sing something that shows off your range." She then twitched to Darius and slipped a gentle hand on his back. "Isn't that what you want, hon?"

Darius couldn't look at Chosen; her touchiness made him

uncomfortable. To Trinece, he said, "Give me something that best shows who you are as an artist."

Trinece began with a broken note but then stopped to collect herself.

"Take your time, girl," Chosen said as she clutched Darius's arm, the two like parents at a daughter's recital.

Trinece's head bowed, shoulders relaxed. She sipped a breath into her diaphragm, and out came heavenly chords that made her listeners' neck-hair sway like sea anemone, and their eyes stretch to nonverbal wows. Trinece gave Mint Condition's *Pretty Brown Eyes* her own personal touch, elevating it to a ballad. Her voice twirled on the higher notes like a Mariah Carey but on the lower keys swooped down husky like a Lauren Hill, the sandy crackles during her transitions brought forth remnants of the soulful moaning from the cotton fields that this very plot of land once was. Finally, Trinece reared back, slipped a hand behind her ear and stretched the word *heart* for five, six measures, her sound growing, ballooning the apartment walls, and then she cut the note razor thin and clean as porpoise's whistle. Just when Chosen and Darius thought she was done, their hands poised to applause, her voice dove on a crescendo of a jubilee hum.

Trinece read the reviews on their faces while silence hung like a stoppage of time. Only the elongated swoosh of a car gunning down the street outside started time again. Her audience of two gave a standing ovation. The young lady gave a ballerina's plié and asked, "You're still droppin' me off at work, right Chosen?"

Chosen replied, "I got you, girl."

Trinece went to the back to get changed.

Darius eyed Whats-her-name. "Chosen… So, *that's* your name." Another answer he couldn't go home without.

Chosen leaned away from his nonsense. "You knew my name, boy. Everybody know me. Trap's lady? But watch when we start churning out these hits, they'll be calling me Queen of Atlanta."

"Honestly, I didn't know your name until just now," Darius said, yet his wrinkled brows questioned his statement. "Or, maybe I did. That was your name on that note."

Chosen slapped her lap. "What'd you *think* it was?" No sooner than she'd asked the question, did she catch an epiphany like a flyball. "Oh… I know… You thought it meant that I *chose* you, or something?"

Darius turned bashful at the thought of how his forty-four-year-old-married-with-children behind, could see himself as her crush. He uttered, "I woke up with lipstick on me." He began to stutter. "And-and, me – as a m-married man – I can't let something like that go unchecked."

Chosen smiled in a gaze. "Funny…"

"Wha? What's funny?"

"The more you show me how loyal you are to her, the more I want you."

Chosen had confirmed this nonsensical attraction. Darius was stuck. He was dumbfounded, but then he realized his eyes were inadvertently trapped in her stare, so he turned away. "If it's my loyalty to my wife that attracts you, won't it ruin your attraction if I betray her?"

"Darius…" Chosen slanted to see him from a new, curious angle and her long hair spilled off of her shoulder. "If you can be loyal to *her*, you can certainly be loyal to *us*."

Darius's hand wiped down his face, leaving a smirk aimed at Chosen. His hand swatted in front of her, "Maaaan, stop playin', Chosen. You can have any man I want – I mean, any man *you* want."

Chosen spotted weakness in the man's stutter and coy smile. She swirled her finger at it and said, "You see, all this back and forth without you shutting me down? It only lets me know that you're open to it."

"I'm *not* open to it, actually. It's just that I can't stomach rejection; neither side of it. So, I was hoping you would simply lay off; that way, we avoid having to have a difficult conversation."

Chosen sighed. "Look, I never wanted a conversation at all. I figured at some point, while doing music together, maybe one day, the stars would align and…" Chosen sighed as she joined her hands and shrugged. "Anyway… Now that chance is ruined. Now that it's out there, we can't even have a friendly hug without seeming like we're either leaning into it or away from this… thing…"

Darius found the remote on the table and turned on the TV as a distraction, but then he thought of something better; he checked his watch and stood in that pose, said, "Looks like half of my lunch hour is already gone so…"

Chosen stood too. She dug in her purse and said, "Before you go. I have something for you." She pulled out a check and approached him. She offered the check but teased it back. Chosen then crept forward, cleavage leading her. She held the check behind her back. "Promise I won't do anything she won't approve of, but indulge me for a second. I have something to tell you." She leaned to his ear and whispered, "Do not tell Trinece about this check."

Darius locked eyes with Chosen, simply to lull her. He even put his arms around her to steal the check out of the hands behind her back.

Chosen marveled at him. "You tricked me. That'll cost you." Her eyes named the price, a kiss plus tax, but Darius turned away. Chosen swayed with him like a bird of prey sight-tracking its scurrying lunch, but then her eyes landed on the television. Her face changed, as if she'd seen a ghost.

Darius asked, "You a'ight?" She was stone. Darius nudged her. "Chosen?"

She snapped out of it. "That's happening right here." It was the Edward Cofield case.

"Crazy ain't it?"

"You know about this?"

"Being that my wife is one of the detectives working the case…"

As if she didn't already know, Chosen asked, "Your wife is a detective?"

"Yes. She carries a gun," Darius winked.

"They say this doctor's been charged and booked? Why, I had no idea... Did your wife tell you if there're *other* suspects in the case?"

Darius's head wagged no.

"No, as in she didn't tell you, or no as in no other suspects?"

"She's not supposed to talk about her cases."

Trinece came up the hallway but stopped at the sight of Darius and Chosen standing so close. The pair backed away from each other, Darius, in shame before a young lady that bears a likeness to his oldest daughter – seeing this married man so close to a woman who is not his wife. Chosen cleared the tension by announcing her departure. "Sorry, y'all, but I gots to go."

Chosen hurried out despite Trinece's protests, the door slamming on Trinece's, "How you gonna do me like that?"

Darius was stuck giving Trinece a lift to work. The ride began in silence. Darius half-turned to engage in small-talk, but seeing Trinece under the hypnosis of her smart phone, he let it be. Trinece turned to his gesture to speak, but saw that her driver was only fixing his collar. Their fidgets made an awkwardness that only conversation could put away, so Trinece shared what she was researching on her phone. She turned up the volume on an old Jaded music video she found on YouTube. She set the device on the console and started grooving, fingers snapping on the end of rolling wrists.

Darius laughed. "You like that?"

"This joint is hot, even today – not that you're old or

anything," she explained. "So, you really produced them?"

"First and second album only. That was the last project I thought I'd ever produce, until now," Darius said.

"You worked with Chosen before?"

"I didn't even know her name until I heard you say it."

Trinece looked away and mumbled, "Some people work fast, I guess."

Darius's eyes came clear off the road to study Trinece's expression. He asked, "What's that supposed to mean?"

"I saw y'all," Trinece said, with a scornful shy-away.

"What you saw was all there was to see: just a hug."

Trinece was not convinced. "Yall's 'just a hug,' seemed to have some drama swirling around it…"

*

Darius waited until bedtime to present the ten-thousand-dollar check from Imperial Records. Aisha was standing on the balcony in her pajamas when Darius hugged her from behind. "It's an advance. Do what you want with it," he said, though knowing she would put most of it aside for Star's tuition.

Aisha stared at the ink, remembering back when they were dating, coming over to Darius's luxury apartment and finding checks, like the one she was holding, lying around on counters and dressers like they were nothing. Also lying around every venue where The Elect played were thirsty women who threw panties on stage, who threw themselves at Darius, even with Aisha on his arm. Random women stuffed phone numbers in his pockets. Old familiars sat poised in the front row. Aisha was also frustrated by exes, having more history with the man than she had, calling him curbside to their car windows or cornering him backstage – Sip, they called him. Two men lived in one, Sip being the alter ego, the showman, the fiery producer, a steep departure from the well-raised son who adores his mother. For Aisha and Darius's relationship to live, Sip had to die. It happened in their second year of marriage. Aisha, the mother of their crawling baby girl, had a fist fight with the lead singer of the female R&B group, Jaded. Their ongoing feud had boiled to a level of blatant disrespect. The singer had tried to sit on Darius's lap and then proposition him, even offering Aisha to watch and learn *from a real woman.*

The ensuing argument exposed Darius's secret, that for the duration of their dating and their young marriage, Darius was working closely with a woman who he'd had a past relationship with. So, it was that night in the studio, with Aisha's shoe thrown across the room, her blouse stretched from the tussle, and a stinging claw scratch on the side of her neck, when she gave Darius the ultimatum.

She'd never found hard evidence of cheating, but she wouldn't have put it past him then. She couldn't connect with him emotionally, when that connection was constantly under threat whenever he left the house.

Ever since Darius left the industry, Aisha had always regretted standing between her husband and his music. The royalty checks dwindled over some years, although the savings they amassed afforded them the lovely downtown home that they never could've afforded without music. It broke Aisha's heart to see Darius eventually pick up a lunch box and ship off to a nine to five, but she wouldn't have asked him if she wouldn't do the same; forsaking all others.

Enough years had passed, Aisha figured. Darius, now groomed by marriage, can better manage the music industry's environment, and with that long of a gap between stints in the music business – from their crawling baby to the fine young lady now touring prospective colleges – Aisha couldn't justify standing in the way any longer. She even vowed to keep away from the studio for fear of seeing anything that resembled the past that might tempt her to try to control the situation, because he'd accuse her of emasculating him.

Aisha decided – with a deep, thoughtful sigh – to trust his love over his past. This, she expressed to him while they were embraced on the upstairs balcony, street lights glowing a melancholy orange.

Her husband nearly collapsed with gratitude, a fist over his heart, then Darius stood straight, as if something stood up inside of him, a renewal; new love sprouting out of their existing love. For Darius, to have a woman of such generational quality and principal bred into her spirit, lay her whole heart in his hands to care for, feels better than access to many women, feels better than the wealth the industry offered him. Standing in the ecstasy of a silky night breeze, hovering in the space between kisses, Darius, responded, "I'm so glad I chose you." Her full trust leaves him nothing left to want for.

*

For days, Darius was busy writing songs. He had a deadline, so this man who had demanded quality time no longer had time to spare. He locked himself in a room to tinker with his synthesizer and scribble bars in his notepad. The interruptions, however, kept coming. The girls brought tight-lidded jars for him to open, and asked him to reach things high up in the cabinet, to fix the wifi router, to capture a lizard basking on the window sill. Darius, always hellbent on dining as a family, would come in late, fumbling to the throne at the head of the table. For Darius, food never tasted so delicious, nor dinner-table sarcasm so hilarious. From the isolation of song writing, dinner was the castaway's reintroduction to society; these other people, his family, seemed to astound him. Out of the dungeon, he had only this half hour's dinner to cram in a day's worth of communication, so the level of engagement he attempted seemed overly gleeful, like the spirit of a Jack Terrier puppy uploaded in the man. Aisha knew, better than anyone, that his over-the-top gladness was manufactured by the guilt of shutting them out. He said he was trying to do the impossible: ten songs in a matter of two weeks.

TERMS OF WAR

The face of the most prestigious law firm in Atlanta believes it's a handsome one, with its sandy five o'clock shadow and array of sporty hats. Maybe it's the tangerine orange Maserati that bricks his confidence. His car, however, can't come inside, and the hat – in keeping with good manners – must come off indoors to reveal a dome that is as smooth and pregnant as a dinosaur egg. The mere sight of the formidable Cornel Law graduate, Thaddeus Broussard, strikes ill feelings with the prosecution. Broussard has made a career of mocking police work, and he is exceedingly good at it, with his Louisiana drawl, which makes every statement ring like gospel.

Sawyer sat at the table with fingers interlocked; silence her only resistance. She was no longer the point-man of the investigation, so it was not her place to speak anyway. Also present was Sergeant Gil, County Prosecutor Joanna Bledsoe, egg-headed Thaddeus Broussard, his client Dr. Cofield and his busty wife, Dianne, clinging to his side.

In time, Travis who was now the lead investigator, ran down the evidence. "We've got Cofield admitting to having contact with Meegan outside of work and within the timeframe critical to the murder, at which time, he threatened Meegan's life. Dr. Edward Cofield then went on to threaten the career of Chelsea Dwyer who witnessed the heated exchange –"

"– Lies," said Dianne. "My husband wouldn't threaten a soul," she added, with her nose dialed at Travis. Dr. Cofield tightened his grip on her hand to quiet her.

Broussard's large head shook. "The timeframe critical to the murder, you say?" The star attorney leaned back and folded his arms like a chieftain. "I've got medical examiners waiting in line to smear your theories on the critical timeframe for one of the least-studied diseases in the modern world. Meegan had a biopsy done on her cervix, which *your* forensics report names as the site of infection, yet not one of you questions whether the OBGYN that did the biopsy could've contaminated her somehow?"

Sawyer didn't dare turn to verify, but she felt eye beams coming from Travis who, day one, raised the concern of cross-contamination.

Joanna squinted with contempt. "Too much time had passed. We didn't know about the procedure until *your client* – the good doctor, here – filled us in," Joanna said, with her statement pointed at Cofield.

"Regardless," Thaddeus said. "The fact that there is a more likely possibility than what you're proposing, will give any jury reasonable doubt. Targeting my client with so little evidence is selfish on the grandest of scales. At best, this is a civil case against the doctor's office that handled Meegan's biopsy. Doctor's offices have insurance for things like this. Through them, you can get an out of court settlement for the family. At least, that way, the family gets something other than the disappointment they'll receive in a court of law against the likes of me. This is rabies, for God sakes. Sometimes people just die, but this office is hellbent on turning as many deaths as you can into murder."

Joanna replied, "We don't make murderers; we uncover them."

Broussard's arms unfolded. "Not with *this* circumstantial bull crap."

Joanna reddened as she proposed, "Murder one for Meegan. Manslaughter for Miller. Take it; it's our best offer."

While Broussard giggled, his client, Cofield, said, "You just don't get it do you? Like I said, I was entrusting my legacy to Meegan, I would've never done anything to her."

"Looks like you were *entrusting your legacy*," Travis finger-quoted, "With a number of young, attractive med students. We're at number four and counting."

Broussard nodded, "I'm already aware. It's not like my client was going around copping feels in the elevator. You'll insult the jury's intelligence if you try to prey upon the headlines, expecting them to lump Dr. Cofield in with the Harvey Weinsteins of the world. I assure you that all of his past relationships – however inappropriate, professionally – were indeed romantic and consensual in nature."

Dr. Cofield's wife snatched away from him and marched out. The husband rose from his chair, but Thaddeus Broussard pulled him down by the shoulder. "Let her go," Thaddeus advised, and then chided, "Let this be a lesson. *All* of my advice – even if marital in nature – is, in fact, legal advice."

Dr. Cofield gripped his face and cried. Jo reached out. "I'll be straight with you, Edward–"

"–Speak to him through me please."

"I'll speak to who I damn well want to," Joanna said to Thaddeus, and then switched to the suspect. "If you put an end to this now, there's no years-long public, legal battle of appeals, no long line of character witnesses portraying you as a predator. This would go away pretty quickly, and for the family who still bears your last name, that name can still mean something... for *them*. We'll reduce Miller's death to *involuntary* manslaughter."

Travis huffed. The fist propped under his chin dropped on the table. "Involuntary-man for the brother... As if *he* doesn't have family, a community, that needs justice for *him?*"

Broussard pounced on the opportunity. "Get your house in order, prosecutor. Take stock of what you have – or do you believe the notion that Cofield's high position brands him as a monster, or that the subordinate positions of his ex-lovers' adorns them with sainthood? I will show you – you and a jury of twelve – how it is no conundrum that a med student who would throw herself at a sixty-year old, married, medical legend is also the type to frolic with a chauvinistic, self-proclaimed gangster, who beats women, such as Mr. Kendall Miller."

Joanna stood and closed her briefcase. "Save your closing arguments for the trial."

"So, you're really doing this…" Thaddeus glanced around, searching for an ally to oppose this madness. "I'll do you all a favor and try my damndest to get this case thrown out."

"Why," Gil shot.

"You wanna build a character case against a man who saves the lives of sick children, who has more pro bono life-saving operations than any other surgeon – a once-widowed single father who raised a daughter up to be a fine wife, mother, and school principle – a son who runs an organic farm? After Dr. Cofield finally made room for love outside of his children, he then remarried to a social worker-slash-Sunday school teacher. Step back a bit and maybe *then* you can see the mountain in front of you. The whole damned country will be watching as I turn your so-called victims into pill-popping, hot-in-the-ass med-students with daddy issues! I, for one, would hate to be the trial lawyer responsible for setting victims back another fifty years."

"Take the deal, then," Joanna said.

Thaddeus rubbed his hands and smiled. "Concede? Well now, therein lies the rub. You see, I have this little thing about winning." He honed in on Sawyer, who hadn't uttered a word during the meeting, which he took as a sign of dissention.

"Detective Sawyer? Something you wanna share with the rest of the class?"

Sawyer gave a sullied, "See ya in court."

The good guys hung back, except for Sawyer who left in tow of the defense team, unable to share the same room with backstabbing Travis for another minute. Dianne, who had been waiting outside, joined her husband as they were leaving, but waft his gesture to hold hands. Sawyer waded in the hallway, watching them. Dianne, after hearing about her husband's affairs, was a mere ghost of the rock-solid woman that came in earlier. Sawyer's mind couldn't even raise an image of herself in Dianne's shoes – the mess she'd be if it were herself learning that Darius had a string of affairs. She'd be forced to leave him, for the sake of her daughters, because staying would undo the lifelong mantras of self-worth and independence she's preached into her girls.

Sawyer wasn't the only one watching Dianne leave. A group of detectives hushed as Dianne strode by. Sawyer knew – by the activity in the men's eyes – that they were admiring her figure, and it made Sawyer sick.

Sawyer felt the weight of a hand on her shoulder; it was Travis, yet another man that made her sick. One side of her upper lip raised in disgust.

Travis smirked and said, "Still giving me the silent treatment?"

"Don't get it twisted, Travis. The silent treatment is for people I actually care about. I simply look at you and have no words."

Travis smiled, "Now, I know I messed up... and I've been trying to figure a way to make it up to you –"

"– I'm good." Her index finger went no-no like a wiper blade.

Travis stared at Sawyer like a fortress about to crumble with these magic words: "I paid Pringle's cellie a visit down at Helms."

Sawyer swallowed hard. Hope made a star shine in her eyes. "And?"

"Turns out that, one night Pringle and his cellie were drunk off of that prison wine, which is canned fruit cocktail fermented in rice and jolly ranchers. Anyway, Pringle was bragging about how he's such a ladies' man –"

"Travis. You're killing me. What happened?"

"Pringle admitted to the murder, and bragged about Vivian taking the fall. He even shared that he kept a tuft of the victim's hair as a trophy, tucked inside of a bible in his mother's attic."

Sawyer was hearing her proof, her vindication. It felt like a thumb-sized thorn removed from her side. She held her head with both hands so it wouldn't topple. "Travis, I swear if this is some sort of joke..." Sawyer pointed at Travis and said, "Interviewing his cellie?" Sawyer's head shook; her pointing hand, heavy with gratitude, dropped and flopped at her side. "How come *I* never thought of that!"

Pringle, serving time for another crime, would finally get pinned for the murder Sawyer always knew he committed. No one could ever again hold her Pringle blunder against her. She couldn't thank Travis enough. Their double high five, interlocked, the celebration turning into what looked like an off-beat dance.

THE STREETS BE TALKIN'

Chosen had planned a celebration, one that would signal the dawn of a new era at Hustle Hard Entertainment and a pivotal shift in the hip hop industry, with Chosen being (to *her* knowledge) the first black female majority owner of a leading hip hop label.

She was at club Savoy (her old job), in the afternoon, examining her 4x6 promo flyers. "This is elegant, Jackson (Savoy's manager), but something's missing. The font needs more texture maybe?"

"But you've already used your two edits, Chosen. My guys are passing out stacks of those as we speak," said Jackson, as he reclined and put his feet up on the desk, but suddenly flinched and took his feet down, caught in the act by the owner of that cherry desk.

Vick stood in the doorway with an eagle stare through brandy colored transition shades. Vick is the type to remove his hat indoors but keep his shirt loose a few buttons to sport the fur on his chest; he is the type to greet someone by simply announcing their name. "Jackson... Chosen..."

Chosen had turned to that familiar voice, surprised, like a toddler's epiphany at a parent's return from work, their return to existence. "Vick!" Chosen celebrated the man with a full breasted hug. "What a surprise," Chosen exclaimed. "All the times I've been coming here, planning this thing, where you been?"

Vick stood pole straight, weathering the hug. "I don't come around as much. I'd lost my taste, honestly, for this new club crowd a long time ago," he said, although he's just over fifty. He then held Chosen at arm's length. "Look at you. Money sure looks good on you, ma. I couldn't be happier about your success."

Jackson slid out of the office. Chosen and Vick sat. Vick added, "I'm here because I knew you were here. I thought I'd come holla at you today since I can't attend your celebration."

Chosen pouted, "Vick... I'm hurt."

"I got two options. *You* tell me which one gets me killed: missing your party or missing me and Gwen's anniversary?"

Chosen's hands dropped in her lap; she smiled fondly. "Where're you taking her this year?"

"No place flashy. A lil spa resort we know about in Asheville, North Carolina."

"The mountains. Nice."

"Got mineral pools, hot stone massages, cucumber water." Vick got up from his desk and offered a hand. "Come out to the bar with me, so we can drink to your success."

Chosen took the gentleman's hand and they went. "You still drinking that Belvedere and grapefruit juice," her mouth, bitter at the thought of it.

"Chilled and strained," Vick sung. "Cosmopolitan for you, right?"

They were out front where chairs were turned over on the tables, daylight glowing softly on all surfaces. Chosen would be Vick's lone barstool customer in a milk white dress with a waterfall of a ponytail down her back. Vick rolled up his sleeves behind the bar and said, "Isabell is stopping by. You've met my daughter, right?"

"She was away, working on her masters when I worked here, but I saw her a few times. She and her brother Jackson couldn't be more different." Chosen crossed her legs and said, "But look at you and Miss Gwen, living out yall's happily-ever-after, and here I am: thirty. Starting all over from scratch." Chosen sighed. "Even Chyna's fat ass got Kelvo to get his shit together. He got her a ring and everything."

Vick's mouth drooped at the corners as he mumbled, "Ole Kelvo ever did like 'em big..." He strained the melon-red drink into a martini glass and garnished it with a coil of orange peel.

Chosen sipped her cosmopolitan, her mouth smacking to examine the flavor. "Ooh, this is *so* good, Vick."

"Starting all over?" Vick's face tightened as he shook the tin mixer. "So, you're dating already?"

The question made Chosen giddy and enchanted. "Well, you *could* say there's someone, a lil boo-thang, if you will. We're taking it slow, though – too slow for my taste, but it's for the best."

Vick then dropped the stirrer in his Belvedere and grapefruit juice. "For the best? Oh, because of Trap's passing… his killer's trial pending and all?"

"Fuck a Trap! *Trap* was dead to me when he was living. Why think about him now?"

"You can't go around Atlanta cursing Trap with a boo-thang on your arm, Chosen. People expect you to be the grieving widow, so you should *be* that – at least for appearances. In *my* humble opinion, you should've run off with that insurance check and relocated; quiet is kept – not purchase the man's company."

"The *only* reason I bought the company is because Miss Lottie had her inherited portion priced to sell. I would've been a fool to walk away from that sure of an investment, knowing how millionaire athletes walk away from the game and go broke in five years. If my money doesn't *make* money; I'd go broke too."

"But when you go and buy the man's company, then throw a party at his favorite club? It's like tapdancing on the grave of the man whose death made you rich."

Chosen's face dipped, as if peering, in judgement, over the

top of imaginary glasses. "Was that a *read*, just now, Vick? Witchyo El Chapo mustache havin', burnt chicken grease complexioned..." Her rant succumbed to knee-slapping laughter.

Vick also laughed, wobbling back a step. "Aw man. See, I wasn't even gonna comment on your spotty knees today. Got russet potatoes for knee caps 'n shit." Absurdity is their brand of humor.

A chuckling Chosen stopped abruptly with an evil eye. "My knees is not no spotty, Vick – or should I say Viquavious. Got people thinking Vick is short for Victor. I should put you on blast. Viquavious: sounds like the name of a paleolithic fruit-bat or somethin'."

They sighed as if laughter wore them out. Vick shook a pointed finger. "I don't know what paleolithic means, but if it's good, I'm that."

"It's a period of prehistory giving rise to the hominid, when we left the trees and began walking upright –" Chosen stopped at the sight of Vick's surrendered palms.

"Look, hon. I could give a good-got-damn about all that. What I'm trying to say, Chosen, is that you're really different. Not just anybody goes around talking about prehistoric bats and such."

Chosen's head-turn threw her ponytail from one shoulder to the other. "*You're* the one who's being different, Vick. Why are you defending Trap all of a sudden? I thought you hated him because of how he treated me."

"Don't mistake me for defending Trap; I'm trying to protect you."

"Protect moi? From what?"

Vick looked down, solemnly. "The streets is talkin' up a storm about you. You know Savoy is like the industry's clubhouse, so I used to hear everything, but now it's Jackson in my place, and he's telling me how these same folks who loved you as a battered girlfriend now hate you as a business mogul. Plus, this freckled punk they call Soda –"

"– His name's Sosa."

"Anyway, that dude's been coming around looking for you like he wants to do you harm. That worries me. On top of that, got people going around sayin' you did it."

"Did what?"

"Murdered Trap."

Chosen drew back, lazy-eyed and heavy-lipped. "Fuck outta here."

"You remember Yaz?"

"Stank mouth Yaz."

Vick grimaced as he stared off into space. "Breath smell like wide open ass…" He shuddered back to his train of thought and continued. "Jackson said Yaz was here about a week ago, drunk as a skunk, talkin' about how the evidence against you and the doctor is exactly the same: both jaded lovers of the victims, both issued threats, and both made contact with the victims within – what these forensic analysts on TV are calling – *the vital timeframe*."

Chosen punched an open hand and said, "But what y'all not understanding is that, although I was never a *named* suspect, police investigated me. They were all up my ass about Trap's death. The evidence just isn't there."

"Yaz is thinking that the only reason the police haven't charged you, is that they underestimate you. She said, if they knew the real Chosen–"

"–The *real* Chosen?" Her nose wrinkled.

Vick countered. "Well, yeah, the real Chosen... The Chosen that throws around scientific terms, the Chosen that peddled homemade organic uppers and hangover tonics to my bar customers, the Chosen that has the skill to put a young lady under anesthesia and give her a new, stout bottom. According to Yaz, you did *her* surgery." Vick pinned Chosen with a glare, adding, "I remember the night o'boy got shot outside, laying in a puddle of his own blood and you put an ear to that boy's mouth and determined, just by the sound of his breathing, which organ was hit and which ones wasn't, and you saved that boy's life with a got-damn ball-point pen and a bar towel."

"Drain the internal bleeding, and put pressure on the wound – that's basic shit, Vick. Plus, saving a life is very different than taking one."

"I'm not saying you did it. I'm saying that when Yaz catches up to you, she'll be standing before you with the ass you gave her, forcing you to pay her a large sum of money to keep her from telling the police about what you're capable of. Best you can do is keep about a hundred bands, cash, stashed in a safe waiting for her."

"Do *you* think I did it?"

Vick's fingers tapped the glazed counter. "I think that, even *if* you did, Trap's life is a small price to pay to have a black female owner in hip hop, at a company of that magnitude." Vick plucked the straw out of his drink and downed it. "I'ma tell ya a story. How a young lady went to Trap with a proposal to be, what's called, a brand manager for his company. She'd oversee advertising, copywriting, some P.R. – things of that nature. So, there she is, this… beautiful, black, educated, female entrepreneur, pitching her expertise, and guess what Trap's response was to this woman of integrity and excellence: Trap told her that before he'd even *consider* her proposal, he'd have to, first, see what that *mouth* do."

Chosen's hand clapped her mouth to smother laughter. "Dayumn that's messed up though."

Vick raised one righteous brow. "That young lady… That was my daughter."

"Oh." Chosen stiffened and glanced around.

"She's done business with franchises, publicly traded companies, even Fortune Five Hundred companies, and *no* one, outside of the hip hop, has ever addressed her in that manner. That type of behavior in the *rest* of the business world, gets your head chopped off, ask Matt Lauer, Charlie Rose, Harvey Weinstein. Yet R. Kelly – because his victims are all black women – is permitted to be a public pedophile – a defiant one, at that. Chris Brown became an even bigger star after he had Rihanna's face looking like Emmett Till. Hip hop is to black women what Jim Crow was to *all* blacks."

Chosen held a look of disappointment. "Trap disrespected your daughter like that, and you still did business with him? Promoting his parties and letting him rent the club?"

Vick's brows raised along with an erect finger. " Had I zzy told me this when it happened, when Trap was alive? He'd still be dead today, but instead of that doctor, it'd be *me* facing trial. I'll tell you something... Despite that incident, Isabell still wants that role – even more so now since the top executive is a woman – a woman of color, at that."

"*Vick...*" Chosen stiffened straight, aghast. "How can you warn me about Yaz blackmailing me, while *you*, from the side of your mouth, trying to use something Trap did to your daughter to guilt me into doing business with her?"

"I'm not trying to guilt you. Even if you *don't* bring Isabell on board, you're still like family to me. All I want for her is the fair chance she was unjustly denied." Vick looked up, finding Isabell peeking through the front door's glass square. He hurried from behind the bar en route to the door."

Chosen said, "So, Isabell's showing up today is just a coincidence, huh...?"

As the door opened, Isabell walked through the cone of daylight cutting into the dim club, her smile revealing teeth too pearly and perfect in the frame of her violet lipstick. Her dress was exquisite yet simple; her only flare being Cinderella puffs at the shoulders. Isabell strides with an air of privilege, where desires and expectations are one in the same. "Chosen," Isabella called. "How have you *been?*"

There was such familiarity in Isabella's hug that Chosen felt guilty for being unable to recall the great friendship they must've had. After Chosen's, "I'm good, girl. How are you?" Chosen had nothing else to say; her smile was frozen. No memories to prompt a line of discussion.

When they finally got down to business, Isabella and Vick were a team, the male and female version of the same face, urging Chosen to make Isabella Hustle Hard Entertainment's brand manager. They were like missionaries trying to convert a wandering heathen.

Isabella promised, "This party is your first big opportunity to appeal to the influencers and tastemakers. I could have you gracing the covers of magazines in a month if this opportunity is handled right."

Vick, checking with his daughter, asked, "Shouldn't she be looking to start some sort of charitable foundation? Or has philanthropy become cliché nowadays?"

Isabell: "As cliché as it may seem, it's still vital, as a tax haven, and to uphold the proper image. Speaking of image," Isabell said as her hands gathered. "What do you plan on wearing to this party, Chosen? Something a little *less* revealing than what you're wearing now, I hope."

Chosen kept looking at them both, bird-twitching between the two, her grin flattening. "Y'all have got to be kidding me,"

Chosen said. "First of all, Isabell, even if I *could* hire you, I'm not fixin to let you or nobody tell me what to wear, but truth is, I don't even have the *authority* to hire you. I have Trap's share of the company, but not his operational role; it's written in their contracts."

Father and daughter looked at each other and then at Chosen. Isabell led, "Show them you can be an asset and you will see that the obstacle is not a paper contract. It's your relationship with your business partners."

"Partners? I go to the office and they act like I'm not even there, so I stopped going altogether."

"Chosen, that spirit of retaliation will be your undoing."

Isabell's nugget of wisdom gave Vick a mini Holy Ghost. "*Preach*, Izzy!"

Isabell did as told. "If you want to become a true partner in the company, Chosen, you must find a way disarm their ill feelings towards you. You do that by bonding over something you all have in common." Isabell folded her arms. "Your party's coming up. Take fifteen minutes out of your program to commemorate Trap. Do a short documentary on the big screen up there, but not without including J Money and Flikka on putting the presentation together." Isabell tapped the back of Chosen's hand, adding, "And that joint project would be the soil from which yall's relationship could sprout from."

Chosen's head shook miserably. "Do you even know what you're asking me to do? You're asking me to honor the man that beat me, the man that cheated on me while I was in that hospital by myself in labor for hours, pushing out a baby that I knew was already dead inside of me!" Chosen was filled with fury, her eyes glassy with tears. "You're asking me to honor the man who, after eighteen months and two miscarriages still wouldn't marry me, but got on one knee for that *white bitch* after just one month?! The same man who told you to suck his dick?"

Vick pounded the bar top. "Now, you *wait* a got damn minute, Chosen!"

Isabell's palm signaled her father to stop – to let Chosen continue. "Pain needs a witness, pop."

Chosen added, "I'll tell you what that mouth *can* do... It can kiss my black ass!"

Vick spun away, steaming. Isabell remained unfazed. "Trap took you through a lot, Chosen. I couldn't even imagine... He may have insulted me, but I know that the responsibility that lay before us is bigger than me. Bigger than you. And, quite frankly, bigger than your pain. You may not have realized it, but when you acquired that company, you acquired the dreams, the hopes, and the *attention* of all black women. You may not be able hire me on with the company, but you can hire me personally, for public relations, at a reduced rate." Isabell offered her hand. "Accept this hand and with it, my guidance, and you will become a catalyst; *refuse* my hand, and you'll become a cautionary tale."

Chosen appeared to be considering the offer, but she was only thinking of how to let Isabella down easy.

Isabella added, "Walking in the right image, Chosen, not only gets you results in business, my dear, but also in your personal life." Isabella offered a limp-handed display of her sparkling engagement ring, an awe-inspiring rock. "You can't project the image of an Instagram chick, and expect Atlanta's most eligible bachelor who will be entering the 2020 state senate race, to take you out in public."

Chosen was astonished like a fan in the presence of a celebrity. "You're married?" Chosen wanted desperately to be a member in that coveted ring of honor. "And a politician, at that?"

"Not married yet, but engaged, and he's not a politician yet; he's a lawyer. I'll be managing his campaign next election season."

"If you're managing your man's campaign, how would you have time for me?"

"Because I must. Like I said, this is too important: too important for women, for *black* women, for progress, for hip hop – in that order."

Vick chimed in. "You talk about image, right, Izzy? Well what kind of image do you think Chosen's putting out there if she's running around with some *boo-thang* and cursing Trap's name?"

Chosen cut eyes at the man and shot, "Dry-snitchin' ass…"

Isabell, wavy with disappointment, imparted, "As bad as Trap was to you, he meant a lot to hip hop. He meant a lot to Atlanta, in the eyes of many. You keep doing things the way you're doing," Isabell warned. "You'll provoke people – otherwise indifferent – to put their heads together and orchestrate your downfall. Even worse, you'll light a fire under those who are already your sworn enemies."

Chosen had thought her worries were over when Cofield was charged with the murders, but with Sosa seeking her out, Yaz conspiring to blackmail her, and the weight of all black women on her shoulders, Chosen was more than worried; she felt small, afraid, lost.

Chosen got a text. She chose to view her phone as a way to delay responding to Isabell's offer. It was that ole bloodhound, Detective Sawyer, her boo-thang's wife, and also an "sworn enemy" with a fire already under her. Sawyer's text read, *We need to have a talk about Ben's death.*

Chosen backed away, her eyes locked on her phone, saying to Isabell and Vick, "I'm sorry. This is all happening too fast."

They tried to calm her, but Chosen hiked her purse strap over her shoulder and ran out in a hurry.

Chosen drove aimlessly, her knuckles tight over the steering wheel, her teeth grinding. She was on the brink of a meltdown. She pulled over. She was shaking, bawling, cursing at the world and cursing Sawyer for being so relentless – but then in light of Isabell's advice, Chosen could only blame herself, for provoking Sawyer during the interrogation, for showing up at the candle light vigil and then showing herself at the expresso shop's glass storefront, staring Sawyer down while she rode away. Chosen's infatuation with Sawyer's husband no longer made sense; exposing the pictures would only make Detective Sawyer more hellbent on revenge.

Chosen pulled over and stared at her phone. She made the call she hated to have to make: to let Darius know that their business was over. Darius failed to pick up, so Chosen told his voicemail the excuse that her business partners turned down her proposal to bring him on as a producer. There would be no resurrection of his music career, at least not with, what she referred to as, her company's subsidiary, Imperial Inc. Chosen added that he could keep the advance, for his time and efforts.

Chosen then scrolled through her phone's gallery and kissed Darius's picture good bye. What started out as a strategic move had turned real; feelings had indeed blossomed for the man. Chosen wanted nothing more than to have made Detective Sawyer eat her words from the interrogation room, where she made Chosen out to be damaged morally, and equally yoked to a man who beat her in the face – *well* below a man as good and wholesome as her Darius. Chosen, being a woman who daily gives married men whiplash when she walks past, was savoring the day when she would've proven to Detective Sawyer that not even her precious Darius is safe from a woman who embodies the images he's masturbated to ever since his armpits were still bald.

Sawyer wasn't Chosen's only worry. She made a mental note to follow Vick's advice to stash away some cash in a safe in preparation for a blackmail from stank mouth Yaz. Ben's attempt to blackmail Chosen for sex made the idea of Yaz blackmailing her seem like prophecy. Chosen took a deep breath, wondering what evidence her old landlord *thought* he had, and if that supposed evidence was uncovered in a police search of Ben's home and if that's what prompted Sawyer's desire to question her.

MAN DOWN

The homicide unit was never called, yet Sawyer showed up for the scene at Ben's home. Latria, a wide-bodied deputy patrol, spotted Sawyer's red Camaro and met her at the yellow crime scene tape. She asked, "What're you doing here?"

Sawyer held up surrendered hands. "I'm not here to step on any toes."

Latria folded her arms. "This is an accidental death, a faulty furnace."

Sawyer turned slightly away. "In the month of June? In Georgia? *That's* the part that doesn't make sense."

Latria hardened her stare and said, "It's brilliant, actually. I couldn't think of a gentler method of suicide."

Sawyer glanced at Benjamin's front door. "One of your guys, over there, isn't wearing any gloves," Sawyer pointed out. "If this is later ruled a homicide, the last thing we need is to explain doughnut-glazed fingerprints to a jury."

"Hazmat is on the way. The body is so decomposed, it's not even safe to go in there."

"You should probably tell that to the guys going in and out of the house, probably taking phone picks."

"Go right ahead. Pick us apart all you want, as long as you're doing it from *that* side of tape."

Just then, Travis walked up beside Sawyer, asking, "What'd you call me here for?"

The moment Latria caught sight of Travis, she forgot that Sawyer even existed. Latria looked the man up and down like a tree she was determined to climb. "Hey, boy," Latria said, with awe and mischief. "Haven't seen you in a while, witchyo your fine self."

Sawyer mimed a *Thank you* to Travis while she snuck away.

She borrowed a cloth from one of the officers and covered her mouth before going in. A forensics examiner and photographer, in bio masks, were huddled around the body. The body was so deteriorated, Sawyer couldn't have imagined it being used for evidence. Sawyer spotted her card on the chair arm, tagged as evidence.

She snuck to the back and found herself alone in Ben's bedroom. There were no evidence tags, as if the room hadn't been checked. A box of bullets was on the dresser with a few handgun shells standing upright next to the box, but no handgun was recovered. She spotted Ben's laptop wedged between the bed and the wall, which seemed odd. Maybe it was hidden, but stashed there hurriedly, as if in a rush to maybe answer a knock at the door; perhaps one of Ben's final acts before dying. Sawyer thought she'd make sure to tell the officers about the laptop, suspecting that they'd overlook it – not that it meant anything to them.

With a defective furnace blowing carbon monoxide, no forced entry, the dead unrestrained, they were set to chalk Ben's death up to accident, which is why the bedroom hadn't been checked. This was a case that would never make it over to homicide, Sawyer thought, so she took the towel from around her mouth and used it to pull out the laptop; officially, tampering with a crime scene. A zip drive stuck out of the laptop's side. She opened the laptop and the screensaver blinked on; the device was still plugged in. Sawyer tapped the mousepad and desktop appeared; no password needed. A video had been paused for probably a month. It was porn, but oddly the video was black and white, and the video quality was grainy, even for a homemade video.

The woman in the video looked like Chosen. The man in the video was not Ben. Sawyer spotted another zip drive peeking out from under a pillow; she lifted the pillow and found four more. Sawyer stuffed them all in her pocket and turned her attention back to the paused video.

Chosen was in a bedroom on top of a man. The bad camera angle told Sawyer that they didn't know they were being filmed. Accidentally, Sawyer tapped the mouse pad and the video resumed; the was volume way up with Chosen moaning in pleasure. Sawyer heard a cop out front say, "What the hell's going on back there."

"Shit," Sawyer cursed, as she tried, frantically, to turn down the volume. She heard footsteps. Sawyer quit with the volume, snatched the zip drive out of the laptop, stuffed it in her pocket, and stuck the laptop back where it was. Sawyer then snapped straight, looking innocently at the officer who materialized at the bedroom doorway.

The man eyed her strangely, "You get off on this type of thing (meaning death)?" He thought the moaning woman was the one staring at him like a deer in headlights.

Sawyer's delay had already confirmed him, but since his assumption was less incriminating than the truth – that she was removing evidence – Sawyer went with: "For the record, the only thing I touched in here was myself." She left the officer there, baffled, yet wildly intrigued.

*

Sawyer was running late for an interview with a Cofield accuser, so she used her blue light to part freeway traffic like the Red Sea. In the city, picketers were on the Jordan Cancer Center's courtyard calling for Cofield to be fired in light of his sexual misconduct. Cofield accusers kept coming forward, which kept the Atlanta double homicide at the top of the newsreel, yet it was Chosen who Sawyer couldn't shake out of her mind. Now swirling around Ben's death is handgun bullets but no handgun recovered; Sawyer's business card found next to Ben's body, and the spy cams Ben must've wired in Chosen's rented house. Maybe Ben caught more than Chosen changing clothes and having sex in her bedroom and was using his finding to bribe Chosen. Sawyer hoped that the hundreds of hours of video stuffed in her front pocket contained the evidence that would explain the murder.

Sawyer was late to the interview. She yawned and sighed through the deposition with the latest Cofield accuser, a now married mother of three, and still-beautiful Theresa Volmer. Unfortunately, Volmer could only characterize Cofield as manipulative and narcistic, but not violent or a sexual deviant like the prosecution had hoped for. Mrs. Volmer had left Sawyer and Joanna deflated in their seats. Joanna, tapping her teeth with a pen, had stopped and then dropped the pen. "Ok, Sawyer," Joanna blew. "Who is the stripper chick and why didn't I hear about her until *after* we charged Dr. Cofield?"

Sawyer stared with eyes that were wise to the deception.

"I swear to you, I didn't know," said Joanna. "Insurance payout like *that?* I would've been all over it."

Sawyer sighed. "You asked who is she? No one can even tell me where she's *from.*"

"Think she's under an alias?"

Sawyer nodded affirmative. "A rental lease is the only thing we could find under the name Chosen, so she's got to be using another identity for her financials. Without that name, I can't even find out where she lives now." Sawyer rubbed her temple.

Jo leaned back in her chair. "To be honest… I think we

pulled the trigger early on Dr. Cofield. I'd like you to try, again, to get me something on Chosen."

Sawyer's eyes widened. "When have I *stopped* trying? I'm out on my lunch hour doing stakeouts in front of her studio…"

"Good… All along, you were right about Pringle," Joanna uttered, from a deep-thinking gaze.

"I'm right about Chosen too. If only I could locate her. The chick owns the studio but she's never there. If I can just find out the name her vehicle is registered under, I think the rest will follow."

"What I need, detective, is more than just her bio. We need to build a murderer from the past up, from their rap sheet, from their troubled childhood. Although Cofield has used his position to help himself to as many med students as he wanted, nothing about those relationships, nor his past, as far as we know, fits the bio of a killer. Even for the people who now hate his guts, the worst they can say is that he's an overambitious workaholic freak who has a taste for blondes younger than his own daughter. I need you to find out just who Chosen really is, please."

Sawyer pinned a party flyer to the table with her finger. "This is where she'll be. I'm going undercover."

Joanna said, "We need something, and fast."

"I'm on it." The two bumped fists like touching girl-power rings. Sawyer still didn't trust telling Jo about the stolen evidence.

Jo said, "It looks like if I continue pursuing Cofield…" Her brows raised as she peered down. "Let's just say, I'm not going to let Broussard make a fool of me again."

Sawyer smirked and said, "To be honest, Jo, you had asked for it."

Wearily, Jo, replied, "Look, I was fresh off a bad relationship; he was there. I may have had one too many margaritas –" Jo stopped and covered her mouth. She'd said too much.

Sawyer, in her shock, was frozen, except for her eyes darting, spying from behind a self-portrait with punched out eyes. "Um… Actually, I was thinking more like the Sam Crowder overturned conviction?"

Joanna reddened. "Not a word of this leaves this room, got me?"

Sawyer, smiling between upturned palms, asked, "Well, was he any good, at least?"

"Freaking marvelous," Joanna said, as she stormed out.

*

After leaving Joanna, Sawyer marched into Gil's office, saying, "There's a hazmat crew down at the home of Chosen's old landlord."

Gil's typing fingers had stopped. "That guy was Chosen's landlord?" He glared at Sawyer momentarily, and then back to his computer screen. "They say his killer is a thirty-year old furnace." Gil resumed typing as a way to blow her off.

"So, you're saying there's nothing fishy about a furnace death in June? My card was next to his body." Sawyer realized that Gil was ignoring her. Sawyer folded her arms. The more Gil ignored Sawyer, the more her anger boiled. The kettle blew when Sawyer snatched the keyboard out from under Gil's hands, the cord knocking over a cup of pens.

"What the *hell*, Sawyer?"

"Do you see me *now*, Gil?" She let the keyboard drop.

"Now, you look here, you …" Gil's lips shrunk tight, sealing in ten pounds of air pressure and profanity.

Sawyer pointed to herself and said, "I am *not* invisible!" Her eyes were ablaze yet searching for more to say, but realized she'd already spoke volumes, like the money-line in a drama film.

Gil walked around Sawyer and closed the door, his head rotating with the beam of his stare. He parked a chair in front of his desk for Sawyer.

"I'll stand." Again, volumes.

Gil's index finger wagged. "All this shit… Yelling, snatching my keyboard… They already think you got me wrapped around your finger."

"Says who?" Sawyer was ready to be amused.

Gil's head shook for a few beats. "The *who* dudn't matter. In order for my authority to hold any weight around here, there has to be a perception of fairness."

"Oh, so *that's* why you were ignoring me," Sawyer said, in grand sarcasm.

Gil pumped brakes with his palm. "Hold it down, will ya… Just listen to yourself. So, not only is Chosen a biologist, but now she's a certified HVAC technician too?"

"As if there's no such thing as how-to videos on YouTube."

"You're coming to me with theory – not evidence. Give me someone witnessing an argument between the two – maybe someone spotting her leaving his home around the estimated time of death."

"Was I wrong about Pringle?"

Gil looked away, smiling and bashful of his own defeat.

Sawyer placed her hands on her hips. "All the hell you've given me over the years about Pringle, I think it's only right that you make it up to me by strolling right on over to Mildred and sweet-talking her out of a search warrant. Ben's death is not the accident they're making it out to be."

Gil looked down to hide his blushing. "Before I make any request to Magistrate Harvey, you bring me some evidence. You should have something by now with all the time you've spent, *still* backdooring the Cofield investigation in pursuit of Chosen." Gil watched Sawyer shrink and smiled at it. "Didn't think I knew, did ya?"

"I *think* you allowed it because you, like Joanna, have your doubts about Cofield."

Gil sighed and said, "Lemme show you something." He swiveled his computer screen. "You ever seen one of these before?"

Sawyer leaned in, squinting. "We're being sued?"

"Sometimes it's civilians, other times it's officers, even if *they* were the ones who put them*selves* in harm's way. Almost all of it can be prevented if we just stick to protocol. This particular case (on his computer screen) was the result of me going against what I knew to be the prudent thing to do; I gave in to the request of one of my tenured detectives, and he turned out to be dead wrong and it put us in a situation to be sued. *I* have to deal with this stuff on the backend. *I* have to type up an explanation that goes to the chief and sometimes even the mayor. This all started with a discussion much like the one you and I are having, right now. I will say this: I shouldn't have ignored you like I did. I was reacting to this lawsuit; not to you. But trust me, there's going to be a culture change around here. We've got a department of prideful, entitled, sensitive assed detectives who get offended when I question them – when that's the *primary* function of my job."

This was Gil's away of apologizing; a long, drawn out speech of a hundred words to cover up the one word he can never say. Sawyer shook his hand, smiling, "Apology accepted, Gil."

COLLISION COURSE

A t home, Darius was not locked away writing songs. He sat on the living room couch drinking from a brown bottle. "Root beer," he clarified, when his wife walked in.

Sawyer replied, "I wasn't going to say anything."

Darius was watching *Frozen* for the hundredth time along with Brianna who had fallen asleep next to him. Aisha had come home late with shopping bags, a kiss and an explanation, "I'm going under cover tonight."

Darius heard his wife, but he was unaffected; his eyes never left the television. He'd been a shell of himself since he'd heard Chosen's voicemail message, which closed the door on the resurrection of his music career.

Aisha went down the hallway towards the bedroom but doubled back, shopping bags still in hand, her face frowning, "You're not making music? What about the deadline?"

Darius spotted a Prada tag hanging out of one of the shopping bags, and in that moment, he didn't have the heart to tell her that the Imperial Records checks stopped at one, and would no longer fund shopping sprees like the one she just returned from. "The deadline," he said with a sigh. "The deadline's been relaxed a little."

Aisha disappeared down the hallway to get ready for her assignment. Darius headed to the fridge for another root beer, but then he stopped when he saw the flyer his wife dropped on the counter. He waited until Aisha left, and then Darius made the call to Trinece, who had also had her music dreams dashed against the rocks by phone. He said, "Get dressed for a night out. We're gonna get some answers tonight."

*

The club lights were low. The black light turned white to purple, even the whites of eyes, so there was a wall to wall gathering of stylish, purple-eyed goblins that Sawyer shouldered through, in order to find a table close to the stage. She joined two women who sat as still as manikins posed cross-legged, one with hair as orange as fire. Both looked away when Sawyer asked, "Mind if I sit?" No sooner than Sawyer sat anyway, in the blot of their shade, did Chosen appear on stage, splitting the curtain where the spotlight shined.

To a hearty applause, Chosen bowed graciously, like a ballerina's curtain call. She wore a clear mage's cape and underneath, what looked like a sheer, skin-colored body suit with rind stone clusters, snow-fallen on the shoulders, embroidered at the wrists and ankles, and swirling at the breasts.

Isabell was in attendance, watching from the bar. When she saw Chosen's outfit, or rather this shameless cry for attention, coming out on stage in the image of a histrionic thot – instead of in the image of a majority owner of a multi-million-dollar empire – Isabell turned away, scowling, and ordered another drink.

Chosen began as her own master of ceremonies, her self-introduction beginning with her origin, a nappy-headed girl from a weed-shod town she failed to name. *But look at me now*, she said, her arms spreading out to the sound of applause. Now a fully blossomed woman, her destiny at hand, she gave honor to God and then the belated Trap, which raised Isabell's brow.

Chosen's self introduction made no mention of a mother or father, no pivotal best friend to call out amongst the audience to give an honored bow. Chosen gave a small speech, promising a thriving future for Hustle Hard entertainment, and then she introduced the first stage performer for the night, Hustle Hard's new protegee Young Boss. She stepped down the front of the stage where squatting photographers flashed cameras, one blinding flash capturing Chosen's glitch when she spotted Sawyer sitting at a table with a pointed stare, Sawyer's finger teasing the rim of a champagne flute.

Chosen swerved and snaked through the crowd. Sawyer got up and followed at a distance, watching as Chosen attempted to hide herself in a crowd of glam. Sawyer saw Chosen backing away from a huddled conversation, unaware that the woman she was trying to avoid was right behind her. Sawyer tapped Chosen on the shoulder. Chosen turned, head and then body, eyelashes appearing to bat against a soft breeze. "Well I'll be damned, Sawyer. Not bad." Chosen said, while eyeing the detective's stylish two-piece crop top, skirt, and high heels. "Prada? At least you tryin', bitch," Chosen said, coolly.

"Look at you," Sawyer said, while eyeing Chosen's rhinestone encrusted body-stocking. "...Out here lookin' like the gingerbread hoe... What'd you do, change your phone number? I was trying to reach you so we can talk about Ben."

Chosen spotted someone coming behind Sawyer and guided her out of the way, "Watch your back, hon. It's a photographer." Chosen shuffled alongside Sawyer and smiled for the series of warm, bright flashes.

Sawyer didn't crack a smile. "Ben had something on you. Coincidentally, he was found dead in his home."

Chosen swat the air, saying, "Girl you late. Carbon monoxide poisoning, they say. Shame." Chosen posed for another flash.

"The furnace was rigged."

"The news report said the furnace was *faulty*, not rigged."

"So, you were watching the news that closely? I find that very interesting..."

Chosen shooed the photographers away like yard chickens. "Wanna know what *I* find interesting? Somebody can assassinate the got-damn president and still you'll be trying to pin it on me.

I swear, Sawyer, you are the hater from hell."

Sawyer replied. "According to the criminal profiler, it's *you* who has a bullseye on *my* back – but wait, there's more: You're a sociopath, manipulative, void of remorse, and display a general discontentment, according to the profiler."

Chosen sighed in exasperation. "You know what, Sawyer? I'm not about to let you ruin my night. Let's you and I have a little talk once and for all. Follow me to the back." Chosen strode towards the back of the club, heading for a door beside the stage, manned by one guard. Chosen whispered something as she slipped past security. The man then slid in behind Chosen, causing Sawyer to bounce off of his large chest. "Sorry you can't go back there," he said.

The man is shaped like a genie, his upper body, large and ominous but legs narrow as if he billowed up from a lantern's neck. Sawyer saw Chosen escaping in the back, but before closing the door behind her, Chosen looked back with a handwave tickling from under her chin, taunting, "Toodles bitch!"

Sawyer flashed her badge to the genie. "I'm undercover. Now, if you'll *excuse* me please." She tried to sidestep him.

He shuffled in defense, and they bumped again. The genie folded his arms. "Damn a badge. Where's your warrant?"

Sawyer pulled out – not a warrant – but the man's unfolded wallet bearing his picture I.D. "I just might have something better."

His eyes stretched with surprise. He pat his backside to

confirm he'd been pickpocketed. "Gimme." He snatched his wallet.

"Mr. Phillip Williams," Sawyer said. "What would I find on your record if I made a simple phone call to have them run your name through the system? Unpaid tickets, back child support?"

The man winced with worry. "I still can't let you back there, miss. This is my job." A bead of sweat inched down his temple.

Sawyer pulled out her phone and started dialing.

By the first ring, the man was willing to help. "Although I can't let you back there, maybe I can help you with some information?"

Sawyer lowered the phone. "What's Chosen's real name –"

"– I don't know these people miss; I just working for them today. What I meant was, I could point out the weed men, the molly boys right here in the club."

Sawyer drained of patience. "What kind of car does Chosen drive? Do you know *that?*" The stage lights flipped on and Young Boss came alive with his second set, at the drop of the beat, which drowned out Sawyer and the genie's conversation. The man had to lean forward and whisper.

*

Sawyer's husband and Trinece neared the front of Savoy's line. It was just Thursday but packed for this special event, attracting the who's-who in the music industry, yet no one recognized the former hit producer, Darius Sawyer, aka Sip. He felt like a refugee in the crowd of self-conscious millennials; the men bolstering their worth in jewelry, with their necks and wrists lit; the women, showing their worth in flesh with their skimpy attire.

Trinece looked womanly in a meshed front, black dress. Darius was sleek in a titanium grey, knit shirt.

A group of skin-tight party girls, fresh off of pregame, was heading for the back of the line when the hand of the one with auburn hair wiped across Darius's belly when she passed by. She had called him a *whole snack*. Darius turned to Trinece. "Whole snack?"

Trinece gave a playful elbow to his ribs. "Don't let it go to your head, big fella." Darius wondered if there was a such thing as a half snack, or an entrée, maybe, just so he'd know where he ranked on the menu.

He and Trinece were there to confront Chosen, who dumped them by voicemail and then changed her phone number. Darius and Trinece came to Chosen's party hoping to talk, like an ex demanding an explanation as an inroad to a second chance.

At the front of the line, the bouncer eyed the pair like outsiders; not a drop of swag for the man in black khakis, and for the young lady, a fawnlike innocence in her small brown face. The bouncer said, "You two must be lookin' for the father-daughter dance." His punchline delivery was penguin-like, short-armed with a giddy tail waggle. Chuckles flamed through the waiting line, this bouncer's nightly audience.

J Money hushed the crowd as he pulled up in the royal blue Rolls-Royce, Wraith. He stepped out in a silk T draped over his gut and a large platinum chain, threatening the valet as he passed the keys. The bouncer stepped back to make a way for J Money, but J stopped and raised a fist to his mouth. "Ohhhhh, shit! Sip? That you bro?"

The two dapped hard and shoulder-bumped. Darius, in seconds, rocketed in status from bud of a joke to mystery celeb.

Darius asked, "You still play from time to time, man?"

J Money's head shook no, in response, and kept shaking no in disbelief for running into an old friend. "What is you doin' standing in line is what *I* wanna know? If Vick saw this, he'd cuss yo ass out." J Money took Darius and Trinece upstairs behind the VIP rope where bottles of Rosay chilled in ice buckets. The entourage, or rather J's security detail, slid down a long sectional sofa, glowing purple eyes hawking the scenery. J Money turned to his honored guests. "I like that short hair, ma. That's hot," he said to Trinece, and then nudged Darius, adding, "Went out and got you somethin' new, ay bro?"

Trinece choked on her chewing gum. Darius touched her hand and explained on her behalf. "This is my business partner. My wife is actually here somewhere."

"Wouldn't know her if I seen her," said J Money. "Same woman, though? The one you left the industry for?"

Darius replied. "I gave up everything, yet I gained everything."

"*Nigga*," J shot, with a smile. "That's, what, twenty years

167

or somethin'? Hell, in that timeframe, I been through two marriages and one long term relationship that went to shit. Why? Because no matter how much they pretend to be about this life, when the babies come, they all want the same thing: they want your black ass at home."

"Ain't that the truth," agreed Daruis.

J replied. "It's *their* truth. Not mine." J Money's head tremored at such nonsense. "So, what brings you to an event like this, you back in the industry now, or what?"

Darius dipped a little. "Maybe... We're here to meet another associate."

"Who?"

Trinece was more forthcoming. "That associate is your boss, Chosen."

"Chosen?" J Money was taken aback; he pointed and said, "But this man here produces music. That's not Chosen's side of the business. *I* manage the music."

"*You* manage the music," said Trinece. "So, *you're* the one we should be talking to, then." Darius gave Trinece a warning eye for her tone, which she idled down when she said, "We were given a verbal contract for one album from the chief executive of Hustle Hard Entertainment –"

"–Wait a minute," Darius interrupted. "Don't you mean, Imperial Inc?"

Trinece sighed like her explanation would be tiring. "The whole reason for this party is for Chosen becoming the majority owner of Hustle Hard Entertainment."

Darius's hands went up as if being robbed. "I'm just sayin' the name on my check said Imperial Inc."

Trinece froze. "Check? You got an advance?"

Darius was taken aback by her greenness. "Because I'm proven."

J Money, after watching the tennis match exchange, dropped a hand on the table. "What the hell's going on? Chosen cuttin' deals behind my back *already?*"

Darius and Trinece explained how Chosen had recruited them as producer and singer and suddenly pulled the plug on the whole thing.

J Money leaned back, reserved, in his chair. "So, y'all in ya feelings right now, thinking because Chosen promised you something that *I'm* obligated to –"

"– Bruh," Darius wiggled a stiff hand. "You know me, dawg. I ain't even the type."

The two then shook hands, J Money explaining, "I know, bro. It's just that I've been sued so many times, I learned not to put it past nobody." Looking out over the crowd downstairs, J said, "The industry now, ain't the industry you left. The industry's fucked up, right now."

Trinece interrupted the peace talks. "Just keep in mind, J Money, that you shook hands with the man who got a check, but what did I get? Something was promised to me."

"Lil girl," J Money said. "Whatever Chosen promised you ain't got nuffin' to do with me."

"My lawyer would beg to differ," said Trinece.

J Money gripped his bearded chin. "So, you talked to a lawyer, huh?"

Trinece's neck swerved and her lips puckered, in a nonverbal, but defiant yes.

"What do you do, ma? Rap, sing?"

"I Sing."

Darius interjected, "And boy *can* she."

J Money said, "I do trap music, yo. I can't do nuffin' wit no singer, but since Sip says you can sing – and I know this man knows his shit – I can put you on with an R&B producer-slash-CEO of his own label who's been looking for a vocalist." J Money pointed downstairs to a young man with an outlaw bandana around his neck and his arms tatted from his short sleeves to his Rolex. "That's lil Duke. He's got a couple hits to his name, but he needs to strike the iron while it's still hot. Brotha needs a vocalist, like now. Go downstairs and introduce yourself, then wave up here at me and I'll wave back, so he'll know I sent you. If he puts you on, my legal obligation is satisfied. Any lawyer will agree."

Without further ado, Trinece shimmied her dress and headed downstairs. She had a sure record deal, according to J Money, while Darius had nothing more than a handshake. With a cheeky smile, Darius looked at J Money and asked, "So, what's up man? You got work for a brotha?" He could use the pay, with a daughter starting college in the fall.

J Money choked his Rosay bottle by the neck and turned it up, in order to delay his response.

A seemingly thirsty Darius added, "Even Trap music needs melody to get radio play, right?"

J Money's head came down with the wine bottle. He wiped his mouth with the back of his hand and said, "The radio mixes used to be Trap's role, a role that was no longer needed, really, because it used to be hip hop seeking play on the radio when it was largely an R&B platform, but now radio is more of a hip hop platform, and it's R&B trying to sound like *us* to get airtime." In short, the answer was no.

They looked down over the balcony to check on Trenice. She had made her way over to Duke. Darius set a hand on J Money's shoulder and said, "Yo, about what happened to Trap, man… That was messed up."

"Fuckin' doctor was trying to kill the girl but messed around and got him too. I had warned him about messin' with them white folks," J Money said, while waving at Duke and Trinece, as planned. The way Duke crowded Trinece's personal space worried J Money. "You know what? I hope I didn't mess up."

Darius asked, "What do you mean?"

"What I mean is, I hope I didn't put ya girl in harm's way."

Darius rotated to face him. "So, that guy, Duke… He's some sort of weirdo?"

J Money nodded yes. "Look at how he's all up in her space, like that. He wants her. There's nothing wrong with wanting, if you're most men. If you're a producer, first you try to charm her. If that don't work, you promise a record deal that won't never happen. You charm. You lie. You ask. This Duke? He takes. I've heard about him tossin' chicks out on the street naked, huggin' their gathered clothes and shit. Nobody outs him because they're afraid of being blackballed in the industry, so he's been getting away with it."

"Not with this one." Darius's fatherly instinct had kicked in. He hurried out of the VIP section and down the stairs to the floor where he shouldered through the young crowd under the spinning disco lights. He approached the pair, nodding at Trinece while extending an introductory handshake to the young producer. "Darius Sawyer."

Duke, with one arm around Trinece, hugged her tighter as if guarding his catch. Trinece cut evil eyes at Darius while his offered handshake died. Trinece said, "Now, I *know* you not trying to insert yourself, after you got that advance and didn't tell me."

Darius replied, "That's not why I'm here. I need to have a word with you."

Duke asked, "Who this nigga?"

"Nobody," Trinece answered as she positioned herself in front of Duke, blocking Darius from joining her negotiations. "Absolutely, nobody."

Darius was stunned by how quickly Trinece had turned against him, by how soon she had let a stranger hug her waist from behind and by Duke's audacity to even try. In the blink of an eye, Trinece went from looking like a woman, to a vulnerable girl costumed in a woman's dress. "Trinece. Hey." Darius grabbed her wrist. "This man is a predator!"

Trinece's eyes stretched at Darius's grip on her wrist. She wrung away and then pointed a two-finger pistol at Darius's temple, yelling, "Do *not* get me confused with Chosen!"

The accusation had Darius incensed. "Come again?" He couldn't believe Trinece, a young lady just three years his daughter's senior, accusing him of wanting her, like she had accused him of wanting Chosen. Trinece had the identities of her protector and the predator crossed up.

Duke, the accused predator, jumped to his own defense. "Bruh, I take care of all my artists. *All* my artists get paid."

Darius sighed over praying hands and said, "You got it all wrong." Wrong about the kind of predator – not a professional predator, but a sexual predator, but the pair wouldn't let Darius clarify. They came at him in waves, tag-teaming their rants, calling Darius everything from a hater to a cornball, with Trinece finally delivering the death blow, *Old washed up ass producer looking for work! Nobody want you!*

They left him feeling his age, and feeling alone in a sardine packed night club of twenty to thirty somethings, a mumble rapper on stage, spitting lyrics over auto-tune that Darius couldn't begin to decipher.

THE NIGHT IS STILL YOUNG

S awyer had located Chosen's hundred-thousand-dollar, matte black Mercedes Benz G-Wagon. The vehicle was not in the valet parking area, but at the club's back door. Sawyer got the license plate number. She called the tags in and got Chosen's true identity: Yvetta Darwin. The real investigation could now begin. Sawyer was about to call it a night, but something told her to go back into the club, and she was right to listen to that voice. She spotted her husband at the bar. On the bar counter beside him, sat a Hennessey shot that he was afraid to touch. Aisha snuck up from behind, put her hands on his body and whispered, "Hey, sexy."

The man hopped up like his barstool was on fire, but then he was relieved to see his laughing wife. Seeing Aisha's body wrapped in that cellophane tight skirt, was all the liquor he needed. Darius replied, "They don't say sexy no more, babe. I'm a whole-snack."

She smiled brightly. "*My* snack." Aisha was loving the way his knit shirt hung over his hero-like shoulders, and how the blacklight gave him the eyes of a nocturnal creature. "We need this kind of lighting for our bedroom." She suspected he was following her again like the last time she went undercover, but she didn't call him on it. It had been a while since they'd went out to a club, so Aisha wanted to take advantage of the situation. She swiped the Hennessy shot and then asked, "Is this yours?"

"I… I wasn't gonna drink it."

"I'll save you from yourself, then." She swirled the glass under her nose, smiling as if on a dare. She'd already had a few glasses of champagne earlier.

"Don't do it babe," Darius warned, knowing that his wife is the worst drinker on the planet.

Aisha put the glass to her mouth, turned it up and then dropped the shot glass on the counter. Her chin tucked, her eyes were teary. She jolted with one suppressed gullet cough; the smothered explosion of a swallowed grenade.

Darius set his hands on her waist and gazed in her eyes, asking, "Who *are* you, woman?"

"It's this atmosphere," said Aisha, as she took his hand and led him toward the dance floor. "Look around you." She was referring to the strobe lights, the skin, bodies jerking to the beat like a mass Tourette's tick. Aisha was in an element Darius hadn't seen in years and he liked it. At a clearing on the dancefloor, she stopped abruptly, causing Darius to rear-end her. Her hips wound back into him, turning the blunder into a dance. She looked back, her red lips poised to speak over her shoulder, eyes slanted at her husband who seemed game for whatever, at the say from his wife. "The carnality," said Sawyer. "It's like I'm in purgatory with my fucking husband," she said, with a backdrop of lost souls, neon-eyed goblins, fuck-dancing.

From the stage, Chosen could've sworn Detective Sawyer was trying to make her jealous, flaunting a love for which Chosen would happily surrender her multimillion dollar empire for. While Chosen was announcing the next item on the program, the tribute to Trap, and calling J Money and Flik to the stage to take over, she spotted Duke escorting Trinece to the back. Knowing Duke's reputation, Chosen figured Trinece was in trouble.

*

Trinece found herself in a backroom that was half storage, half office, with chairs stacked along the back wall and an office desk at the front. Duke took the lemon garnish off the side of his glass and gave it to her. "Suck on that. It'll clean your vocal chords."

It would be a back-office audition and the first day of the rest of Trinece's life. She bit the lemon wedge and frowned. The club speakers beat faintly through the walls and floor; the soundtrack to Trap's montage, the audience's cheers, sounded like a distant block party.

Duke leaned back on the desk. "Ever performed in front of a crowd?"

"I used to, on Sundays."

Duke seemed disappointed. He said, "Church folk are obligated to show love, no matter how you sound. You gotta prove to me you can sing under pressure." Duke eyed the length of her slim body, licking his chops. "Sing something low and sweet. Show me some control."

Trinece cleared her throat and drew still. She wrapped herself in the spirit of Lori Lieberman, like a shawl around her shoulders. The head leaned, her eyes unblinking, as if gazing out of a passenger train window, watching her lover shrink in the distance. Killing Me Softly lyrics fluttered out of her like lovely butterflies.

I heard he sang a good song, I heard he had a style.

"Keep going," Duke said, as he approached her. A confident smirk snuck into Trinece's cheek. If the producer staring her down, in her personal space was what he called pressure, she teased him with her readiness, venturing to role play, making him the romantic subject of the sweet lyrics.

And there he was, this young boy. A stranger to my eyes.

"No matter what. Keep going," Duke whispered, and then he touched her breast.

Trinece clenched with the shock of betrayal, the note *life* ran through a grater.

Duke taunted, "Is that a crack in your voice, I hear? You want this record deal, don't you?"

Tears blossomed from the lashes of her closed eyes. Still Trinece sang, but from a register of stress more deep-seated than her four-year-old Easter recital.

I prayed that he would finish, but he just kept right on.

Duke's hand went up her dress.

Trinece clamped her thighs and gripped his forearm. "No," she said, officially.

Duke had no ears for the word; he muscled against her. "Your career takes off, babe? You'll be glad you did this."

She couldn't release her grip to slap him; it would free his hand to violate her a thousand times worse. Trinece shuffled backwards, whimpering, "Please. Duke." Even in a full-blown sexual assault, Trinece tried to protect her dream of being a singer by not screaming. Her back hit the wall.

"Mm-hmm… Where you gon' run to now? Umma get dat lil' snatch, just you watch." Duke wedged his shoe between hers and began forcing her legs apart, and then his knee between her knees. He relaxed a little, but did not let up completely. He looked in her eyes. "You may not believe it now, baby, but you gon' love it," he said, with a lightening vein thumping at his temple.

Trinece, now negotiating mercy with her attacker, replied, "If you want to be with me, this is not how." As if she could possibly be with him after this.

He twitched and frowned, as if any route other than rape was ludicrous. "Fuck I'm s'pposed to do, wine and dine you? Bitch, this is all I got *time* fo'." His hand shoved between her thighs like an uppercut.

Trinece squealed, "No! Don't!" She'd learned, too late, that the brief exchange of words was a lull tactic. His fingers, like spider legs, began manipulating her panties to the side and he bore inside of her down to the deepest knuckle. Trinece slapped Duke so hard, he staggered back and tremored twice to shake the bees out of his head. He licked the dipped finger while eyeing her; the sting from the slap and the taste of her nectar, fueling his lust. His head jerked on the words: "Ooo-*wee*, that pussy tight!"

Trinece's arms spread against the wall just to hold herself up. Her mind thought *run*, a command her body ignored.

There was a knock at the door. "Duke! I know you're in there." The voice was Chosen's.

Duke looked at Trinece, his eyes burning as he warned. "You don't say *shit*, hear me?" He pointed to a chair in front of the desk and yelled in a whisper. "*Sit* yo ass in that chair and act normal." Duke remained planted until Trinece followed his precise command. Her body had ignored her desire to run, but followed Duke's instruction, as if he were its new owner.

Duke opened the door. Chosen gave a hug and air kisses. Duke appraised her at arm's length, seeing woman's full fruition – twice the woman of the young lady he was assaulting. Chosen waltzed in on the bounce of her hip, stopped in front of Trinece, and spun around. "Duke! Are you trying to steal my artist? Is that what you're doing?"

Trenice crossed her legs tight and blushed quite normally, considering what she'd just endured.

One who'd never experienced what Trinece just experienced would've missed it, but Chosen knew that look. She could see shimmers of the emotional effort that it takes to hold normal together, like glue to a broken vase. Chosen didn't think – she *knew* – what evil had occurred. Chosen remembered – as a prepubescent girl under her uncle's side glances – playing casual in front of the family while a fire smoldered between her legs.

"Are you *sure* this is your artist, Chosen? I mean, here we are – Trinece and me – conducting business and she never even mentioned you," he said, as he sat behind the desk.

Chosen replied, "I'm keeping her under wraps until it's time." She dangled her Mercedes Benz key chain. "Trinece, take my car. I'm parked by the back door. I'll call you in a few."

Duke's palms turned up helplessly. "Is this really happening right now," he said, as he watched Trinece pluck the keys from Chosen's hand, like an olive from a branch, and then hurried without question or hesitation.

Chosen backed against the door, closing them in; just Duke and herself, one on one.

Duke asked, "So *this* is what you wanted? You and me, alone?"

Chosen stomped a heel into the floor. "Yes," Chosen said. "Just so I can tell you that you ain't shit!"

The man turned coy with guilt. "Oh *that?* That was just–"

"–This is my big day, Duke, and yet you don't make your way over to me? I've heard congratulations from everyone tonight but you."

180

A relieved Duke spread his arms in grand fashion. "Congratulations babe."

"Save it." Her pointer finger pushed his forehead.

Duke staggered exaggeratedly and flopped into the seat behind the desk. "Hell, I ain't know you was checking for me like that."

Chosen sat her rump on the desk in front of him. "Duke, wasn't you the one trying your damndest to get with me when I was still with Trap?"

Duke's sly eyes fell to the swell of her butt on the desk top, plump and covered only with what looked like a sheer body stocking, sparkling with rhinestones. "I tried, but you didn't budge, though."

Chosen's eyes narrowed. "Because I'm loyal. No man of mine would ever have to worry about me stepping out."

Duke licked his smoker's lips and said. "That's good to know, babe."

Chosen asked, "Why do you act so standoffish still – watching me from across the room, like Trap is still here or something?"

"It ain't really *that*. It's just that… Well… you *got* money now."

Chosen never heard such foolishness in her life. She spun around on the desk, playfully lifting one leg on a rainbow arc over Duke's head to the other side, so she was facing the seated Duke, her legs parted before him, chest level. "Ok, so… *Now* what," Chosen said.

Half the air in his lungs fell out in a long, "Woa..." He spread his hands on her inner thighs, a thumb reaching, pressing, rubbing in circles over her rhinestone encrusted vulva.

Chosen was well aware that, unlike Trinece, she was too wise, too experienced to appeal to Duke's lust for power, but she could take advantage of his lust for pleasure. She moaned as if his caressing thumb was actually doing something for her.

Duke stood up between her legs so eagerly that the wheeled chair rolled back and crashed into the wall behind him. They kissed, his tongue licking into her mouth. He stopped, confused since there was no skirt or dress to lift out of the way but a one-piece that he didn't know how to get into. "Damn, babe, how do you go to the bathroom in this thing?"

Chosen's head reared back and her mouth opened like a lioness tasting the kill even as she stalks. Her eyes fell level with him. "As bad as I want you, right now. I'm not about to have sex in the backroom of a nightclub; I know my worth."

Duke was offended. "So, you came here just to tease me?"

"No. Take your ass to the valet and have them bring your car around."

"How are you fixin' to leave your own party?"

"I'm not due back on stage for quite a while. We're coming back." *One* of us, Chosen thought with a half-smile.

Duke was stuck between decisions, go or stay, like a pup torn between his master's call and a squirrel in the bush.

Chosen helped him make up his mind by running her hand down the front of her body, apparently, antsy with desire; she made her butt come alive, quaking with stripper twitches. "Pick me up in the alley; I don't want people in my business."

Chosen watched while Duke shut the door behind him. She dug in her purse for her phone to make a call. "Trinece," she said. "What happened in here?" The girl was choking on her sobs; she could hardly make words. Chosen urged her, "Go to the hospital right now and get a rape kit done... Say what? He *didn't*?" Chosen sighed and paced. "What exactly *did* he do? Because I know, for a fact, that *something* happened!" Chosen listened while marching out to the alley. She responded, "I'm gonna make that bastard pay, I promise you... No. Don't go to the police. Girl, he's rich and you're not. They'll treat you like you're after a check. Listen to me! You can't rely on the police. You can't even rely on *God!* The many times He sat up in heaven watching me get raped and didn't do shit?" She's in the mouth of the dark alley, her shadow stretched long and witch-like as she preached her dark sermon into the night. "Justice is a steak knife to the fucking throat with blood pissing from my uncle's neck like a lawn sprinkler. I'll do even worse to Duke."

As Chosen gave Trinece the address to her home, Duke stopped cattycorner in the alley in his pearl colored Bugatti. "Don't leave until I text you," Chosen said into the phone, ending the call as she approached the car. She then said to Duke, "I'm driving." With a smirk, Duke climbed over to the passenger seat, and Chosen got behind the wheel. She put her hand out. "Your phone?"

Duke's brows raised; his head bounced. "My *phone...*"

"So, you can't take any pictures." Duke hesitated. Chosen gave an ultimatum. "Do you want this pussy or not?"

Duke handed over the phone. Chosen revved the engine and tore off into the night, Duke's head whipped back against the seat.

Chosen wove through traffic as if fleeing a bank heist, punching it on straightaways, and screeching around curves. Duke's hands pressed the dashboard, his eyes peeled wide, mouth wailing in protest. "Hey! Yo! Wait! Help! *Laaawwwd*," he screamed, as they roared through a red light.

Only by grace did they arrive at Chosen's place in one piece and without a speeding ticket. Inside, Duke sat on the edge of the plush sofa, unsettled from the roller coaster ride, his hands wringing.

Chosen was at her kitchen's island counter, her back turned, shielding the syringe that she was slowly, carefully, driving into the cork top and emptying clear poison into the champagne bottle. While extracting the syringe, Chosen was as careful as a bomb expert; an imperfect angle would break the needle. The needle broke. "Shit," she said and then covered her mouth. She hovered a fingertip over the broken needle and felt the slight breeze of pressure leaving the bottle. She had little time.

Duke called from the living room couch. "Everything alright?"

"Yeah, baby. I'm just getting us some wine," Chosen replied, as she scampered around the kitchen, searching for a pair of pliers.

"Hell if you *is*… Sounds like you're re-organizing the cabinets or something. Ya-boy stiff as a bone over here, ma." Duke got up and went to the kitchen. Chosen had her back turned, wrestling with the wine bottle to pull the broken needle out of the cork with a pair of pincers. Duke eased up and grabbed her from behind.

A fraction of a shriek escaped Chosen. It wasn't a restraining hug, but a lustful one. He held her tight, pressing her rear end with his boner. He asked, "Why so uptight, babe?"

Chosen was 'so uptight' because the syringe had fallen to the floor. She positioned her shoe in front of it. She churned in Duke's grasp, smiling at the man that she has marked for death. "You scared me, silly. I can't seem to pop the cork. Can *you* do it for me?" Chosen thrust the bottle to him, in order to busy his hands; by reflex, he took the bottle. She handed him the wine opener, spun him around by the shoulders, and she slyly back-kicked the syringe out of sight. She nabbed a wine glass, and then pushed Duke towards the living room with a hand on his back, like a two-member Locomotion dance. Chosen sat him down on the couch.

While Duke fought with the cork, Chosen fought with his belt. He sung, "Yeah baby, that's what I'm talkin' about. Lil nasty self…"

Suddenly Chosen's horny man turned into a thinking man, perplexed by the cork in his hand. "What," Chosen asked.

His eyes strained on the thought. "There wasn't no pop or nothing. This is champagne, yet there was no pressure in this bottle."

Chosen confiscated the bottle, poured Duke a glass of wine and said, "Happens sometimes."

He swirled the glass under his nose. "Where's yours?"

Chosen wiggled her hand in front of her throat. "I can't."

Duke reared black and gave a hard blink. "Fuck you mean, you *can't?*"

"I'm on a fat burner. I drink anything carbonated and I get bloated – and when I say bloated, I mean like…" Chosen inflated her cheeks and then chuckled.

Duke slid his glass on the table. "*I* ain't sippin' on this shit."

"You're tense. It'll relax you."

"Didn't you just hear me?"

Chosen's eyes maddened, offended. "What… You think I put something in it? You popped the cork your*self*, Duke."

Duke smiled. "That's the thing: there *wasn't* no pop. And to be honest, word on the street say you be druggin' niggas –"

"–The streets? Keep following up *the streets*. The streets is gonna get you bounced up outta my house with a chumpy."

"You see, that's that bullshit right there," Duke said behind a pointed finger. "I had a feeling you was gon' renege."

Chosen pressed into the back of the couch with her arms folded. "Maybe somebody should teach you about romance; you don't run up behind a woman, poke her with your dick, and expect her to respond to that."

The man stared Chosen down. "You can have all the attitude you *want*, but I'll tell you what: I'm *gon'* fuck tonight. I don't give a good-got damn if it's you, your housekeeper – if ya got

186

one – pet cat? I'm fuckin 'fore I leave here tonight."

Chosen didn't want this man's aggression. She put on a quite convincing laugh, hoping to bring his stress down. She backhanded Duke in the chest. "Boy you stupid – talkin' bout some damn 'pet cat.'"

Duke laughed along. "I'm tryna tell you, babe. I gots to get mines tonight; hell, I already been teased once."

Chosen snatched him by the outlaw handkerchief around his neck. "Boy, bring your silly self here." Chosen kissed his mouth. "…Talkin' bout I'm trying avoid sex when I sped all the way here because I want it so bad." She kissed him again, steamier this time, grunting in passion. "I need mines too," she said. "I ain't been with a man since months before Trap died."

Duke squeezed her bottom and said, "Enough talk."

Chosen backed off. "One more thing: this outfit is kinda tricky to get out of, so I'll be right back." She left the man on the couch holding himself, his knees flapping in heat.

Chosen returned naked under a black silk robe. She straddled him on the couch, opening the silk robe and feeding her breasts to Duke, the material was like curtains around his face, blinding him to her right hand that was drawing a newly prepared syringe out of her robe pocket. The needle snagged the material. Chosen shook the syringe loose.

Duke felt the hurried movement. "Anxious lil thang ain't you… The dick ain't goin' nowhere."

Since Duke wouldn't drink the poisoned wine, she'd have to inject him herself. Chosen pretended to caress the back of his neck, but she was really feeling out his spine notches like braille. The injection had to go into the spinal column to work as fast as possible. Chosen sighed to brace herself. She'd have a whole minute and a half, give or take, to deal with a grown man, bucking in rage. She prayed, internally, to be spared a broken nose or punched out teeth as she jammed the needle in the space between two vertebrae.

Duke wailed like a tree ape and threw Chosen clear over the table. "*Bitch!?*" He stood, pulled the needle out the back of his neck and looked at it in utter shock. "Aw *hell* fuckin' no!" He tried to hurdle the table in pursuit of Chosen, but tripped and tumbled. Chosen scrambled like a crab, but Duke yanked the hem of her robe, stopping her in her tracks. "*Get* yo ass back here," Duke yelled. He stood with the robe and pulled. Chosen braced forward like a strongman pulling a bus, but then she let her arms back, and the robe slipped off her shoulders; the release slingshot them in opposite directions, Duke stumbling back to the couch; Chosen's momentum shooting her into the kitchen. She went for the knife rack but heard the centrifugal whistle of the airborne wine bottle. She dropped on all fours. The bottle exploded on the wall above her, showering wine and glass shards, and in the quick moment from the bottle's flight and impact, Duke had run into the kitchen.

Chosen found herself on opposite sides of the island counter from Duke. Duke drew a knife from the rack, his eyes blood red. "I don't know what you stuck me with, but if *I'm* dead, bitch, *you* dead too!"

He tried to cut her from across the counter. Chosen leaned back, the blade smearing an arc of silver, an inch from her windpipe. She pat her throat to make sure she wasn't cut. "You raped that little girl!"

"That bitch knew what she was doing when –" He stopped. His face clenched and shook, as if to start again. Sensing death coming ashore, he wouldn't let a lie be his final note on earth. "You don't know *shit* about a man, Chosen," he said, pointing the knife. "We can't repress everything!"

She moved around the island like a dial in direct opposition to Duke's movement. "Repress? What about respect? What about boundaries, decency!"

"I'm talking 'bout *man!* Not just man, but *male* – on two legs and on four – killing baby cubs to just to send the mother into estrus. That's how it is out in nature, but nature ain't just out there. Nature is *in us* too. But man? Oh, we s'pposed to be *civilized*."

"Cubs? Estrus? You spend *way* too much time in that head of yours–"

"–Trying to make *sense* of this shit, can't you see? I'll take your curse over mine. I'll take the curse of a baby nine months. Man's curse will break you in just *one* month."

"Break me?" Chosen almost smiled. "Nigga, *because* of it, I *am* broken!"

Duke's nostrils flared. "You ever walked around with a migraine in your loins, huh? Did God give you wet dreams? Got adolescent boys worldwide rendered powerless by sleep, nature forcing sex upon them in their dreams – the very definition of rape…" Duke's eyes narrowed evilly at Chosen's dismissive gasp. He countered, "Yeah, that's right… Wanna talk about rape? Rape is a part of a man's fucking life cycle. Who's responsible for that?"

Chosen folded her arms and studied Duke, wearily, seemingly through eyes too old to see new ideas, for the recognition of the age-old principles they're rooted in. "When o' when will Evil ever answer to its name," Chosen said. She was biding her time with the debate, figuring she could mouse-chase around the counter for another twenty seconds, give or take, and Duke would be stretched out on the tiled floor. She did not, however, expect Duke to leap on top of the counter, saying, through grit teeth, "Evil? I'm 'bout to *show* yo ass evil!" In the bat of an eye, the landscape had changed. With Duke atop the counter, any escape route available to Chosen became also available and unobstructed to him. Chosen dashed. Duke dove, landing on Chosen's back and riding her to the floor like a mare.

Duke turned Chosen on her back, wanting to see her agony at the plunge of the knife. Chosen's head turned to the side, eyes closed, shielding with forearms crossed, screaming, fully expecting to be pecked to death with a stainless steel, Cutco knife.

Two beats passed. Her eyes opened. Duke had the knife still drawn back, but his face was drained of life, drool strung off his bottom lip as thin as a spider web. He fell forward; the knife coming down with him, still on target for Chosen's breast. Chosen heaved and twitched like turning in bedsheets and the knife hit the floor an inch from the tip of her nose.

The doorbell rang. Chosen shimmied out from under Duke's dead weight and ran to the door. "Get in here," she said to Trinece who came to the address Chosen had texted her.

Trinece shuffled backwards. "Girl, you better put some clothes on! I don't even go like that."

A naked Chosen yanked Trinece in and shut the door. Chosen hurried towards Duke, swiping her robe up off the floor, yelling back, "C'mon, Trinece, I need your help!"

Now inside, Trinece saw Duke's lifeless body, the knife, and suddenly she was standing in a murder scene. She was inside of a mansion with a man dead on the marble floor with his arms pinned under him, and Chosen, barefoot, was tying her robe while standing over the man's body, asking for help to dispose of the body.

Trinece's head shook. "Oh no. Uh-uh…" She pedaled back toward the door, but Chosen outran her. Four hands fought for the door knob, Trinece crying frantically.

Chosen yelled, "That man ain't dead!" She put Trinece in a bear hug, picked her feet up off the floor and spun her around. Chosen backed against the door, guarding the exit as if with her life.

"He ain't dead?" Trinece crept near, hypnotized by the lifeless man. "He drunk? Is he knocked out, or what?"

Chosen hurried over, kneeled next to Duke's body and

rolled him over on his back. "He's in a deep state. He can see us. He can hear us. He can think. As a matter of fact, he can go on thinking about man on four legs killing cubs, or whatever the hell goes on in that deranged mind of his."

"Say what?"

Chosen added, "He's a prisoner in his own body. He can't much blink an eye."

Trinece's face swung back to Duke. "He can hear us talking, right now?" In that case, she kneeled to have a word with the man on the floor. Just above a whisper, Trinece asked, "Who do you think you are? Huh?" Tears fell from the well of eyes that will never see the same after tonight.

"There you go," Chosen encouraged from the background. "Don't hold it in."

Trinece began pointing a finger on Duke's forehead with each stressed word. "Who are you, to *think*... that you don't need... my *permission!*" Trinece was huffing, her finger jabbing harder in Duke's face. "You fucking *monster!*"

"Let him have it, girl!"

Trinece slapped Duke's deadened face. "How does it feel, huh? How! Does! It! Feel!" She showered him with palms to the face again and again with one hand, and then both hands. She went berserk, screaming and wailing on him.

Chosen pulled her up by her armpits; Trinece threw kicks as she was dragged away. Chosen held Trinece from behind, restraining her, yet consoling her. "Enough, sugar. Enough. No amount of punishment can undo what's been done. For what he did to you… Beating him – even killing him – will never make it go away. That violation is now forever your shadow. It'll follow you when you walk to your car, when you're home alone, when you meet someone new. It follows you into the most intimate spaces in your life. The more anger you give it, the bigger that shadow becomes. If you're not careful, it will grow bigger than you. And suddenly you realize that, the thing is no longer *your* shadow, but that you have become *its* shadow."

Trenice sobbed miserably in Chosen's arms. "It's not fair, Chosen. I didn't ask for this…"

Chosen, staring into the depths of her past, answered. "Me neither." But then Chosen remembered the time. "We've got to hurry. Help me put him away. We need to get back to the club, like *right* now, okay?" Together they drug Duke's body into the basement, letting his head thud every stair step on the way down.

Chosen disappeared down a hall and returned dressed in her sheer rhinestone encrusted bodysuit, fanning her light sweat. "Follow me," Chosen said.

Chosen drove off in Duke's car. Trenice tailed in Chosen's car. They sped down the interstate, a Mercedes behind a Bugatti until Chosen finally pulled over. Trinece followed suit and waited for what felt like a year compressed into a minute until Chosen hurried over and got in, a passenger in her own car. Trinece dropped the vehicle in gear and sped past Duke's car, which was filling with smoke. "We're going to prison," Trinece cried.

Chosen gripped her arm. "No, we're not! Nothing destroys DNA like fire."

"What if someone saw us."

"These people are flying by eighty miles an hour, girl. They eyes is on the road." The half-million-dollar car exploded in the distance, the orange flames illuminating the rearview mirror.

*

Aisha and Darius were still at it, dusting off of their Cha-Cha lessons from a decade ago. Aisha high-stepping and twisting; hips one way, torso the other, the disco ball spinning constellations all around them. The younger crowd was awed as if they'd never seen anything like it. Darius spun her out to arm's length, then spooled Aisha back in, the two stopping bosom to bosom, face to face, smiling, panting, as the song faded down. There was a round of applause; the elder couple had stolen the night for themselves.

The stage lights faded down and there was a hush among the crowd. There was a delay. Chosen was scheduled for the stage, but apparently, she was nowhere to be found.

J Money approached them on the dance floor. Looking back at one of his boys, but pointing at Darius, J Money said, "I'm sooo jealous of this dude, right now. This your old lady, bro? You married to po-po?" Just as J gave Sawyer a half hug, a member of his crew threw their arm around J Money and whispered in his ear. Hearing the report, J Money's smile faded. "Get ya man's and them. We gon' have a lil talk with this nigga."

Sawyer asked, "What is it, J? What's happening?"

J Money thumbed over his shoulder and said, "Got some bidness to take care of." He then took off.

Darius asked, "How do you know J Money? You arrested him or something?"

Distractedly, Sawyer watched the group's movement, how they were rounding up soldiers with hand signals, like a silent resistance. Something bad was about to go down.

Darius took Aisha's hand. "Babe?"

Sawyer came to. "Oh, I questioned J Money once, while I was investigating his business partner, Chosen."

Darius's head nod dropped his mouth open. "Investigating *Chosen*, for what?"

Her eyes came off of the crew to look into her husband's face. "You say that name like you know her." While Darius stammered for a reply, Sawyer noticed a familiar face, and suddenly she knew why J Money and his crew were grouping up. Sawyer gripped her husband's shoulders and looked in his eyes like life depended on what she was about to say. "I need you to stay right here, ok?" She retreated backwards, watching to make sure her husband stayed put.

Anyone who knows Sosa would recognize him on sight because of the galaxy of freckles in the T of his face, showing a richer contrast under the violet club light. Sawyer hurried towards him, but Sosa was also coming to her. "Sosa," Sawyer called. "You gotta get out of here." She put a hand on his shoulder, but he shrugged it off.

"I tried listening to you once before, but you tried to screw me," he said.

Sawyer jerked him by the arm. "You're drunk."

His arms raised like wings. "How the hell is this Chosen's party but can't nobody find Chosen?"

"Chosen is the least of your worries, right now."

He blinked hard and his head shook. "The club's packed and the main attraction not here?"

"Sosa! Take a look behind me!"

He leaned and saw J Money's crew, two men leaving them, trotting down the steps from the VIP section, necks stretching to look in Sosa's general direction. Sosa knew they were coming for him. He and J Money had bad blood ever since he'd stolen that gold Desert Eagle.

Sosa skipped backwards a few strides but then turned and ran. Sawyer ran after him to help him escape. The two shot out of the building, Sawyer with her high heels in her hand. "This way," she said and turned him toward Popular and Forsythe and ran for a hundred feet. "Back there!" She took him behind the club to the back-parking lot. "Look! There's a break in the fence. Go! I'll hold em off."

As Sawyer retreated around the corner, a duo of goons came to a running stop. The one in skinny jeans and white sneakers yelled, "Where he at?"

"He's gone," Sawyer answered, defiantly.

The other, with a face tattoo and a gold grill, walked up on Sawyer. "Hold up. You helpin' this nigga? You his bitch?"

Sawyer took a defensive stance. "Take another step, and I'll make you *my* bitch."

Skinny jeans squinted in the distance. "I see that nigga Sosa right there."

He pulled out a gun and aimed. Sawyer darted over to him and bat the gun hand upward. The shot fired at the moon. Sawyer, with a shoe in each hand like a pair of martial arts Sai, chopped the gun hand, and the pistol fell. Skinny Jeans took a swung. Deftly, Sawyer spun under the punch, the other shoe arcing out in a backhanded high-heel stamp on the forehead. Skinny Jeans retreated in pain, his screamed *Fuck* doubled from an echo off the side of the building.

A sneer on her upper lip, Sawyer smarted, "You like that?" She heard the grit of sneakers wheeling to her rear. She spun around. Tattoo face had closed in. Sawyer threw both shoes as a diversion. The moment he popped up from ducking the shoes, Sawyer met him with a leaping roundhouse kick to the head. Tattoo Face fell over the hood of a parked car, setting off its alarm.

With each man somewhat subdued, it bought Sawyer a moment to pull out her badge. "Atlanta P.D., bitches!"

She heard feet running and turned to defend herself, but it was Darius, using all of his running momentum to shove Skinny Jeans in the back. The boy snatched forward with such force, his body whipped as if a car had plowed him in the back. The impact propelled Skinny Jeans into a run that he couldn't sustain nor stop until he tripped over his own feet, tumbling and rolling on the pavement. Darius, in chest-pounding authority, yelled, "That's my wife, bro!"

The goons were leaving, limping and groaning in pain, powerless against Sawyer's kryptonite badge. As they walked past, Darius made Skinny Jeans flinch with a jab-step feint, and then taunted, "Yeah, that's what I *thought*."

Sawyer tried not to laugh at her husband's effort. "You've done enough, babe." Aisha hugged her husband from the side, patronizing him. "I don't know what I would've done without you."

There was something else Sawyer needed to investigate: Chosen's disappearance. On the way back toward the club, she saw Chosen's SUV parked by the back door, and figured she was inside after all.

Darius strutted over to the vehicle. "The hood's still hot. She must've left and came back." He then brandished a smile. "I saw that on TV once."

Aisha Sawyer gave her husband, her buddy detective for a day, a thumbs' up. "Good work, partner."

WHEN IT
ALL FALLS DOWN

Only Detective Travis would halt his turning world just to show interest in whatever Sawyer was interested in, even if it undermined the case. He tuned into Sawyer like his favorite show, hearing how she'd uncovered that Chosen was born Yvetta Darwin of Walterboro, SC. Travis seemed hungry for more details on Chosen, even though there were more Cofield former med students to interview and more records to obtain subpoenas for. As the lead on the investigation, he'd come into Sawyer's office to pile more onto her workload, but instead of *telling* her about the work that needed to be done in pursuit of Cofield, Travis was *listening* – but not listening from a position of weakness.

Strategically, Travis knows that the only current, female homicide detective, has an appetite for affirmation, and if Travis wanted more mornings like this: sitting in a swivel chair beside her, close enough to see the window light scatter prism colors in her eye lashes, and to observe her pretty hands animating her ideas, he'd have to be all ears and astonished eyes. Hearing about Sawyer's tussle the night before, Travis reared back in his chair, chuckling. "Really? You took out two goons by yourself?"

Sawyer was all smiles. "You should've seen it. I felt like I was in The Matrix, but I wasn't *all* by myself. Here come D–"

"*D?*"

"After it was all over, he ran up and shoved Skinny Jeans in the back–"

"–From *behind*, though?"

"You should've seen him. Chest all puffed out like he saved the day," said Sawyer, punctuating with twisted lips and cut eyes.

Travis laughed himself into a daze. "But what about Chosen though? Did she resurface?"

"She came back to the stage, in her lil' see-through outfit, child – looking like a gingerbread hoe." Sawyer was a comedian all of a sudden, or at least Travis's laughter made her feel like one. "I later saw her arguing with this woman. I say argue, but it was more like Chosen *explaining* herself to this woman. And Chosen doesn't seem to be the type to explain herself to anybody. This woman looked like a lawyer or something… I thought, well, whoever she is, she seems to have some influence over Chosen so, naturally, I was interested in her. The bartender says her name is Isabell, the night club owner's daughter. And guess what high-profile lawyer she's engaged to?"

"Who?"

"None other than your boy, Thaddeus Broussard."

"Egghead Broussard, you mean?"

"The one and only."

"Wow." Travis rocked his chair back on two legs. "Sounds like you had fun last night. But in a hostile environment like that, you shouldn't go undercover by yourself. You should've called me."

"Good thing I didn't – since Darius showed up. Imagine if he saw us together, after that scene at the coffee joint?" Sawyer's hand swatted limp.

Between the lines, Travis read that if Sawyer could be assured anonymity, she *would* go out with him, to a club – if only to investigate – perhaps. That perhaps was like saltwater taffy in his mouth, as he slipped into a daydream.

Daphne came to Sawyer's door, frantic, as if someone was in labor down the hall. "Sawyer? There's someone out front making a formal complaint against you."

Sawyer waved it off. "Won't be the first time."

"This one's rich. She looks like she's somebody important."

Sawyer stood. Travis stood. The two turned to each other with puzzled looks.

Sawyer came down the hallway, not so much in a hurry, but every stride quick and determined. She was nearly floored by who she saw out front: Chosen, with her hair tied in a bun, wearing a skirt-suit, as if she's dressed for a day in court.

Sawyer's fists drew to her hips. "You have no idea what you're doing, do you?"

Chosen tucked the clipboard under her arm. "Your relentless stalking leaves me no choice, detective. I feel like I'm under twenty-four-seven watch. And here you are, trying to intimidate me, even as I file the complaint."

Sawyer's head shook. "A murderer complaining about unfair treatment..."

Chosen turned to the secretary. "She's using that badge to carry out a grudge."

Sawyer called the name her investigation uncovered. "Yvetta."

"What." Chosen's eyes shut and she mouthed *damn* at her error.

"Gotchya." Detective Sawyer's pointed finger shook at Chosen, while she let Travis pull her back towards the door. Sawyer added, "The investigation on you has only now begun."

"Whatever you say, bitch," Chosen said, but at the same time, Chosen was texting. Next, she watched her text arrive at its destination: Sawyer's hip.

Sawyer felt her phone buzz, and would've thought nothing of it until she saw Chosen's finger descend on the send button, and again, Sawyer's phone buzzed. "Are you texting me?" Sawyer pulled the phone out of her belt clip and found a slide show featuring her very own husband, mounted by Chosen in a room with neutral colors and impersonal furniture; a hotel room.

Sawyer's phone dropped. She rushed like a mad woman.

Chosen shuffled back in fear, saying, "Y'all better get her!"

They tried, but so much happened in that split second. Sawyer sweep-kicked the inside of Chosen's right leg. Chosen would've dropped into a full split if Sawyer hadn't caught her by the throat, strangling with both hands. The clipboard fell, papers swirled. A strangled Chosen's scream was just a long wheeze.

Travis and Daphne rushed to Sawyer, trying to pull her arms away, but Sawyer had a pit bull's hold on Chosen, whose eyes bulged under strangulation. Callahan and officer Brown came in and dove into the melee, bodies scrunched, like five adults wrestling in a phone booth, barking, Stop! Wait! Sawyer!

Finally, they pried her hands apart and Chosen poured flat on the floor like a puddle, gasping with her skirt scrunched, panties peeking. As they were corralling Sawyer out, Chosen sat up into a sitting position, frowning and massaging her throat as she said, "Thank you, bitch."

Sawyer was inconsolable. She fought to get at Chosen again, but they walled her off. The commotion brought Gil out of his office. Seeing Chosen on the floor holding her throat, Sawyer irate, hellbent on fighting through her fellow detectives to finish what she apparently started. Gil calmed everything with his hand out and his heartbreaking request, "Sawyer. Hand 'em over." All faces turned solemn, except for a delighted Chosen, while Detective Sawyer handed over her badge and gun. Gil said, "I'll hold onto these for now. You sit tight at home until further notice."

Slowly, regretfully, she followed instruction. Travis shouldered through and handed Sawyer her phone. She stormed out, speed walking in rage. Travis ran behind her, calling, "Sawyer... Sawyer..."

Out in the parking lot, Sawyer stopped and leaned back against her car, arms down by her side.

Travis grasped her upper arms like bars. "Don't you worry Sawyer. Everything's gonna be ok. It's not over."

What's not over, Sawyer wondered. Her career; the investigation on Chosen; her marriage? Either one, or all, could be at an end, directly. Sawyer had stormed out to hide her tears from her male colleagues, but outside, standing in front of her car, she let tears fall in the presence of Travis who'd consoled her before, and who has become closer to her ever since. She leaned into his embrace and wept on his chest.

THE MOMENT
OF TRUTH

Aisha's personal handgun lay on the living room table beside her crossed feet. She sunk back on the couch with her arms folded. Darius entered with a casual *Hey babe*, realizing there was nothing casual about this day. "Why is your gun out on the table like that," he asked, frowning.

"The girls are at your mothers," Aisha replied.

His wife's glare ignited Darius's guilty conscience. He remembered that, just the night before, at the club, Aisha said she was investigating Chosen; he feared maybe her investigation had turned up surveillance of him entering Chosen's hotel room. "Everything alright babe?"

Aisha released the gun clip and ejected the bullet from the chamber, maybe to save them both from a snap decision. "That's precisely the question I want to ask you. *Is* everything alright?" She had no tears left to shed.

"–Babe…" Darius had turned ill. His sigh embodied twenty years of sighs. "C'mon now, you're freaking me out."

"In the beginning, I never, ever had proof… I even thought maybe I was being unfair for not trusting you." She held her phone up. "*This?* This changes everything… This makes me think that everything I ever *thought* you did – you fucking did!" Aisha walked over and shoved her phone into his chest.

Darius took the device and turned it around in his hands. The images buckled his knees. "Hold up… I was there only to sign a contract. That's all. This ain't… Dude in the picture is supposed to be *me?*"

Aisha was appalled that he didn't respect her enough to come clean in the face of clear evidence. "Oh, it's *you*, you son of a bitch," Aisha said, as she wound back and slapped the features off of Darius's face.

At impact, a light pulse scattered into stars. Darius's eyes popped wide. "Ay!"

Aisha went at him again, coming down on his ducked head with openhanded wallops screaming, "You son of a bitch. I deserve better!"

He scurried back, pleading. "Babe! Yo! Go'head on, now!"

For such a skilled fighter, the two times she's wailed on him, in all their years including this, she'd fought like a teen girl.

Darius caught her hands. "Babe. I didn't do this. *This?!*"

Aisha's eyes widened and her fists tightened. "Who is that in the picture, then?"

"Babe, look at my eyes." Aisha looked at him, but Darius redirected her to the phone. "In the *pictures*. In all these pictures, my eyes are closed!" He thumb-swiped between the pictures. "See? Closed! Another one. Closed!"

Aisha took the phone. "Your eyes are only showing on a couple–"

"–And they're *closed*. Don't you think there's a *reason* for that!" An epiphany hit Darius in the chest; he looked like he was suffering a heart attack.

"Darius… D…" Aisha was talking to a manikin.

Whispering to himself, he said, "No. No. This can't be."

Aisha wanted to shoot him in the penis, but instead she offered this verdict: "I have the girls at your mother's house so they wouldn't have to witness you packing."

"Babe. I was drugged. I smoked some weed and the next thing you know I was out. I thought it was a bad reaction because I hadn't smoked in, Lord knows how long."

The possibility rinsed over Aisha and she was left stunned. "Chosen gave you weed? You smoked it! What about your sobriety?" Aisha immediately thought about how Chosen put Sosa to sleep using weed, and what she did to him while he was asleep. Her husband's eyes were closed in the photos; it made perfect sense. "My God," Aisha said, her arms out to balance her in her spinning world. "You're not the first, Darius. You were raped." Aisha threw herself into her husband and held him. "I'm so sorry."

Darius seemed confused. "But remember babe, that night..." Aisha's head tossed back from the embrace, she looked in dire need of whatever information he could share. "What about that night?"

He was going to remind her that on the same night, he came home begging for pity-sex, so maybe Chosen was only staging sex for the photos, because Darius was never relieved of that *need* until later with Aisha. He'd started talking too soon, however, because if he's no rape victim, he's just a married man in a single woman's hotel room. "That night? Um..." Darius swallowed a lump in his throat. "I was gonna say – or rather ask – do you think that the drug she used might still be in my system, like maybe we could do a toxicology?"

Aisha touched her chin with a finger, thinking. "How long ago was this?"

"A month?"

"Too much time has passed." She slipped into deep thought again, some new horrible thing to consider.

Her concern worried Darius. He asked, "What is it?"

"Do you remember feeling tender back there?

"Back where?"

"The last guy she did this to, she sodomized him, so do you remember if you felt any tenderness, or rawness back there?" A silent discomfort loomed. Aisha thought her husband needed clarity. "I'm referring to your booty hole."

Her husband just stood there staring at her like she was stupid. "No."

"Are you sure?"

"I'm sure. And ain't no doctor or nobody else going in there peeking around neither. Not *this* ass."

"Too much time has passed anyway." Aisha grabbed her husband's hand, channeling her strength to him. "We have to report it. She needs to be charged with this rape."

"But there's no evidence. It becomes word against word. Who will they believe? Man or woman?"

"You really need to check that ego of yours."

"But I'm sayin' I don't even *feel* raped."

"Only because you slept through it. That doesn't mean you weren't."

"It was you she was after. Since I'm the dearest thing in the world to you. She raped you *through* me."

Aisha's anger felt like a wave of heat washing down her face, springing tears. "If you want this marriage, you're going to call the police and you will report this. Or we're done!"

Darius wanted to argue the point, but figured words would only dig him a deeper hole; he was already waist deep in his own grave.

"Wait –" said Aisha. "–Don't call, actually. You know what? Don't tell anyone," she said, a hand knifing the air.

Darius was all too ready to put the phone away, but then his worry changed tracks. "What's changed all of a sudden?"

"The law can't give Chosen what she really deserves."

"Don't do nothing crazy, Aisha. You have a family to think about."

Her head cocked sideways. "Don't you start thinking about family *now*. Did you think about *family* when you went to that hotel room?" Aisha turned away, distracted by her loathing. "The audacity of this bitch," Aisha said. "Chosen fucked my husband! You picked the right one now, Chosen," Aisha said, her eyes bleeding tears. Darius tried to console, but Aisha halted him with the white of her hand. "Don't you dare!"

"I thought *I* was a victim, here." He shrugged.

Aisha flexed claws, showing her first mind to gouge his eyes out, but she relaxed and said, "She didn't drug you until *after* your weak ass went to her hotel room."

Drenched in disgust, Aisha walked slowly to the table. She couldn't even hear Darius's heart-pouring apologies, not that anything he could say would've taken affect. She picked up the gun just to return the clip and holster it. Her mind raced as she stood there, shoulders slack, her head tilted, madness settling in her bones. No other suspect had ever tried to ruin her in this way. Chosen raped her husband and was bold enough to come down to the police department to goad Sawyer with the pictures, in hopes that Sawyer would do something to get herself removed from the investigation and maybe even ruin her career.

Aisha's hand ran back through her hair, thinking she should've known Chosen was at least this evil, since she used her never-to-be-born fetus as a bargaining chip for a life insurance policy, the payday for Trap's murder. Even when she showed up at Meegan's candlelight vigil it didn't seem, to Sawyer, like Chosen was there out of remorse for the unintended casualty; she was there for intel. Sawyer remembered their stare down, with Chosen at the coffee shop storefront and Sawyer riding away; Sawyer now knew the depths of malice in Chosen's glare.

Chosen had managed to contaminate the most intimate and sacred space in Sawyer's life. The memory of what Chosen did, would be an elephant in Sawyer's bedroom. Never again could she make love to her husband without being reminded of Chosen. Under the weight of these thoughts, Sawyer buckled at the knees and screamed at the top of her lungs.

Darius jumped into action, to comfort his wife in her mental breakdown. He was quick to hold her tight, to kiss her cheeks and forehead. His eyes shut tight to seal off tears as he whispered, tenderly, *It's ok, babe. We're gonna get through this.* They held each other and cried.

Sawyer then sat motionless in her husband's arms. After a stretch of minutes, her eyes drying while staring at the taupe wall paint, she said to her husband, "I guess you'd better get packing."

MEANWHILE

Under normal circumstances, with school out for the summer and Sawyer on suspension, Sawyer would've taken full advantage of the opportunity to spend quality time with her girls – maybe a little shopping, a matinee, a trip to the city aquarium. Instead, Sawyer continued to drop the girls off at their grandmother's while she pursued the investigation on Chosen aka Yvetta Darwin. Sawyer's life was repurposed to one ambition: putting Chosen away for the double murder and for raping her husband. On sleepless nights her bedroom ceiling tormented her with scenes of that hotel room. Although she doesn't blame Darius for what happened to him, and him going to the hotel room of a beautiful woman isn't divorceable, it was the fact that meeting with Chosen was so important to Darius that he left work early and kept it secret that was so unspeakable; therefore, she stopped speaking to Darius altogether. Internally, Sawyer acknowledged that maybe her time would've been better served working on her marriage, doing couples therapy, as Darius suggested. Sawyer decided against pursuing her own happiness in order to pursue Chosen, knowing full well that it could cost Sawyer – not only her marriage – but her career, if Gil learned that while on suspension, Sawyer was conducting a rogue investigation against the woman suing the department over damages caused by Sawyer herself.

By Wednesday, they called Sawyer in to let her know her fate. She stood numb in the office with Gil and the captain as they handed her a week suspension, counting her three workdays missed while awaiting that verdict.

Before Sawyer made it out of the building, Jo caught up to her. They ducked in Jo's office like secret agents. Jo said, "You can go ahead and kill the investigation on Chosen."

"Kill the investigation on Chosen," the woman who drugged and raped Sawyer's husband. Sawyer folded her arms and sneered. "No."

Jo dipped forward in disbelief. "If a suspension teaches you nothing, will you process this: she's suing us for harassment and for your assault, so anything we do is now will be perceived as retaliation. Chosen has also put out a restraining order against you. So, please tell me, Sawyer, what in the world could she have said to make you put your hands around that woman's neck?"

"She came at me first," Sawyer said.

"Your self is the only person you could tell that lie to."

"Well, Chosen has two selves: one who has degrees biology and chemistry where she finished at the top of her class."

Unfazed, Jo replied. "Education doesn't make a killer."

"A twenty-million-dollar insurance policy does."

"A policy of that amount is not unusual for someone of Kendall Miller's wealth, but aside from all of that," Jo said, as she waved her hands. "We've actually got some goods on Cofield now: he had an abusive father, a devoutly religious man, community pillar type, but behind closed doors he was an abusive alcoholic who beat his children with belts."

Sawyer laughed. "Was Cofield's daddy named Richard Livingston too?"

"If your dad also stripped you and your siblings naked, chained you to a radiator and beat you while reading scriptures, maybe."

Sawyer leaned away scornfully.

"So, the thing that was missing on Cofield, we now have. That level of violence doesn't just pass through someone. It takes residence inside of you. Hurt people hurt people."

"And that's the gist of your defense? Unlike the Crowder overturned conviction, this time it won't take years. Cofield will be pie on your face by jury deliberation."

Jo backed away, brows raised above a straight face. "Again, Sawyer, what did Chosen do to you that made you attack her?"

Without a reply, Sawyer left, slamming the door behind her and speed-walking down the hallway, panel lights streaking above. She heard footsteps behind her, faster than her own.

"Ay! Sawyer!" It was Travis, running her down until they were shoulder to shoulder, his head turned to her determined silence. "Do I even need to ask? What'd you get," he asked, his eyes darting, looking for the slightest guide to become whatever Sawyer needed, sympathy, empathy, a listening ear, a comforting shoulder, whatever.

"They gave me a week. The incident goes on my permanent file." Sawyer kept walking fast. She was still embarrassed by having let Travis see her cry three days earlier.

"Hey, can you slow down for a second?"

Sawyer slowed, she sighed, she stopped. "I'm ok, Travis. Really, I am."

"Breakroom's right over there. The coffee's still free."

"Remember what happened the last time we had coffee," Sawyer said, but still followed Travis into the breakroom.

They were leaning against the counters, stirring in their creamers and sugars when Travis asked, "Are you *ok?*"

"I'll live."

"Those pictures. That was fucked up."

Sawyer faced him, squinting. "What?"

"When I handed your phone back to you. I saw those texts from Chosen. That's why I'm asking if you're ok."

"Don't mention those pictures to anyone." Sawyer put her lips to her coffee cup but remembered. "It wasn't consensual, by the way. Chosen drugged my husband."

Travis's brows raised only because his head dipped. "Is that what he's telling you? And you're buying it?"

"It's her M.O., Travis. Darius didn't want what he got any more than Sosa wanted what he got."

"But what's a married man even doing alone with her?"

Sawyer looked away in disgust. "Walking his naïve ass into a trap."

"Is *he* the naïve one? Traps have bait, Sawyer. What do you think a woman like Chosen *uses* as bait?"

"A recording contract, Travis. I know my husband."

Travis slumped in disgust. "Maybe you *forgot* you knew him when you put your hands around Chosen's neck." Instant regret surfaced. "I'm sorry, I... I just don't want to see you hurt." All this time Travis thought Sawyer was a woman of absolutes – light-switch judgement – on or off, guilty or innocent, honest or crook. Now suddenly, she was seeing levels, blaming the blindness of naivety, and the lure of a contract, ways to minimize the fact that her husband entered a hotel room of a woman with a body that put's a Nikki Minaj to shame. Travis figured Sawyer wasn't being real with herself, but then being honest with himself, Travis was in denial that from a small, primitive place inside of him, he was angry at Sawyer for not abruptly leaving her marriage and seeking comfort in him.

"Don't apologize, Travis. Your tough words come from a tender place. You're the one person here that I can call a friend."

Travis's heart filled with pride. "Won't be the same without you here."

"It's only a couple more days–"

"–Plus, the weekend."

"Besides, I'll be in contact. I can't log into the database. Can I call on you if I need anything?"

Travis smirked. "I'm really failing as a friend if you think you even have to ask." Travis bit down and said, "You're a good woman, Sawyer. All around..."

"Good..." Sawyer said with a contemplative smirk.

Travis stared at Sawyer, trying to get a bead on her emotion. "Is there something wrong with being good?"

Sawyer sighed and set her Styrofoam cup on the counter. "Old church ladies are good. I don't wonder if I'm good. I wonder if I'm *hot*. Or has Darius been telling me lies for the last twenty years?"

Travis rubbed his chin and looked down at his shoes, then looked up, inspired. "Let me put it this way: A man looks at a woman like Chosen, and his thoughts go no further than that night. A man looks at you and he starts seeing his happily ever after."

"You suck, you know that." Sawyer gave Travis a soft, chummy punch to the solar plexus. Travis caught the fist at impact, with a slight grimace. He felt Sawyer's fist soften in his grasp. Sawyer pulled back her hand, not so urgently, yet not so reluctantly either. "Thanks, actually. I needed that," she winked, and then turned to leave. While walking away, Sawyer wondered, for the first time, if Travis was watching her walk.

BLACK MAGIC

What made the prosecutor decide to stick with Dr. Cofield as the prime suspect was information about the violence in the man's past. Jo said that education alone doesn't build the narrative of a murder; their past does, violence does. So, Sawyer went exploring Chosen's past. Basic research revealed that by the sixth grade, Chosen's – or rather Yvetta's – mother had died of an aneurism. She had two older siblings, brothers. Chosen was Randy and Babette's successful last try for a girl. Out of the family of five, only the father, Randy, remained at the aqua blue, bricked-in mobile home with black shutters, in the county of Walterboro, SC.

The prow of Sawyer's car nosed into the yard where two men in overalls stood under a shade tree. They leaned against a pickup truck, listening to its radio. One chewed a straw and the other whittled a wood block with a pocket knife, like a living stereotype of rural complacency.

Neither man moved to greet Sawyer; something untrusting about city folk. The man whittling the wood block, flicked his head and said, "This here Oinest. He a'ight."

"Earnest?" Sawyer shook his hand first, and then said to the man who introduced them, "And you must be Randy, Chosen's father." Sawyer saw Chosen's lake reflection in the man's face, the sharp M arch of the upper lip, the blunt brow and the deep seam edging the nose and cheeks like a jigsaw puzzle.

Randy pointed a thumb at Sawyer while saying to his friend, "I told this 'oman here that me and Chosen don't talk. Still she came all this way."

"It's not that I don't believe you," Sawyer said. "If you and Chosen were close, you'd have a brand-new truck instead of this old thing, but this isn't about the here and now."

"Drove *all* this way," Randy mused.

"Chosen's your daughter, isn't she?"

"*My* daughter named Yvetta. Chosen is the daughter of Faye."

Sawyer frowned. "Say what now?" His backcountry tongue too quick.

"*Faye*, I said… Faye."

Sawyer's research says Chosen's mother was named Babette. "I take it you don't like this Faye."

Randy nudged his buddy. "*You* like Faye, Oinest?"

Earnest adjusted his hat. "About as much as I like a hole in my head."

The whittling block slipped out of Randy's hand and he bent over to retrieve it.

Sawyer asked, "What does this Faye have to do with Chosen and why do you hate her?"

Randy began dusting off the whittling block he'd just picked up from the ground, ignoring Sawyer.

Earnest leaned forward off the truck, looking down the row. "Miss? His ears is ringin' in perpetuity. Too many years of them TNT explosions down at the rock quarry. If he ain't lookin' right at ya, he can't hear too tough."

Randy turned to Earnest. "Whatchya say hoss?"

Earnest answered, "The lady axed why we don't like Faye."

Randy swatted the question like a gnat. "Who *would* like a real-life witch –"

The quick spurt sentence blurred past Sawyer. "A what?"

"A root lady… Thought it was all rumor 'til Yvetta went ober there to live with Faye."

"After your wife died?"

Randy dumped the whittling block in the truck bed and pocketed the knife. "1989. Hell raised up, ya hear me? Babette, out yonder in the field pullin' sweet grass, fell and died. Yvetta's period came while standing before her mother's casket. Year wadn't half over when Yvetta stabbed the man who *s'posed* to be my brother – I would've kilt him *myself* had I knowed what was going on…" Randy massaged one hand with the other. "The moment Faye got in that child's ear, Yvetta went from bad to woist."

Sawyer spent an hour leaning against the truck, shootin' the breeze with a couple of old timers; hashing out the timeline and details of that trying year – the year that Chosen's innocence died and a killer was born. Sawyer couldn't wait to inform Joanna of the things these country men were saying – all true. Cofield's past didn't compare; the chains, the belts, the paternal monster justifying the abuse with scripture – was nothing compared to Chosen's past, with her mother passing, the incestuous rape, and Chosen, at age eleven, murdering her uncle, who they say was the spitting image of her father, her point of reference for *all* men.

Randy gazed into the distance, his mouth narrating the haunting memory, first describing a festive day out in the yard, celebrating the generous creek with a fish fry, when the youngest son went inside to fetch another pan of cleaned fish from the ice box, and found his uncle twitching in a pool of his own blood, the brother's eyes then following his sister's blood-stained shoe tracks out the door where she played double Dutch with the other girls, like it was nothing. When the adults rushed the scene, the question the shell-shocked brother kept asking was, *But why uncle pants down like that?*

Randy believes, down to the marrow of his bones, that Faye groomed Yvetta for murder because when Yvetta was questioned, as Randy described, *the mouth of a child spoke the mind of an adult.* She didn't blame herself, as children do. When asked how, after killing her uncle, could she play outside like it was nothing, she replied: *same as uncle rape me*

221

and go play cards with daddy and them like it's nothing.

The Department of Social Services took Yvetta, citing that neglect allowed the incestuous rape; they later released her to Faye, who was next of kin outside the home. Randy said he argued to have his daughter go to strangers instead of Faye because she dabbled in dark arts; DSS wrote off his claim as gibberish, so Yvetta shipped off a few counties over, where no one knew the face of the child who – as rumor had it – bathed in her rapist's blood. Beaufort County didn't know her face, but the name had traveled by newspaper and word of mouth.

Sawyer was surprised to learn that the name *Chosen* was not some sizzle title for social media, nor was it the stash-house for bad debt it later became. The name Chosen provided the young Yvetta a social disconnect from the killing. The court had granted Randy and Faye's petition for a name change. For the eleven-year-old who had so many life changes happen outside of her control, they gave Yvetta power over at least one thing: her new name. A young, depressed Yvetta picked a name that reminded her that she was here for a purpose, and that despite her heavy burdens, there is a shepherd tending from the heavens. The name Chosen also reminded her of her mother, Babette, who insisted into Yvetta's understanding, that she was *chosen* by God.

That's the story Sawyer left with, but it was only half the story. She looked in her rearview mirror, eyeing two rural sunbaked men in overalls, leaning against a dull colored pickup truck, like a Glenn Simmions painting.

While driving down a barren stretch of highway seventeen, heading toward Faye, Sawyer heard the crack of a distant thunder, dark clouds filled in the sky, l ike smoke trapped against a glass ceiling. Her windshield broke out in pox, the light rain sounded like a vinyl record sizzling under the needle. Sawyer remembered arguing with Chosen during the interrogation, saying how she pitied Chosen for what love-depraved childhood groomed such an empty vessel of a woman, the bottomless void of self-worth that Chosen kept trying to fill with implants and material things. Sawyer began feeling guilty, realizing that Chosen, in many ways, is still that motherless, raped child crying out. The rape made her feel worthless and ever since, she's been doing whatever she could to make herself feel like she *is* of worth.

As tree shadows rushed over her speeding car hood, like rapids, it mixed with reddened hood reflections of grey-bellied nimbus clouds, and then with the confusion of the rainfall and it all began shapeshifting into new, decipherable images. A bead of water blowing back on her red car hood like a tear, became the bead of red blood running down the child's leg while she wept over her dead mother who was stiff as cement in her casket. A cloudy image of Faye appeared and whisked the child away to the bathroom. Church organs coming in softly through the tile walls, she helped Yvetta tend to the same blood that bonds them as kin, and as women, when perhaps, Faye examined the area from which Yvetta bled and discovered something unspeakable.

Sawyer turned down a dirt road, littered with signs that read Keep Out and Private Property. Randy's theory that Faye influenced Yvetta to wield a steak knife against her rapist didn't seem so farfetched. A root lady living in the remote sticks of Shelby County, South Carolina near the self-governed African Village, might view the idea of a rape conviction giving a man who *should* be stoned to death, a roof over his head and three-square meals a day, as no law in which she could abide. Even Sawyer, an officer of the law, would agree that in the wake of such a vile crime against a child – a *child* – there is no balancing the scales of justice through such a humane penal code.

Faye's yard is fenced off with wood posts and wire mesh. A grey wolf barked on the end of his chain. A hatchet was stuck in a tree stump with chicken feathers glued by blood. Chicken snooped about the yard with their wings tucked behind them. A big-breasted rooster was perched on the porch rail, master of all he surveyed.

From the bottom of the porch steps, Sawyer looked through the screen door and saw the shadowy shapes of two women. Faye had company, a heavy woman getting up to leave. Faye got up to usher her out, reminding her, "Remember, once you break the seal, it spoil in a week, ya here?"

On the way out, the woman refused to look at Sawyer, as if she were ashamed. Sawyer watched Faye's outline approaching the screen door and saw what side of the family gave Chosen her curves. Faye asked, "Who is you?"

Faye's salt and pepper dreadlocks were Randy's age, but her

face is twenty years younger, except for a few poppy-seed moles around her cunning eyes, which gave the impression that Faye was guarding a secret inside. Sawyer replied, "I'm Detective Aisha Sawyer."

"*Detective…* What business the law got on my property?"

"It's about Chosen."

"She in trouble." It wasn't a question, but rather Faye seeing chickens coming home to roost.

"I can't quite say," Sawyer replied.

Contrary to expectation, Faye is beautiful, in the most natural way imaginable. She wore no bone necklace nor gypsy piercings like any self-respecting witch; she wore a tank top and a wrap skirt made of mud cloth. There were no ritualistic stone altars on the property, no hanging garlic, nor ceremonial masks on her walls, but picture collages, displaying her wealth in kin, like the typical rural grandmother. There were no shrunken heads on the window sill, but there were finely crafted wood sculptures – an African Queen on a throne, a faceless drumming man, and a griot sculpture. The only oddity was coming from the kitchen, a cast iron pot bubbling with something that smelled nothing like food, but more like the smell of wax and dog musk.

Sawyer sat with her ankles crossed. She looked down at her fidgeting hands and sighed. She used the wood sculptures to break the ice. "Those come from the African Village?"

Faye nodded yes.

"You go there often?"

"I'm exiled from there. The king's three wives found out about me and they husband. I'da been burnt at a stake had it been *Africa*, Africa."

"There's an actual *king?*" Sawyer blazed at Faye's nod, and then added. "Aimed high, didn't you?"

"King, prince, president of these United States of America – no matter what you call him, child, he is but a man."

Eventually, Sawyer questioned Faye about Chosen, and Faye spoke freely, volunteering all details, as if she'd been waiting all her life for someone to ask. Faye said she found the home in disarray just a week after Babette's passing; she coached the men on how to wash laundry and cook some basic meals. The father and the boys couldn't believe the things they were expected to do for themselves. "They were spoiled by a woman's love," Faye added. She taught them how to do Yvetta's hair and established, for the household, boundaries of respect and privacy for their maturing, post-menstrual baby sister.

Sawyer, knowing the pathology of a raped child, imagined how Yvetta would've been attracted to her aunt's – her surrogate mother's – independence.

"She said I wadn't fearful like Babette," Faye said. "I didn't make like God's standin' ober there, lightenin' bolt in hand waitin' to strike if you do wrong. I tell her, 'if that's so, why God ain't struck Walter?'" Faye's head twitched on the logic as it did twenty years ago. "I ain't keep scripture on the tip of my tongue; I have a different tongue."

Sawyer, covering her nose for the smell from the kitchen, said, "Randy says you're a root lady."

Faye's head fell forward and she chuckled. "And that's supposed to mean what?"

Sawyer imagined pinned dolls and Ouija boards. "Isn't it, like, voodoo?"

Faye was fully amused. "You just as fool as the rest. If you' lookin' for voodoo, go see Dr. Buzzard."

"Dr. Buzzard?"

"He's a shaman. Can speak to the dead and cast spells. Man named Mr. Ginther had a run-in with Dr. Buzzard. They say Dr. Buzzard blew a powder in Mr. Ginther's face and, to this day, Mr. Ginther neck stiff as wood, gotta lay down to drink from a cup. Can't much turn his head at the sound of his name – gotta shuffle his *whole* body around, eye balls slam in the corner lookin' for who called his name." Faye laughed out loud. "Me and my girl Sissy each take a side, taking turns callin' Mr. Ginther's name and watch that man shuffle 'til he tired."

Sawyer laughed too, but she felt herself getting queasy and the rims of her eyes were stinging. "Excuse me Faye, but… whatever you're cooking – I think it's…" Sawyer stood.

"Oh. You must be having a bad reaction." Faye took Sawyer by the elbow. "Come on outside, get you some fresh air. I got work to do out there anyway." Saywer's stinging eyes were shut. Faye led her down the porch steps like a blind escort, Sawyer groaning in discomfort. Chickens scattered, beating their wings and clucking.

Faye took her out in the backyard and had her sit on a pile of logs, facing a garden, and then Faye went back inside. From the brief rain, the ground under Sawyer's feet was wet and soft like a sponge. Whole rain drops clung to the tips of grass. Faye returned in a pair of boots and gloves. She grabbed a garden hoe from the side of the house. "Figured I'll put a row of scallions next to them turnips."

Sawyer asked, "What in the world are you cooking in there?"

Faye had tiptoed through the garden rows like a minefield. She raised the hoe and hacked the ground next to the row of turnips. "It ain't food, I can tell you that much. Have a bowl of that for supper, you'll be in bad shape."

"If it's not food then what is it?"

"Leaves from a popcorn tree, along with some other ingredients. Popcorn trees are poisonous."

"Poisonous?" Sawyer panicked.

"Not poisonous like that. You let me know if your throat start closing on ya," Faye said, as she chucked the hoe into the ground.

"Why would anyone need to make poison?"

"Not to harm, to hep." Faye kept chucking the ground, breaking the carpet of grass. "See how easy that is? The ground gives much easier after rain."

Sawyer snorted and spat, her mouth still bitter when she asked, "How is poison supposed to help anything, Faye?"

Faye stopped with the pole standing in one hand, the other hand on her hip. "This lady I know, gets a check every munt.

Every now and then she have to go downtown to see them disability people. So, I give her that mix I'm cookin' in the kitchen right now. She rub huh legs down with it because it breeds inflammation. Next day? Lo and behold, huh legs done swole up fat as that log you sittin' on. Them people down at the disability office see that, and they keep on writing checks."

"You taught Chosen how to make poison?"

"Whuther I taught her or not, she know just by livin' with me."

"That's all she was? Someone living with you?"

"She *became* that." Faye resumed her work, chucking the hoe, more determined, the tool raising straight overhead, armpit hairs flashing as she punished the ground. *Thump... Thump...* "She make war with me cause I won't fix her. She can't carry to term. She return with them white folks education in her head, thinkin' she know more then me, yet them folks who got more education then huh, can't get huh to carry to term. Modern medicine caint do what I do. Ask them scholars how putting moss in the bottom of your shoe give you long life; how a cast of mud from the marsh can heal a broken bone in half the time, or how standing with your back against a pine tree for a while everyday cure asthma. I can fix Chosen if I want to. I did it for Tanya, I did it for Margo, I did it for Audrey, but Chosen? She ain't fit to be no mother. She put money ober everything. She'll sass God for that dollar. A tree bear fruit of its own kind – it says that in the bible." *Thump... thump... thump...* "I love her the same. Ask me: she *my* daughter. But when the daughter can't humble herself before the mother?" *Thump... Thump...*

Sawyer dared, "Randy thinks you made his daughter into a killer."

"Me?" *Thump.* "Not Walter? Not the rapist! You's a fool to entertain that nonsense, miss." *Thump.*

Sawyer still felt the ill effects of that smell from the kitchen. Sawyer tested her airway restriction with a few deep breaths. The rain-moist air was too fresh; it induced a euphoric dizziness. The sky yielded prism colors in swirling tie-dye rings around the soft-white bulb of sun. Sawyer's eyes blinked and stretched to see whether the kaleidoscope was a register of the eye, or a figment of the imagination. She heard windchimes from afar. Every thudding blow Faye hoed, felt like the earth's heartbeat radiating underfoot. Sawyer closed her eyes and breathed deeply to clear her mind – breathed deeply to temper her natural inclination to fear what was happening to her, and while listening to the airy hiss of her own breathing and the earth's heartbeat, the overlay of Faye's voice streamed like consciousness:

Chosen ain't normal. I ain't fixed her mind to kill no man; I showed her how to gut a pig." *Thump... Thump...* Sawyer found herself in a dream state, immersed in Faye's rendering of the past. With lifelike clarity, Sawyer imagined the pinkish white piglet, hair as fine as corn silk, its hooves jostling with no ground to run on because Faye held it on its side, the silver knife exiting its throat, blood pumping from the wound. *Pig just a squealin' and a kickin'.* Faye dug two fingers into the throat-slit and pinched the carotid artery, her fingers slimy and paint red, manipulating the spurt of blood. Chosen watched, appalled yet interested. *Pig's throat ain't no different than a man's. No matter how big and strong, just know that his life is on a string, ya hear me? This lil handy knife here is David's sling.*

Faye switched scenes, back to not long after Babette's death, when she was helping the men get adjusted to her absence. Faye recalled a day-trip away from Randy's home and back to her own, to tend her neglected chickens and goats. The king met Faye with a bushel of okra. Faye prepared a meal and left Chosen at the kitchen table while she and the king went out to the feed shed. Chosen, in time, wondering what was taking the adults so long, went to the shed and saw his highness's cloak fallen down to his sandals; his hat, tall as a wedding cake, tilted on Faye's head, her legs hugging his waist. Faye said to Sawyer, "Child, I ain't never been mo' shame in my life. Later that day, Chosen talking 'bout: she thought kings only messed with queens. I tell her, if you look at a man like you look at candy, and then lower the shoulder of your blouse, any man with a ding-a-ling will follow you to the shed. Guess Chosen took the lesson to heart. That's how she lured her uncle. She pull up her dress in the front, let him get close. She punched that steak knife into his throat and watched him wallow in his own blood – like a pig in mud."

Sawyer's head shook in disbelief. "You taught that child how to seduce. You showed her how to slit a throat. You planted those seeds in her. You knew if you killed Walter yourself, you'd go to prison, so instead you coached Chosen because you knew that, given the circumstances, that eleven-year-old child wouldn't go to jail. The man you wanted dead was dead and no one had to answer for it." Sawyer paused, lost for words, but not because of Faye, but because she was hit with an epiphany: Sawyer found herself being an advocate for the woman who raped her husband.

Faye offered both wrists. "Here you go. You gon' lock me up?"

Sawyer's hand back-flicked at Faye's nonsense, her lack of conscience.

"Talkin' about I planted seeds," Faye said. "Hell, planting seeds is what I'm fixin' to do right now. I'll bet you one thing though: I put scallion seed in this ground, in due time, scallions gon' get up out this ground. See, the earth is consistent, but man? Plant the identical seed in a hundred men, it manifest different in each one – according to his or her *own* nature."

Sawyer stared Faye down. "Chosen was being raped. As an adult, you *protect* her. You don't give a child a steak knife and send her out to battle that kind of evil. Ordinary folks call the police. But you... You're out here chasing your lunch around the yard and wringing its neck... Brewing poison... There's a different world outside of this... this..."

Faye stood upright, peering. "You alright, girl?"

Sawyer realized that she was damp; a salty sweat bead melted at the corner of her mouth. She took a deep breath. The feeling of rain essence filling the chambers of her lungs turned in her stomach, and Sawyer bent forward in an arc and vomited.

THE WATCHMAN

D uke *still* lay comatose in the basement; therefore, Trinece couldn't ponder anything outside of that fact – couldn't see around the rump of that elephant. "We gotta do something, Chosen."

Chosen came away from the blinds. "Not yet."

"Police came to *my* job! What if they come *here* looking for him?"

Chosen sighed over pleading hands. "I'm suing them for harassment and assault, Trinece. Coming here would only bolster my case against them. When police questioned you, did you mention what Duke did to you?"

Trinece stared blankly. "No."

"Good," Chosen said. "A half-million-dollar car was burned down so, yeah maybe they suspect insurance fraud. Maybe they think the fire was accidental. They probably thinking he's around, but that he fled the scene because of the unregistered gun in the car. Eventually, though, as days go by and Duke still doesn't surface, this *will* become a murder investigation."

"How long will Duke be a zombie like that?"

Chosen went to the blinds with a pair of binoculars, answering with a striped face, "In another week or so, Duke will be twitching and moaning at the most. We're trying to wait-out the world's sorriest spy over here."

"What?"

"Yup. My house is being watched."

Trinece's jaw dropped. "Your house is being *what!*"

Chosen squinted harder in the binoculars. "Look at him: leaning against his van, smoking a cigarette." Some darkness fell over Chosen. "But then again, maybe he ain't spying. Maybe he's here for intimidation."

Trinece's hands clasped over the top of her head and she paced away. "This is not happening. I am *not* going to jail behind this–"

"–Pull. Yourself. Together."

Trinece's fists struck down by her sides. "Here's what you don't understand about me, Chosen! I was put on this earth to sing – not to rot away in nobody's prison! I am *going* to be famous. I am gonna marry another artist, a rapper – not no thug rapper, but one of the socially conscious ones – and we're gonna be a power couple in the industry, and – well – after that, I don't know," she shrugged. "But what I *do* know, is that it can't happen if we don't tie blocks to that nigger's ankles and drop him in a lake!"

Chosen was shocked at Trinece's recommendation, but

Chosen's shock began entertaining this sort of maternal pride. "Look at you."

Chosen may have been smiling, but Trinece's emotions swung the other way; she began crying.

Chosen, consoling yet businesslike, said, "As I was saying earlier, this will become a murder investigation in the near future. Now that we're together in the same room, we need to get our stories straight for when they put us in *separate* rooms." The advice didn't break Trinece's cry. Chosen lay a consoling arm over her shoulder. "Darling, darling. Nothing bad is going to happen to us. Wanna know why?"

Trinece looked up, awaiting some restoration of faith.

"The universe is on our side, girl," Chosen smiled. She put a hand on Trinece's back and said, "Let me show you something." Chosen guided Trinece to the adjoining mother-in-law suite, where there is a second fireplace and living quarters, a kitchen, or rather a laboratory; test tubes and syringes lined the counter and the back of the sink.

"Stinks in here." Trinece mouthed, under a wrinkled nose.

Chosen opened the fridge. Nothing under that frigid light looked consumable to Trinece. The crisper was stacked with petri dishes, the shelves with tear droppers and vials containing liquids in undrinkable hues, like pond water and pink sludge. "You were wondering what happened to Duke? He got on the wrong side of a root lady."

Trinece leaned forward, peering into the refrigerator. "Girl, what are you into?"

"I'm the beneficiary of a very special inheritance – passed down generations dating back to tribal West Africa. Traveling in the belly of slave ships were not only human cargo but intellectual cargo. Myself, and those like me, are the diaspora."

Trinece drew back, but still staring into the refrigerator, rubbing her upper arms, though not from the cold. "So those are, like, potions, huh…"

"To call them potions is degrading. They're as legit as meds on the shelf, the products you use for hair or for your headaches; some as lethal as cyanide. My mentor never dealt in spells, but in tonics, astringents, elixirs, psychotropics; even poisons, all derived from plants, mainly, but also from minerals rinsed from clay, from fungi, from excrement."

Trinece asked, "What did you give Duke?"

"A chemical produced from the gland of a poisonous newt, which is a type of salamander."

Trenice was blown away. "Who comes up with this stuff?"

"It was the so-called heathen, subhuman slaves who brought their knowledge from the motherland and began an extensive oral catalog about north American taxonomy and herbology." Chosen hopped up on the counter, her heels tapping the lower cabinets. "To do what they *did,* with what they *had*, I believe, it is very essence of Black Girl Magic."

"How do you know all this?"

"I learned from a very wise woman. Too wise for her own good, so I don't fuck with her no more. But my point is this: we're going to be just fine. As long as we're on the right side of the universe, we'll come out alright just like those before us. Nothing we do will fail."

Trenice sighed and her head shook. The potions, the comatosed man in the basement, the spy outside, was overwhelming. "You say the universe is on our side, right? But are you sure the universe says that Duke really deserves *death* though?"

"Ask not what *he* deserves, but ask if his past victims deserve justice – if his future victims deserve to remain free from the bondage of rape."

Trinece, staring into the depths of the universe, awaiting inspiration, replied, "*I* deserve to never go through anything like that again."

"That's my girl." Chosen handed Trinece an amulet, an oval moonstone enclosed in burnt wire, the face like a wiry gate in the shape of an eye. Chosen closed Trinece's hand over the amulet. "If you find yourself in danger again, twist the face, aim at your attacker's nose and mouth, and then pump the top."

"What does it do?"

"Actually, it's just a fancy perfume bottle I got from the African Village, but I filled it with a mist that causes instant muscle spasms. Inhaling this will give an attacker an asthma attack, so you'll have time to escape."

With the acceptance of that gift, Trinece had become Chosen's protégé, like Chosen was to Faye, like Meegan to Dr. Cofield.

In light of learning about Chosen's particular skill, Trinece said, "You killed Trap, didn't you?"

CO-CONSPIRATORS

T ravis sat at a hotel bar hunched over a frothy mug, pretending like he didn't see Chosen enter and drop her purse on the bar next to him. "You said *a* drink..." Chosen's lashes fluttered with impatience. "That's exactly what it's gon' be: *a* drink, and then I'm out." It was Happy Hour. Chosen ordered a cosmopolitan, and then said, "Is this how Atlanta Police Department do: send some eye-candy in hopes to get the victim to drop the lawsuit?"

"What?" Travis frowned and smiled at the same time.

"They could send Michael B. Jordan if they want to; I'm still suing they ass. Your girl nearly choked me to death – you saw it."

"I saw you thank her for it. She did what you prompted her to do," Travis said and then turned up his beer mug.

"I thanked her for letting go, for sparing my life."

Travis tried to shake off the entire conversation. "Forget the lawsuit, a'ight. That's not why I called you here."

Chosen looked him over in mockery. "If it's not about the lawsuit, then what? Obviously, it's not about *us* because you should know I ain't got time for the likes of your broke ass. I mean, you fine – I give you that. But no thank you."

Travis cut eyes at her. "I see why you're single: that mouth."

"Boy please… Not long ago, I was almost married."

"Almost married," Travis giggled. "That ain't special. Every single-woman who's been strung along and dumped was almost married."

Chosen sneered. "What makes you think *your* lonely ass can shame me with my singlehood? What about *you?*" Chosen leaned forward, taunting the side of his face. "How come nobody want *yo* ass? Ever wondered about that? What are *you* lacking? Nobody never taught you how to be a *man?* Huh? Can't keep your dick in your pants, so you're searching for a docile chick who's afraid to question you, or go through your phone – a chick who makes cheating more convenient for you?" Chosen then pointed a long, blaming finger. "That's why, at the candle light vigil, you were all up in that white girl's face."

Travis frowned and tugged his earlobe. "So, you *were* there, at Meegan's vigil?"

Chosen sipped her cosmopolitan, pleading the fifth.

"Anyway. What's the deal with you and Sawyer's husband?"

Chosen pulled the stirrer across her tongue. "Sawyer think she slick… Using you to get information outta me."

Travis's head shook on the words: "No she's not. This is all me. She thinks Darius is innocent. She's buying his every word that you drugged him."

Chosen's lips shroomed. "I'm not even gonna go there."

"I know guys come for you all the time – even married ones – when they see a woman like you, they curse the life they chose, because," Travis swallowed hard over a fist. "Because they made their choice without knowing there was a woman like you walking this earth. Had they known, they would've kept their options open." Travis turned in his bar seat, eyes aflame. "I look at you and I realize just how limited the word beautiful is."

Chosen looked away, fanning herself. "Am I blushing?"

"Sawyer's in denial. She denies that Darius came sniffing. She thinks you lured him and drugged him – end of story."

"And so, *you* need Sawyer to believe that her husband was intent on cheating."

"The truth is what I need. Because, as a man, everything inside of me tells me that that man wanted you, that he pursued you. Look at you. What man wouldn't?"

Chosen's smile spread flat. She didn't trust the flattery. "Before I say anything, first I have to check you for wires." Chosen laid a hand flat on Travis's chest and wiped slowly, left and right, across and back, inching downwards. She reached his tiled abs. "Fuckin' *ay* bough…" She was face to face with Travis, her lips wet and parted, her eyes charming him like a snake, her hand crawling down to his crotch where she discovered an erection. "Weak ass. How are you turned on by the enemy of the woman you love?"

Travis's phone rang. He showed Chosen an index finger to his lips and then answered. "What's up…" He covered the non-phone ear to blot out the bar chatter. "Do what? Videos? *What* videos? … Can it wait?" Travis got out of his barstool and wandered off for privacy. "But… but… No, Sawyer, you, of all people, cannot be in possession of evidence. You're on suspension. You know I would if I could, but like I said… How about tomorrow morning? Did you hear what I just said?" Travis took the phone from his ear and studied the screen, seeing the blinking timestamp of the moment Sawyer hung up in his face.

When Travis returned to his barstool, Chosen asked, "All this talk about evidence… If Sawyer can't touch it, then it must be about me, since I'm the one who has the restraining order against her."

Travis's eyes dimmed. "Get over yourself."

"Don't tell me that wasn't Sawyer. I know it was her."

"That wasn't about you, though."

Chosen nodded with a thumbs-up. "Yeah, sure-ya-right."

Travis's eyes sliced at Chosen as he asked, "So, did you find any wires?"

"I'll give you all the information you need. After you give me what *I* need." Chosen was disgusted by Travis's smirk, believing he was being blackmailed for sex. She gave an exasperated sigh and said, "Nigga…" Next, Chosen slipped a picture on the bar top, a picture of the man who had been staking-out her home. She got a shot of him standing outside by his vehicle. "Who is he?"

Travis asked, "Who do *you* think he is?"

"I'm still investigating."

Travis was amused, but with a sparkle of pride. "*You?* investigating?"

"Don't forget, I deal with rappers – rappers fresh out the trap house; some still got one foot in the streets. So, I was asking them if they recognized the cop in this picture –"

"– Cop?" Travis raised brows at the picture. "Don't look like no cop to me."

Chosen sucked her teeth. "Now, who else would be staking out my house but y'all? Probably a friend of Sawyer's. *She* put him up to this. Because she knows it'll be her ass, once and for all, if she got caught stalking me herself."

Travis turned the picture and squinted at it. "Never seen him before. I doubt he's a cop."

Chosen snatched the photo, palmed it to his chest and said, "Damn a doubt, Travis. I need you to be sure. You don't know every cop in that big ole building. Ask around. Only then, will I show you what I have on Sawyer's husband."

Travis went blank momentarily. "Nah I need you to tell me, like, now, Chosen. But I'm not talking about more of those same pictures. I need texts, voicemails, dick-pics –"

"– Oh really," Chosen interrupted. "You want dick-pics, you say?" Chosen was loud enough for the whole bar to hear.

Travis drew stiff with the fear that the dip in bar chatter volume meant that the patrons had heard and that he'd suddenly turned gay in their eyes. Likewise, Travis was loud enough for everyone to hear. "Quit playin, girl. Ain't nobody said nothing about no –"

"– Are you sure about that?" Chosen's eyes popped wide and she turned an ear to him, saying, "I could've sworn you just asked for a dick-pic."

Travis could see, out of the corner of his eye, that the bartender thought Travis's sexual orientation was just outted, so the bartender outted himself by fanning his face while gleaming at Travis. Travis got out of his barstool, jaws rippling in anger. "Ay, Chosen! Go 'head with that, girl! Fuck I look like? You're up here playing. But this is important."

Chosen giggled. "Important to whom? Ya see, rich people don't say who, we say whom. But yo broke ass don't know nothin bout that." She laughed again and then tipped her glass. "I was in the bathroom that night at the coffee shop when Sawyer's husband busted you two together. I heard everything. Did you and Sawyer ever…?"

"We *checked* the bathroom."

Chosen's non-drink hand bloomed open, offering, "Wrong bathroom."

Travis's head tilted. "Why hide – if you're so innocent."

"You saw what that crazy woman did to me the other day? Hell, I was right to hide, and I'll hide again." Chosen sipped her drink and swished a little. "I swear though… I don't know what yall *see* in Sawyer." Chosen's face soured both from the bitter alcohol and from the thought of Sawyer. "To be honest, there ain't much *to* see."

"This: coming from someone who is nothing more than what there is to look at."

Chosen had a tough swallow, from the alcohol and the hard pill Travis had just given her. "Oh really? What happened to all that sweet-talk earlier? You mad because I won't give you the information you want, until I get the information *I* want? It's a mutual fuckin' exchange. I tell you… *Niggas*," Chosen pouted. "Always wantin' somethin' for nothin'. And got the audacity to get offended when you ask them to play fair."

"You don't know the first thing about me."

Chosen eyed him through slits. "I know that you reek of dysfunction. Obsessed with another man's wife…"

Travis countered, "What about *you* – obsessed with that same woman's husband?"

Chosen leaned back in her barstool, her legs crossed, her eyes squinting in judgement. "You come here often I b et… Hanging out at hotel bars located near the airport, feasting on lonely travelers who don't mind getting a little hard body before flying back home – while you, on the other hand, get you some empty sex to tide you over until you can break up Sawyer's marriage and have her for yourself."

Travis bit down and said, "You are one cynical woman."

"One cynical woman who turns you on." Chosen began walking away, her hips swinging on a pendulum. She turned a glare over her shoulder, and caught Travis eyeing her. Chosen stopped and asked, "Hey, Trav. Do you really think I did it?"

Travis's eyes were glassy with shame. "If that's what she needs me to believe…"

DAUGHTERS

Aisha went to her mother-in-law's home to get the girls. She was a whole two hours late but received no grief from her waiting husband. Darius greeted her at the door as if he'd been standing there waiting all day, as homesick as a seaman. He smiled with all of his teeth and said, "Long day?"

Aisha acknowledged him with a straight face and walked in.

Darius turned as she passed him. He asked, "Are you okay?"

She'd felt queasy ever since visiting Faye.

Darius knew he had little time; he had until the girls gathered their things to plead his case yet again. He said, "Being apart doesn't help us, babe. We need to be together."

Aisha replied, "If only I could stand the sight of you."

"Babe, I'm living out of suitcases in my childhood room, a fleet of toy Hot Wheel cars still in the top of the closet. And I ain't even do nothing."

"Maybe you should stay here until you figure out that what you did wasn't nothing."

Sawyer's mother-in-law ignored the adults and went to corral the girls. Darius kept pleading his case. "Do you even care what this is doing to the girls?"

Aisha honed in on the television. CNN was on, a group of panelists discussing the Cofield case with a Breaking News banner along the bottom. It seemed as if the prosecution finally got the break they were looking for.

Two new witnesses came forward, an old friend of Cofield who witnessed an incident back in 1979 where Cofield choked a stripper at a friend's bachelor party. The other witness was a former escort claiming that Cofield used her services as recently as six years ago, paying an upcharge for a little 'rough stuff' but went overboard, beating her bloody and unconscious and later paying her forty thousand dollars in hush money. The former escort held onto the payment receipt and medical records documenting injuries consistent with her story.

Sawyer ignored her husband while watching two panelists duel over the implications of the new developments: a beady-eyed conservative journalist with an off-color toupee versus his intellectual opposite, a frizzy haired free-thinking academic. Cofield's violent acts, in the conservative's opinion, were not as damaging as they seemed since it only proved that the righteous and wholesome Dr. Cofield, understandably, has a disdain for sex workers, which is inconsistent with violence against Meegan, a career focused well-bred, blue-eyed American girl.

The frizzy-haired professor, however, argued that Meegan's sexual relationship with a misogynistic millionaire rapper was financially beneficial to such level that allowed Cofield to see Meegan as some sort of unsanctioned sex worker, which led him to take Meegan's life, as he had already verbally threatened to do.

The case had been so effectively tried by the media that the prosecution could copy and paste CNN's transcript for their closing arguments. A Cofield conviction, whether by trial or by plea, seemed imminent. Sawyer's only weapon to prevent the wrong man from being convicted, was a pocketful of tainted evidence; the storage drives containing hours and hours of spy videos that Sawyer has scoured nightly without yet finding the footage that Ben must've been using to blackmail Chosen.

"Are you even listening," said Darius, who'd been talking all along while Aisha was glued to the television.

"I heard you just fine," Aisha said. "The problem is, all you're doing is talking. You know me by now, D. If you want this behind us, stop talking about it and do something, and you'd better make one hell of a show of it. And I mean *fireworks*," Aisha said, just as the girls came out.

On the car ride home, the youngest, Brianna, asked all the questions while Star sat with her head leaning against the backseat window, staring at the moving city in her teenage indifference. Brianna was up front, toying with a braid like she does when she has something on her mind. "Are you and daddy getting a divorce, ma?"

It was the question Aisha feared. She hadn't yet rehearsed an answer to give her daughters. She passed the steering wheel through her hands during a turn, asking, "Why? Because daddy's spending more time with grandma?"

Brianna, careful not to sass her mother said, softly, "Because most of his *clothes* is at grandma's."

Aisha should've known she couldn't pull one over on Brianna so easily. She took her daughter's hand. "Do you think there's anything that could stop me from being your mom – or your dad from being your dad?"

Brianna took her mother's response to mean that everything's fine, but her older sister, Star, pointed out, "She said they'll still be mom and dad; she *didn't* say husband and wife."

It was later that night when Aisha went to Star's room and the two lay belly down, heads resting on forearms. Star asked, "Is it *that* bad, ma?"

Aisha knew she had to be more direct with her eldest. "It could be. Or maybe not. It's one of those things where the intention behind the thing is more important than the thing itself. The difficulty is, you can't see someone else's heart."

"You don't know dad's heart by now?"

"I do. I just don't know where his heart was in *that* moment."

The child's head raised, her face small under her thick hair. "I thought it was music, but you're making me think maybe dad cheated."

"He didn't. If he did, there would be nothing to think about. And that should be the same for you and *your* little boyfriend."

"Woman law," the daughter said and then their fingers fanned out and tickled, their private sign of endearment.

Aisha said, "I'm surprised you're taking this so well."

Star's eyes thinned slyly. "Nah, I cry in private, ma."

Aisha threw an arm around her and they touched foreheads. "Just know that you don't have to."

"I know, ma. But the thing is, my role model doesn't stop for anything. She keeps on going; she doesn't blink. And since I'm trying to be like you, ma, I gotta start practicing now, right?"

To hear that from her most disapproving daughter was the greatest prize Aisha could ask for in life. They held each other, chins over shoulders, eyes clenched and leaking tears.

Bri happened by the doorway and stopped. She came in and did what they were doing: holding each other tight and crying.

*

Once the girls were in bed. Sawyer stretched out on the couch with her laptop on her lap, a chilled bottle of Moscato and the storage drives on the floor beside her.

Sawyer fast forwarded through hours of Chosen turning in her sleep, brushing her teeth, getting dressed, sitting Indian style in the center of her bed while filing her nails. Whenever Trap came into the frame, Sawyer watched in real time, looking for a syringe.

She'd see the couple make love on the shower cam and then again on the bedroom cam with the same date stamp in the corner. Trap was only slightly taller than Chosen and he had a soft body, but the man was a savage in bed, often slapping her butt, front and backhanded. He had complete dominion over Chosen and she seemed to prefer that. She'd lay there mewing like a cat, eyes glazed, pleasure transporting her to galaxies unknown. Chosen only took control when he directed her to. The vixen treats sex like a performance, how she moves like an erotica actress, riding him with her hands up in her hair, bouncing up and down just to give him a visual of juggling breasts, but then Trap would steal the show, plowing her from behind with a fistful of hair or deep stroking her missionary with a chokehold. Although Sawyer was watching a dead man and a murderer, the sex had her tingling in her chair. There was no husband there to soothe her. She took her cold wine glass and rubbed it across her face and throat to cool down.

NAUGHTY SAWYER

The next morning Sawyer drove to Travis's home without hesitation. Her husband had went to see a sexy woman in secret for something work related, therefore she could. Sawyer's don't-care attitude that she felt while modeling a tight dress in her bedroom mirror, must've stayed home. Standing in her much-exposed legs at Travis's door, Sawyer felt self-conscious. Suddenly she cared how tight and short her dress was.

Just when she thought to leave and return in sweats and flipflops, the deadbolt clicked. Travis was shirtless. Sawyer frowned. "Ewww," she said, as her open hand stopped short of palming his face. "You didn't have time to put a shirt on?"

Standing in the frame of the doorway, Travis's head swiveled as Sawyer went in, her trail of perfume made him follow with a smile glazed clear across his face. "I thought I had a few minutes to spare. You must've been speeding." His lame excuse for being barebacked. He eyed the Ziploc bag Sawyer held, and asked, "Is that your evidence you were talking about?"

Sawyer hesitated. She came to this weird realization of what it felt like to be alone and behind closed doors with a man who wasn't a plumber or maintenance man, or delivery guy, but also not her husband. Travis was wearing only pants, his chest full and tight, his waist thin and tiled with muscle. Sawyer shuddered and came to. "Oh this? Well, Ben was spying on his female tenants; Chosen was one of his tenants."

"Sick fuck," Travis said. "So, what'd you find?"

Sawyer bowed slightly. "Nothing yet. This is hours and hours of video, it could take up to a week to find out what it is, but I assure you, there's something; otherwise, Ben would be alive today."

Travis dipped aside and said, "Pardon my manners. Have a seat."

Sawyer put a hand up, declining the offer. "Look, I'm hating myself for asking you this, but... well... You used to work in narcotics, right?"

"Oh, you' talkin' about the *war on* only the *drugs* that black people use, department? The mass incarceration of the people who look like *me* department? That's why I came over to homicide."

Sawyer was fidgeting. "Travis... I've never asked anything like this before..."

Travis was blindsided by the potential gravity of Sawyer's request, considering how her head hung in apparent shame, along with the fact that she was standing under his roof in *that* dress, wanting something. "Never asked anything like *what* before," a shirtless Travis asked, her answer threatening to detonate his heart like an ink bag.

"I know guys in narcotics usually have a good rapport with the folks who work in evidence." Sawyer was leaning and twisting like her own daughter asking permission for a sleepover. "So… I was hoping you would be able to call in a favor, and get this checked in?"

So, she wasn't offering herself, Travis realized. The letdown nearly killed him; it took everything out of him to just to raise his brows in mach surprise. "But Ben's death was ruled accidental. The scene at his home was no crime scene."

"As if you couldn't find a way, regardless of that…"

"Not every guy from narcotics sneaks in evidence, Sawyer."

"I'm not talking about 'every guy' I'm talking about *you*."

"This isn't some petty drug dealer and their public defender we're dealing with. Chosen's got deep pockets. One of the victims is a rap legend. I wouldn't even consider tampering with evidence on a high-profile case like this one. It's not worth risking our pensions." Travis paced away, covering his face and groaning, but then he turned and dropped his hands. "I can't do this anymore with you. Let's stop this, ok?"

Sawyer seemed to have suffered a gut punch. "Stop what…"

His arms folded; his jaw rippled from grinding teeth. "You don't really believe Chosen did it, do you? You're using this investigation as a way to get revenge, if you're being honest. That's a new level of petty, Sawyer."

Sawyer's hands drew to her hips. "So, that's what you *really* believe." Sawyer's finger stirred at him. "You think Chosen's innocent? You've been pretending all this time?"

Travis sighed and looked away. "You were down. You needed an ally more than you needed the truth, but now that you're trying to sneak in evidence, I feel like you need the truth more than you need an ally–"

"–So you *have* been pretending."

"While hoping you'd come to your senses at some point, but you're spiraling even further... *On* suspension, yet here you is, driving all the way out to South Carolina and shit? Look, number one: Cofield did it, okay? And number two: your husband cheated."

"Number three: fuck you! How about that!" Sawyer pointed, as if to fire a death-ray from her fingertip. "I know my husband."

"I may not know your husband like you do, but you don't know *men* like I do. If a man comes to the hotel room of a woman that looks like Chosen, best believe, he's got more than a contract on his mind."

Sawyer, in refusal of Travis's theory, maintained, "She raped my husband!"

"Sawyer, you're too good of a detective *not* to figure out that *if* Chosen drugged him, it wasn't because he wouldn't consent to sex; she drugged him because she knew he wouldn't have consented to the pictures."

Sawyer was breathing heavily, but from a center of hurt. Her head flicked up, eyes hardened. "But *who* does it with someone's husband and sends them the photos? Someone trying to get the only person coming after her, taken off the case; someone who knows she's guilty, *that's* who."

"Think back to the interrogation room when you taunted her with your happy family, your prized husband and her lack of one. Just for your *mouth*, she wanted to show you that your husband is still a man."

Sawyer paced past Travis, her eyes cutting back. "If I were to think about men in the way you're suggesting, nothing can be taken as innocent – like you coming to the door with no shirt on. *You*, Travis, are but a man."

"Sex doesn't control me anymore. I'm woke."

"*Are* you, now..." Playing devil's advocate, Sawyer planted a high heel on top of the living room table; her already short dress hiked up her thigh.

Travis held up a hand to shield his eyes. "Sawyer? I know you're frustrated... You're hurt... But coming here in that dress... what do you think you're doing?"

Sawyer approached with slow, linear strides, her high heels clocking the wood floor until she was up close. She sucked her teeth. "So, you're one of the exceptions, yes?"

A smile and frown drew conflict in Travis's face. "Ay, Sawyer... Quit playin.'"

Sawyer's smile vanished. Her face angled upward slyly; they were face to face, breath to breath. Travis suspected a ruse, that Sawyer was doing this simply to prove a point. His eyes rolled north, and he sighed, as if unaffected, but the moment turned real when Sawyer placed her hands on his chest.

Travis kept stark still, as if not to startle a butterfly. Pride gathered in his throat. His hard swallow bobbed his Adam's apple.

Just when Travis was convinced that Sawyer was, in fact, serious, she revealed the prank. "See, you're no different," she said, pitifully, as her silky fingers glided off of his chest. "You say sex has no power over you, when it has you paralyzed right now – afraid of what rejecting me might do to your chance of ever having me. Afraid to *act* on it and prove that you're no different than the man that you say I shouldn't trust. The only thing you're proving right now is that men *do* have restraint. Because even for a man, what's more important than sex is the thing sex might destroy."

Travis's head shook. "Are you sure it's me you're trying to convince? You're the one coming to the apartment of a bachelor, in a body dress that's just screaming extramarital revenge."

"That's ridiculous. I have children to think about."

Travis's head shook no. "That's maternal guilt talking – that part of your mind that urges you to lose yourself in the needs of your family. What do *you* want?"

"What do *I* want?" Her brow wrinkled and unwrinkled, her eyes stayed up; any glance below the neckline would give the wrong impression. "Boy please."

"No, really. Block out everybody but yourself... Now tell me... What do you want? Just you." Silence measured a few beats. "You can't even do it," Travis said while making his chest twitch.

"First of all, I'm not even entertaining your question. Number two: about this dress. I..." Suddenly, she was hit with a flash of Trap and Chosen from the video that made Sawyer hold her cold wine glass to her throat. "Well, it's like this..." Again, Sawyer's mind held up the image of Chosen cupping her breasts, the arch in her back as deep as a letter U, but this time Sawyer's mind replaced the man lying under Chosen, from Trap to her husband, Darius. The only reason why Sawyer was able to place her hands on Travis's chest earlier – even for play – is because her husband's bad judgement gave her permission. Sawyer now found herself in too deep to back away in an air of one-uppance, no. With the fresh image of Chosen and her husband in her mind Sawyer wouldn't back away.

Travis was rock still, but unabashed; poker eyes staring out of his devilish beauty. "You were saying?"

Sawyer felt a hand settle in the curve of her waist; she thought *no*, but the word wouldn't come. She was suffering a moment of dementia, interrupted by images, forgetting how she'd gotten there, or what point she was trying to make. Made vulnerable by forgetfulness, and stilled by the want of remembering, Sawyer suffered a lapse, which Travis took for desire, so he went for a kiss, but stopped an inch before the point of no return, his lips hovering at the slot of hers; the decision still unmade, his breath seething from the inferno within.

A mere kiss would be revenge enough, Sawyer thought, but she feared that that decision would domino out of control.

She'd only imagine: the soft, warm compress of the kiss, the pinch and pull of the lips, shut eyes opening only to verify that it's all real; the view, up so close, his shaved face porous like an orange. Sawyer's imagination was viciously real – real because it wasn't her imagination; the kiss was happening. Their embrace tightened, each grappling the other to station the self; every breath heaving in desperation.

There was no turning back, it seemed; only the wonder and anticipation of what's next. Travis lifted her; his hands powerful and sure. It was what Sawyer wanted, suddenly, for him to take over; she wanted to be manhandled. He walked her across the room with her weight in his hands, buttocks plush between his fingers. He set her down on the windowsill's ledge. The kiss unplugged. Sawyer couldn't believe what was happening – what she was doing. She couldn't believe Travis's body. She was in awe of him, his powerful chest inked like a tribal warrior. She arched back against the window, the blinds mashed behind her. Even with her head back and eyes closed, she saw with her hands, massaging information through her fingers caressing his round marble shoulders; her hands traveling down his biceps, which tightened and thumped under the weight of her legs. Sawyer looked like a gymnast on balance beams, with her legs' V spread, her high heels flexed upward. Travis reached in her dress and began inching her underwear down, which triggered Sawyer's moral consciousness to swim to the surface. Her eyes popped open. "Travis… Travis…"

Travis looked up, asking, "You good?"

Sawyer ran her hand back through her hair and sighed. The glare of Atlanta's yellow morning fought through the window blinds behind her. "This isn't right."

Travis, with his reasoning curbed by lust, misinterpreted the concern. He hoisted Sawyer up in his arms like a damsel. "Couch should be more comfortable."

She lay weak in Travis's arms, her legs lapped over his forearm, the room spinning as he turned to take her to the couch. Travis lay Sawyer down gently. Sawyer felt the weight of her own body pressed against the couch. Her eyes were closed and her head trembled no. Travis saw the pool of tears in Sawyer's eyes and backed away from it, his hands up and saying only, "Oh."

Sawyer couldn't look him in his eyes. She tugged the hem of her dress to cover herself. She laid there for a few minutes, weeping and feeling quite basic. She mourned the death of the woman she was before showing up here: a faithful wife. She'd crossed the line of infidelity since the kiss. What she did felt nothing like revenge, she thought. What good was balancing the scale when her platform is weighted with shame.

SECOND
THOUGHTS

S awyer went home sulking. While stewing over the ways in which Chosen has caused her misery, Sawyer became suddenly energized to search Ben's video files for the evidence that would put Chosen away for life – if the footage even existed. After only a few minutes of watching, however, Sawyer shut her laptop, unable to bear the sight of the woman who raped her husband, which has spurred Sawyer's downward spiral, such as weaponizing an investigation and then offering herself to Travis. Sawyer hated herself for enjoying it before her conscience kicked in. Sawyer needed to get her mouth moving, to hear her own voice instead of the voice of the little prideful devil on her shoulder, justifying what she'd done.

She called her husband, the man she just betrayed, knowing she couldn't discuss the true thorn in her spirit, but to discuss other things as an indirect way to purge the poison of depression. "You got a minute," Aisha started out, as if the call was about a common household matter. Just a few words in, though, Aisha was bawling. "I can't be with you," she kept chanting.

Darius was discerning, even as Aisha's words stabbed him repeatedly in the heart. "I know it's hard, love… I know… But how does our love, for so many years, be so right, and then suddenly be all wrong? I'll tell you how: by feeding the damage my indiscretion caused. We should be feeding our love, instead. We have to tarry, babe, and be patient. On God's time, our storms roll on into the distance; our midnight-hour gives way to morning." He sounded lifetimes wiser and Godlier than Travis. The comparison of the two men seemed so unevenly matched, but the fact that there was another man to compare at all made Aisha's stomach turn.

Aisha cried. "Was God on your mind when you were with that bitch! Huh? What you did was irresponsible… It was selfish…" Aisha was using her husband as a way to rebuke her own doing.

"I can't have you hurting all alone like this babe. Where're you at? Are you at the precinct?"

"I'm under suspension."

Darius glitched for a second, but didn't pursue an explanation. In that moment's silence, he heard something. "Are you in the car? Sounds like you're driving."

"I'm driving towards you right now," cried Aisha.

Behind Darius's workplace, there is a slice of a park that

looks like an afterthought, or a stalled beautification project; no clear dividing line from the dense pines that the park's landscaped scene fades into.

Darius waited in front of a picnic bench. Aisha approached, looking downward, managing high heels through soft grass. Darius thought the tight dress and fresh makeup was for him. "You didn't have to get all dressed up to show me what I stand to lose." He gazed at her and touched her face. "So beautiful I can't stand it."

They hugged tight as if each had escaped a burning house and found each other safe out on the front lawn. Aisha avoided the kiss, though; she felt unworthy.

Darius said, "You were saying you can't be with me, right? Well, if it saddens you this much, that means it's worth another try, ya think?"

"I thought we *were* trying, or am I the only one?"

"Living apart ain't trying, babe, that's just weaning us off of each other," said Darius.

Aisha slipped out of their embrace. "I've got to put Chosen away. It's the only way."

"Aisha, don't do that. Do not use the fate our marriage as a way to amplify the importance of the investigation. Our marriage is on *us*. You'll end up compromising the investigation anyway by making it personal."

"I'm *not* making it personal," she replied, when not long ago, she privately admitted shame for the reason she now denies. "It's just that I'm doing it all alone. I'm the only one investigating

Chosen because I'm the only one convinced that she's the genius behind a murder that has – not only our medical experts, but – this whole damn nation, scratching its head."

Darius giggled, but the giggle was not humor; it was spite. "Just lovely, put it on you being the angel, the lone unbiased cop. Or is it that you're the only detective obsessed enough to spend every waking hour on a case even while your marriage goes to shit?"

Aisha showed the brown side of four fingers. "Like, maybe four freaking days, at the start of this investigation, yeah, I zoned out. But since then, I've been all-in and you know it. *You*, Darius, were the one who zoned out – locking yourself in a room to write songs, without a clue as to what I was going through emotionally – what it took for me to trust you returning to music. And I'll be damned if history didn't repeat itself. Music, again, put a woman between us."

Darius leaned back and frowned. "It was your *investigation* that put a woman between us. You wanna talk about history repeating itself? Again, you inspired so much hatred in a woman, she took-on the karma of coming after a married man just to be the woman that personally delivers you *your* karma. Remember Tianna?"

The sound of that name triggered rage, which Aisha bit down and yielded. "Keep going," she warned.

Darius's right hand hammered out syllables on the palm of the left, like a Ginsu knife chopping out the words, "I'm living with my mom, Aisha. What else can you threaten me with?"

Aisha's eyes fixed on her husband and burned for a few beats. "Be my guest."

Darius hesitated, unsure which twin was aiding him in battle: bravery or foolery, but he went ahead anyway. "Before you and Tianna bumped heads, she used to say to me, all the time, that you were a lucky woman. Only *after* you two bumped heads, did her comments change. *Then* she started asking me if you were handling your business at home, or if I was happy."

Aisha's smiling cheeks shined with sarcasm. "All *my* fault, right – when yall's little secret had me looking all stupid. It's like I was the butt of a year-long joke. Everyone knew Tianna was your ex but me."

He looked up at the sky, mumbling a prayer to the God beyond it. "You ever asked yourself why I didn't tell you?"

"We've had this argument ninety-nine times, and for the hundredth time I'm *telling* you, I am *not* insecure."

Darius's arms flopped at his sides. "Tianna sensed it. She knew that *all* she had to do was make a comment loud enough for you to hear, to upgrade that insecurity to paranoia, keeping you up at night. Twenty years later, the same thing with Chosen."

Facetiously, Aisha responded, "So profound, Mr. Smarty Pants. But what you're forgetting is that with Chosen, it's *not* the same thing. Chosen fucked you, actually. Remember knocking at her hotel room door?" Aisha nearly seized up when her own words reminded her of herself knocking on Travis's door.

Darius grabbed his head for its forgetfulness. "Oh yeah, about that, babe… There was no sex. It never happened."

Aisha turned away, hiding behind outward facing palms, shielding against his blaring nonsense. "See, that's why I can't even talk to you. When you can look me in the eye and deny obvious shit?"

Darius grabbed her hand to keep her from walking away. "Babe. I tried to tell you–"

"–*Tried* to tell me? That statement only makes sense if your jaw's broken."

"On the night I was drugged, I was never, um… relieved. I came home begging *you* for it, remember?"

Aisha was horrified. "*That* was the day? The day you left work early?"

He nodded yes.

Sawyer was stumped; his explanation made sense. Thinking back to that night, she remembered his hunger. "Why did you let me go on thinking Chosen had you?"

"You seemed more forgiving when you thought I was a rape victim."

Aisha backed away, horrified, tears spilling under the realization that what she'd done with Travis. "No… No, no, no!"

Darius came forward trying to pull her into him. "Babe, that's a good thing, right?"

Aisha reeled away. Her cry showed more teeth than laughter would. "You shouldn't have lied." A timid finger went forward. "You shouldn't have lied." His lie had led her outside of their marriage. The truth – that her near-sex encounter with Travis avenged nothing – swarmed Aisha with guilt; she couldn't get away fast enough. She sobbed, "Oh God!" She then hurried to her car and drove off.

BLACK GIRL MAGIC

S awyer went home and sat on her couch, inflamed with sorrow. For what she did to her husband, with Travis, she felt there was nothing that could be fixed, she was an animal caught in a snare, night falling; resigned to her fate. She cried her eyes fat. She cried herself into a somber nap, blaming herself even for her husband's transgressions.

Sawyer later woke up of a different mind; she was energized and blaming it all on Chosen, the woman whose scheme to make Sawyer believe that her husband cheated, had, in effect, made Sawyer believe that she could do the same with Travis and still live with herself. Realistically, Sawyer *could* live with herself, just not with Darius because after kissing Travis, she could never experience her marriage the same again. The foundation of their marriage was cracked and left Aisha and Darius on facing cliffs too far apart to leap across. All because of Chosen.

Sawyer was rejuvenated by vengeance. She went to her laptop and continued viewing Ben's videos. No more than five minutes in, miraculously, Sawyer was watching Chosen harvest the murder weapon.

The bathroom camera captured Chosen in long rubber gloves and a surgeon's mask, thrusting a kitchen knife through a wire cage into a racoon's breast, and then harvesting rabid saliva (the murder weapon) with a tear dropper and a petri dish. This video evidence would provide enough to have Chosen charged with murder. The evidence was so damning, even a hotshot lawyer like a Broussard would have to swallow his pride and come groveling to the prosecution for a plea deal. Still, the question the prosecution would have to answer for a jury, is how Chosen infected Trap without a puncture wound on his body. Sawyer went to the bathroom and ran a hot bath. She sat on the edge of the tub trying to think of how Chosen might've infected Trap in such a way that a medical examiner would miss.

Sawyer's hot baths are magical. It is the precise location where Sawyer has solved many cases. She burned lavender candles and sunk deep in her porcelain lake, suds tickling her chin as she waited for it: the outer body experience that puts her in the window of a killer's eyes, however, this time was different. There's no murder *scene*; no blood spatter, nor chalk outline where the body fell, to help Sawyer speak for the dead.

Sawyer scrutinized all the facts and evidence. She searched her spirit like steering a y-branch in search of ground water; it's by feel, by chi, that Sawyer entered the world of her imagination and found herself at Savoy, clothed in Chosen's flesh, wearing Chosen's sequin dress. Staring back in Savoy's bathroom mirror is the girl raised by Faye, the root doctor who never punched a clock a day in her life, so Chosen was never groomed into the logic of working for a third of your existence just to stay a few paychecks ahead of homelessness.

In her mind, Sawyer was Chosen. In the world, Detective Sawyer was still in her bathtub, as if she'd died there. Her head laid back, candle light flickering on her damp face. Behind those eyelids, she was standing in front of Savoy's bathroom mirror, and staring back at her was Chosen's reflection. Sawyer could feel the additional mass of her thighs; she blinked and her eyelids felt the heft of fake lashes; she could feel Chosen's motive beating in her heart: scorn and money.

Had Chosen carried the pregnancy to term, she wouldn't have needed Trap's death to cement her financial freedom, and she would never again have to fear living her life like the woman who raised her, living off the land fucking a dirt-village king next to the same bushel of okra that they later preserved in jars and ate throughout the year.

Trap had umpteen times more wealth than the so-called king, and he provided far more lavish gifts than picked vegetables – like shopping sprees in Paris, copping bags with comas in the price sticker, a birthday in Morocco, walking along the white sands of Mediterranean beaches – the life Chosen wanted so desperately to secure, that she bought her own engagement ring to pressure marriage.

Sawyer believes that Trap tried to give Chosen a child as a financial pipeline, to honor the sacrifices she'd made. Chosen couldn't bear the child; Trap couldn't bear the alternative of marrying Chosen when Meegan had his heart. Trap's transition from Chosen to Meegan was poorly executed. After Chosen's second miscarriage, Trap somehow figured that the following Tuesday, he could take the good life out of Chosen's grasp and place it at the feet of a med student he hardly knew, a woman who *hadn't* miscarried his children, nor committed a felony in order to keep Trap's hands clean.

All of these thoughts Sawyer processed, in order to manufacture the rage Chosen must've felt towards Trap. Sawyer was looking through Chosen's eyes in the club's bathroom mirror, modeling a waistline as thin as her own, but stacked with curves. Sawyer was Chosen on the night that she told Trap that he was already dead. She placed her hands on the side of her breasts, fluffed them, and then left the ladies room in search of the man with the twenty-million-dollar insurance policy on his head.

Although Trap was the abuser in the relationship, on this night, the roles were reversed. According to the video's timestamp, it was just fourteen hours after she harvested rabid saliva, so Chosen was the hunter and Trap the hunted. She flirted with men to lure Trap with his own jealousy.

She predicted that Trap would try to protect his reputation by abusing her behind closed doors. When he tossed her on the floor and doused her with champagne, Chosen used the tussle as an opportunity to inject him with the rabies. After spraying Trap in the face with pepper spray, he didn't see the syringe stick him in a place where a coroner or medical examiner might not think to check, like maybe his scalp, which is covered with hair, Sawyer thought. Her eyes were steely with confidence in this new rendering, but on a second thought Sawyer was no longer feeling the idea. Trap would've felt the jab of the needle, and suspected something from a woman known to drug men.

Then it hit Sawyer. Sawyer sat straight up in the tub and said, "The pepper spray!" Maybe Chosen somehow infused the rabies in her pepper spray, Sawyer thought, but then wondered if rabies could be transferred if ingested, since Darlene, the forensic examiner, had talked about how hard it is to contract rabies, so this was a concern for Sawyer. She dried her hands, reached over the side of the tub for her phone for a quick Google search. The top result revealed the answer, under the heading Non-bite Route of Exposure, it read ... *except for laboratory workers, most people won't encounter an aerosol of rabies virus...* She read the entire article which detailed how rabies can infect through the mucus membranes like the eyes and the lining of the nasal passages and throat, the very sites that pepper spray penetrates.

So, the spray bottle was the murder weapon. Clever, Sawyer thought, but also familiar. Sosa and her very own husband was put to sleep from something Chosen made them inhale. Ben's death came from inhaling carbon monoxide, and Trap's death from inhaling Chosen's rabies-laden pepper spray. Sawyer's next challenge was to cleanse the video evidence she'd already contaminated, so that it can get filed as evidence that would put Chosen away for the deaths she brought to Trap and Meegan, and frankly, for the death of Sawyer's marriage.

COFIELD DOWN
TO EARTH

Sawyer was awaiting her midday return to duty with the evidence to exonerate Dr. Cofield, but Dr. Edward Cofield was set on a path of destruction. He'd just left the suite of Broussard, Saxon & Hurley, where his attorney vowed to overcome the new allegations and still make a mockery of the prosecution. The embattled doctor couldn't see a reason to continue fighting if he could no longer lead the Jordan Cancer Research Center into the future that no one else has the audacity to strive for. The board, in response to the negative press and picketers protesting on the sidewalk outside, held a meeting to officially oust their leader. Cofield realized that with the public shame that now preceded his name, he had no hope, at his age, of starting over at ground zero and taking his calling to another hospital.

Cofield stood at the back entrance of the Jordan Cancer Research Center and looked up the twelve-story rear of the building, the moving clouds giving the illusion that the building was tipping over on top of him. He slipped in while a vendor hauled in a dolly stacked with soft drinks.

Heads turned at the sight of him, but no one gave a mumbling word. Either they did not know he was banned from the building, or maybe his reputation and status still held him above reproach.

Dr. Cofield took the stairs to the top floor where the board meeting was just beginning. He drank at the water fountain as a way to hide his face as someone walked by. He waited on a staff member to swipe their badge at the security door. He charged through the door, tossing aside a brunette half his size and age, and ran full sprint, knowing he had little time before security would come storming through the elevators.

He burst in. Board members braced. A sharp *Woah!* shot from Cavanaugh. Amanda shrunk behind Ted, but Cofield was armed with only a laptop. He came asking for grace, his face red as a tongue. "You're not answering my calls, Jack? Owen? Will ya hear me out please?"

The only response was, "How'd you get in here? You're not supposed to be in here."

Cofield said, "What we're trying to do here is way too important for you to let that dang mob outside dictate to us."

Ted straightened his necktie. "What do you expect us to do?"

"Allow due process."

"So, leave your seat vacant for a year-long trial to end?"

"Let me *work!* What will happen to the Africa initiative (focusing on breast and cervical cancers in Zambia, Tanzania, Ethiopia). Who, but me, has the clout to pull off that kind of collaboration?"

Ted set his fists on the table as if anticipating a steak dinner. "Collaboration? Or charity?"

Cofield, red-faced and wearing the smile of a madman, growled, "You still don't get it do you? Your so-called charity gives us a seat at the table of the international medical board, Ted! Worldwide sponsorship! Of course, I'm explaining this in *your* terms, Ted, since all you comprehend is money, but truth be told, this is nothing short of God's *will,*" Cofield yelled, while eyeballing all board members. "It's helping people who don't have the resources to help themselves."

Cavanaugh announced, "Security's on the way up."

Cofield didn't waste an instant. He darted out of the room and hit the stairs. He came up through the roof access, wear the unobstructed sun was bearing down; the atmosphere smelled like hot tar and roared with the sound of A.C. units the size of work-sheds. He sat with his back against a vent that stuck out of the roof like a giant periscope. There is where he pulled out his laptop and hit send on his pre-typed, preaddressed suicide email.

He stood on the ledge, his mind beset on flying. He looked down over the tips of his shoes, seeing ant sized people and toy cars below. Security came bursting through the roof access door. Dr. Cofield tipped forward and dropped into that misnomer they call free-fall; there's nothing free about it. The wind's power pinned his arms to the front of his body. Breathing was stifled with the acceleration of gravity, the surge of atmosphere ripping across his face. To the sound of pedestrian screams, wild, yet in concert, like a rollercoaster's plunge, Dr. Cofield's spirit left his body the instant he smacked the sidewalk like a dropped jelly jar, with lines of blood spreading out from under his mangled corpse.

THE CONFESSION

Sawyer and Gil didn't see the breaking news. They were in Gil's office watching Chosen harvest rabid saliva on the computer screen.

"So, you stole this from Ben's home…" Gil's head shook. "One day you gon' learn, Sawyer."

"The *evidence*, Gil… What do we do," Sawyer asked? "I'm not going behind your back, nor around you, sarge. I came *to* you –"

"–With tainted evidence, though? Asking me to get my hands dirty too?"

"Albeit, Gil… Will you?"

Gil paused, a moral storm waging inside of him. He offered a handshake. "Chosen is a murderer. And it's our job to put away murders, isn't it?" All four hands piled-on in a brethren's pledge.

Travis barged in with his thumb pointing back over his

shoulder. "Y'all ain't heard? Fucking Cofield… The sombitch jumped off a building… Left behind this confession."

Gil looked like he'd seen a ghost. "No shittin'? Cause if you are, Travis, Umma knock the hell outta you."

Travis handed over the printed suicide email. "He CC'd a lotta folks to this email, including me."

Sawyer twitched. "*You?*"

"I guess because I'm heading the investigation. On that paper is his confession."

Sawyer's hands pressed the sides of her face, feeling her own goosebumps. "You said confession. You mean *suicide* note, don't you?"

"A confession," Travis repeated.

Sawyer: "What'd he confess to?"

"To everything."

Travis read the letter aloud, and the three eyed each other in silence.

Sawyer snatched the letter. "Lemme see that." Her eyes scanned down the letter and then she lowered the paper by her side, her head shaking. "He confessed, but he didn't confess to murder."

Travis asked, "Are you under the illusion that the man offed himself out of guilt for cheating on his wife?"

Sawyer answered, "The *hospital* was that man's life. The moment he lost that, he was already dead."

Sawyer and Travis then squabbled to Gil like they were his children. Gil, the determining voice, snatched the printed email and said, "Confession or no confession.... Not you (Travis), nor you (Sawyer), or even *me* is gonna determine how we proceed from here." With that, Sergeant Gilliam took the letter in the direction of the chief.

Sawyer waited until Gil was at a safe distance, turned to Travis and said, "That confession is hardly a confession. He wrote that he was guilty of hurting people – not guilty of murder. It's too blurry to stand as a confession."

Travis's head shook as if he were tired. "So, you think bad semantics is a good enough reason to keep the case open?"

"I've got Chosen on video harvesting rabies onto a petri dish."

"A video that is tainted evidence against the person who's suing the department. This confession – however badly worded – is their chance to close a case that never should've been opened, and I'm all for it; this case is destroying you, Sawyer. Putting Chosen away can't undo what's been done to your marriage – on *either* side."

Sawyer folded her arms and studied Travis. "What if I told you that I don't regret what we did; that I... I only regret not finishing."

Travis glowed, as if he were holding a Lifetime Achievement trophy in front an admiring audience, humbled by the gift just bestowed upon him. "Wow... But you were crying..." He sighed and hooked his thumbs in his pockets. "What're you doing after work – I mean – so we can talk. There's so much to talk about."

Sawyer's smirk held a dare. "Or maybe we don't need to talk at all."

Travis smiled. "Sounds like a plan. I gotta take care of something really quick, though. Call me," he said, while backing away, his thumb and pinky making an imaginary phone.

"Where're you going?"

"Got an interview. It's about Duke's disappearance."

Sawyer covered her mouth. "Duke's missing person's case was turned into a homicide while I was on suspension? Was a body ever recovered?"

"It's still a missing person case; that hasn't changed, but I peeked in on the flat-foot who has the case. He complained that he couldn't do anything with the case because the main person he needed to interview, was now off limits."

"Chosen!"

Travis winked and shot a finger gun. "It doesn't matter if Cofield's confession stands or not. I'm gonna take Chose down *for* you. I'm meeting her at the studio, in a few."

"But like the other investigator said, she's off limits – to *all* of us."

Travis smirked. "I can get away with it. I've built some rapport with her."

Sawyer's brow raised. "I see a *lot* has happened in the week I've been gone, huh."

BEING CHOSEN

Travis left his bullet proof vest sitting on the front seat, and he strolled into the studio with his pecs twitching.

While following Chosen to her office, Travis passed by Trinece who was leaving. He remembered her face from a picture paperclipped to Duke's missing person's case. "You know her?"

Without looking back, or breaking stride, Chosen answered, "She's a new artist on the label."

They sat in Trap's vacant office, Chosen, behind her dead fiancé's desk, her hands together, eyeing Travis as if she'd noticed something odd. "I'm waiting…"

Travis's brows wrinkled. "For…?"

Instead of going off on him, Chosen took a calming sigh, and said, "After the hell you all put me through, and now I see on the news where they say the doctor confessed in his suicide letter? I'm waiting on my apology."

Travis's clasped hands opened in plea. "Honestly, I always knew Cofield was our man. Going after you was more of a Sawyer thing – not a department thing."

There was noise in the hallway, the entourage playing a spirited game of spades in the lounge. Chosen got up to close the door. She looked over her shoulder and noticed that Travis was not eyeing her body as if hoping to invoke x-ray vision; he was smiling at his phone (perhaps a text from Sawyer?). When Chosen sat again, she reclined in her chair, smiling as if she'd solved a riddle. "Something's different about you."

Travis tilted away, amused. "I got a haircut this morning."

"No, seriously," said Chosen. "It's your eyes. Couldn't take em off me at the bar, but now?"

Travis shrugged. "You haven't stopped being fine as hell."

"Damn... I bet I know what it is: Sawyer finally gave-in to you, didn't she?" Chosen's top and bottom lashes closed like Venus fly traps.

Travis's suck-tooth reply: "Now, you know better than that shit."

Chosen sighed relief. "I was about to *say*..."

Travis avoided the topic by setting the picture on her desk. "This guy? He's *not* one of us. I went asking all around the department. Maybe he's a private investigator."

"A private investigator?"

"Got any enemies?"

"I would've answered yes, until recently, but my relationship with my business partners, J Money and Flikka, has done a complete one-eighty. Ever since we put together that memorial for Trap, they now seem to hear me when I speak. Suddenly they're making *me* the face of Hustle Hard entertainment, to shakeup the industry, they say, to diversify the brand."

"If not your business partners, then who else would want to spy on you?"

Chosen offered a handshake as if their business was done. "Thank you, Travis. You've done what you could. Let me worry about the rest." Chosen noticed how Travis scoffed at her handshake offer, and she remembered. "Oh, I almost forgot. Now you can go ahead and ask me anything you wanna know about myself and Sawyer's husband."

With Sawyer now willing, Travis no longer needed the information, but for good form, he asked, "So, it was just that once? A one-night stand?"

Chosen wore a smirk as she said, "Let me tell you something about me... I don't do sex outside of a relationship. He promised to leave her, but got cold feet. I took those pictures to try to force his hand."

Travis leaned back in his chair, eyes wide as if he'd been shot. "Wow... So, you two had a full-blown relationship, then. You've got text messages confirming what you're saying?"

"I don't share a man – at least not knowingly. That is *not* me. Maybe I allowed it to happen this time because I was depressed over Trap's death–"

"–Which made you filthy rich, by the way."

Chosen's fingers flicked out at his comment. "As I was *saying*,

I was depressed over Trap's death. Darius was persistent..." Chosen drove her pointer finger down on the desktop. "And you make sure that that heifer, Sawyer, knows that her man pursued *me*."

Travis went with sarcasm. "I see your logic. Laying with a married man is ok as long as *he's* the pursuer."

Chosen crossed her legs and folded her arms tight under her breasts. "Says the man in love with a married woman. Don't think for a second that I don't stare long and hard in the mirror – wondering what's missing in me that allowed me to actually go forward with it – wondering that if maybe my mother didn't leave this earth when I was so young... I was just eleven when she died."

Looking down at his fidgeting hands, Travis said, "My mother died when I was fourteen."

Chosen lit up with surprise. "Don't you see, Travis? As a man who lost his mother: loving a woman you can't have is just a manifestation of you loving the mother you couldn't have. As fine as you is, don't you think you can do a lot better than Sawyer? It's her being unattainable that makes her irresistible to you."

Travis exhaled from the hit to his gut, of having his internalized altar for Sawyer burnt down to the slag and rubble of his dysfunction. He asked, "What about you, Chosen? Do you really find *me* attractive, or are you attracted the fact that I've got it bad for Sawyer?"

Chosen's head shook as if there was nothing more wrong

in life. "Travis… You and I, we love alike. It's the way we fixate, it's our blind loyalty, it's loving someone simply because it's them. *That*: I'm attracted to, way more than I'm attracted to your looks."

Travis went back in his chair. It shook him to his core to hear these revelations about love's connection to his dead mother, and this psychological connection to Chosen, who also lost her mother at a young age. As he had said in the coffee shop, about *thinking of love, instead, in the terms that they're rooted in, for any given person.* These given persons, he and Chosen, lost the most stabilizing thing a child could have, their mother. Relationships have been like spending their adult lives trying to cup water in their hands. Every moral judgement Travis had held against Chosen went away, and he saw her, for the first time, in the same light as he sees himself. How is he any different? Because he used the gym, rather than a surgeon's table, to reshape his body? Travis placed his palms over his eyes and wiped back, his fingers locking behind his head. "You're blowing me away, right now, Chosen. It's like you can see right through me." Travis had even forgot that his sole purpose for coming to the studio was to grill Chosen about Duke's disappearance.

"Can't you see," Chosen asked, as she came around the desk. She leaned over a seated Travis, gripped his shoulders as if to shake some sense into him, but joyfully, like celebrating a milestone. "You need to forget what you want. You need what I need – a love that'll love you back just as fiercely."

There was nothing more either could say. Eyes locked, smiles faded, and then there was the readying gulp, putting away inhibition, the shedding of titles – homicide detective, murder suspect, millionaire executive – leaving only man and woman, two half-jagged hearts willing to mend into one, like the puzzle of their profiles drawing near, but a half beat before the touch of lips, they heard a commotion out front – not card-game banter from the entourage, but panic, like a robbery in progress.

A single gunshot rang out, and then another deafening bang. Chosen covered her mouth, trapping her scream. Travis shushed her and pulled out his firearm. They heard a male voice out front yelling, *Where is she! I said, where is she!*

Trinece was gone. Chosen, the only *she* in the building, ducked behind the desk, with frightened eyes peeping over the desk edge. "It's Sosa," she whispered.

Travis put his back to the wall next to the door. "Who?"

Chosen was crouched and whimpering *Lordy Jesus, Father God*, and a few of His other names, over and over, but then she remembered the gun in her purse: Benjamin's gun, which she began toting when she'd discovered that her home was being watched.

Travis stilled himself and listened. Outside, he heard the smack of metal on flesh; an entourage member, pistol whipped by Sosa, perhaps, the victim pleading, *She in there, man! Second door on the right!*

Travis took his ear off the door like it was hot. He stood

off at an angle and cut the lights. The room turned shadowy and ominous, as if they'd glitched into a parallel universe. The sound of Sosa's footsteps stopped in front of the door. Travis looked over at Chosen and saw her stand, defiantly; she too now aiming a gun, an ivory-handled cowboy style revolver that even looked like it had been picked off of a dead man's body.

Sosa jiggled the door handle, finding it locked. "Gotchya now, *Chosen!* You gon' pay for what you did! You killed me inside. I'm dead. But I just... keep... fucking, waking up every morning! And I hate that shit!" He banged the door. The man was crying. "You think this door can hold me?"

Travis had heard Sosa shuffle back and knew he was looking to shoot the lock. Travis aimed chest level at the door, his veiny hand tight around the gun. Sosa couldn't have known there was a cop in the room, guns aiming at him from their side of the door, which worked to the advantage of Travis and Chosen, but it was Travis's duty, as a cop, to announce his presence. "Atlanta P.D. –"

Chosen fired. Three guns fired – each deafening bang giving the door dime-sized shafts of light beaming in from the hallway – nineteen ear-ringing shots in five seconds, when Travis heard Sosa hit the floor outside. "Got em," Travis said, as he bent over, hands on knees, taking deep sighs of relief.

Chosen ran over to Travis, and said, "Oh my God! You hit?"

"I'm good," Travis assured. "Can't say the same about dude."

Chosen shoved Travis in the back. "Don't just stand here! Go check and make sure."

Travis put his back against the wall next to the door, reached over to turn the doorknob and pushed the door open. There was no Sosa in sight, just the man's blood – lots of it, trailing towards the back. The emergency alarm sounded; he must've escaped out the back door.

Chosen pinched the front of her dress and high-stepped over the puddle of blood and then followed Travis, who followed the red blotches. The building seemed empty, the entourage escaped and some maybe hiding. Chosen caught up to Travis and they were side by side. Chosen slipped her hand inside of Travis's, and said, "Did you see me in there?" She followed Travis into the lounge, toward the increasingly deafening emergency exit alarm. "We got his ass, didn't we?"

"Sure did," replied Travis. They were strolling as if in a park but they were following a blood trail under the sound of a war siren.

Chosen skipped ahead and turned, going backwards a few steps until she stopped and said, with a shy grin, "Now, where were we, before Sosa so rudely interrupted us?" Both knew the answer; minutes ago, back in the office, they were but a moment from a kiss, a moment that Chosen wanted back. She bit her bottom lip in anticipation. Travis did not bend; Chosen tiptoed. They pecked. They kissed again just to confirm that the first was no accident. Chosen smeared the lipstick off of Travis's lips with her thumb.

Travis beamed at her, surprised at how pleased he was, and at how quickly his heart for Sawyer was challenged, and then there's the logistics; Chosen is unmarried, beautiful, no children. If he still couldn't will away his love for Sawyer, he could at least take comfort in the fact that with Chosen, money would never be an issue. Travis turned away, his head shaking in denial of his thoughts.

Chosen, with the hand not holding the gun, caressed his face back to face her.

"Sawyer will never leave him." Chosen, who was looking forward, noticed a second trail of blood. Sosa may have pushed the emergency door open, but didn't leave. He must've doubled back. Pouring blood from his body, and nearing death, Sosa had set a trap.

Everything slowed down. While Travis's slow-motion lips, replying to Chosen offering her heart, gave a doubtful, *I just don't know…*

Chosen tugged Travis and yelled *Wait!* She looked around and spotted Sosa seated at a table in a dim corner, woozy, but aiming his gun. Chosen backed against Travis as she raised her pistol, her eyes closed as she pulled the trigger. The shot that fired was not hers. Her gun just clicked, the revolver already empty of its six bullets from the first shootout. Her eyes widened as she felt the donkey kick to the gut. Travis caught Chosen's fall with one arm wrapped under her armpit while his gun-hand rotated out and pumped three shots into Sosa, who jostled and then slumped forward, face on the table.

"*Chosen*," Travis cried out as he went down to the floor with her. She bled and quaked. Quickly, Travis phoned in for an ambulance, barking out their location and giving the situation in a three-digit police codes. He felt something warm and metal. Still communicating with the operator, he looked down and saw Chosen pushing her gun to him. "Hide this," she said. Travis lowered the phone; the operator talking to no one. Chosen was giving him her gun – Ben's gun, asking, "Hide this. Please."

Travis stuffed it in his belt. Hiding a gun couldn't repay half the debt owed to Chosen for taking a bullet that would've struck him. Once again, a woman had saved his life, but this time, likely at the cost of her own.

Travis could hardly see through his tears. He cradled Chosen's head and looked into her eyes, away from the blood spreading through her dress, pooling in the bed of her stomach. "Stay with me," Travis cried. "Stay with me, Chosen."

Chosen was heaving and crying and coughing and clenching against the pain.

"Relax." Travis urged. He ran his hand back through her hair. "Breath." Chosen was noticeably calmer. "That's right," Travis coddled.

Chosen gulped and said, "I'm scared," her words blurring in a sob.

Travis's head shook slowly. "No, Chosen. You are a survivor. It's not your time." He lifted her limp hand up to his lips and kissed it. "Don't you dare leave me, Chosen. You and I... we're just now getting started. I'm going to make you so happy, baby." His face tightened to suppress his cry and then he released a calming sigh. He lowered face to face with Chosen and said. "I love you." He then kissed her like a wife, when just moments before, Travis was either unsure, or in denial of what he felt, but with Chosen dying in his arms, he was never more certain about anything in his life.

Chosen was coughing and feverish. She was slipping away from this realm, but Travis's words, the sincerity behind the profession of his love and his kiss, was something Chosen had never felt before. It helped Chosen open her eyes a little wider, breathe a little steadier, for the time being. She smiled slightly. Even with life slipping away, she became cognizant of the transition that happened at the core of her being, from simply bearing the name Chosen, to *being* chosen.

SPELLBOUND

S awyer stood by, waiting and calling throughout the day to check on Travis. He was rattled, as any officer would be, after taking a life in the line of duty. He'll do mandatory counseling, for having to use lethal force on Sosa, but first and foremost, Travis had to get his story straight in a closed-door interview with Gil, the captain, and the chief who will face the media about the shooting at an Atlanta studio that is associated with big names in the industry, and formerly owned by the recently deceased Trap Miller.

Sawyer had been through a similar ordeal when she saved Travis's life by using lethal force on the man who tried to run him over with a truck. She remembered being grilled in the chief 's office, being bombarded with questions, her responses dissected and picked apart when all she could think about was the moment in which she'd taken someone's life, a mother's child, a child's father. Since Travis had killed someone in the line of duty, it was now his turn.

The moment Travis texted that he was home, Sawyer rushed to his aid. Already they're facing crisis, yet it's an opportunity for Sawyer to show Travis how dedicated a partner she could be.

Sawyer had become so caught up in the sheer fantasy of a new future that it curbed her past. Sawyer looked back to the beginning of this case, when she and Travis were partnered, and realized how supportive Travis was, how, with all the pressure surrounding the case, he had still encouraged Sawyer to pursue Chosen while he picked up her slack on the Cofield avenue of the case. More than the other men in the department, Travis respects her. He listens to her, heeds her ideas, and doesn't minimize her. Even when he disagreed, he hid his doubt and went along entertaining Chosen as he would a legitimate suspect, just to validate Sawyer, until he realized that his validation of Sawyer was leading to her destruction. He was then man enough, gentle enough, to give it to her straight like a true friend would.

But the way he looks at her, though... Travis holds her in his eyes as if she is the source of all gladness in the world. It's all new, yes, Sawyer reconciled. Undoubtedly, the butterflies fade, but it's thrilling to consider the promise of a clean slate, no ugly scars like the past with Darius that she now looks back on. The past is now, with Sawyer almost forty, now wise enough not to repeat the mistakes she's made with Darius. Now at a crossroads, she could decide – in this very moment

– to envision a future with someone other than Darius, and to where even co-parenting after divorce would seem like a badge of honor, that it could even strengthen the bonds with her girls.

Sawyer knocked on Travis's door. He answered before she could knock a second time. They embraced.

Travis was feeling the effects of having someone, a woman, gunshot on his watch, and Sawyer knew what he was feeling. Words could only complicate the levels of understanding channeling within their embrace, so they broke away wordless, and headed to the couch.

His brows leapt and next his voice. "She jumped right in the way."

"I'm sorry you had to go through that, Travis." Sawyer let the emotion rest a moment before asking, "Was she trying to escape? Or was she shielding you, or...?"

"If Chosen wasn't in the way, it would've been me."

"I see it differently, hon. You just happened to be standing behind her. Sosa didn't come for you; he came for Chosen. And he got her."

Travis heard the tone of redemption in Sawyer's voice and didn't like it. He swiped a shot glass off the table and headed to the kitchen. Sawyer fought the urge to follow him. Travis raised a bottle of whiskey. "One for you too?"

Sawyer declined.

Travis, looking not at Sawyer, but watching the whiskey fill the glass as he poured, said, "Just because Chosen's a bad person, doesn't mean she deserved to be shot down like a dog. She might not make it." Chosen was in intensive care. She was receiving blood from the blood bank. Twice, she received defibrillator shocks to bring her out of cardiac arrest. The surgery was ultimately a success, but success was still a tightrope walk. Chosen was still unstable, nurses checking on her double time, walking on eggshells at her bedside.

Sawyer eyed Travis as if he were three years old. She replied, "Ask the parents of Kendall Miller and Meegan Appleton about what Chosen deserves and see what they say." Sawyer knew that a debate was touch and go. He didn't need an argument, considering what he'd been through; he needed consoling. Sawyer added, "Chosen is guilty. And if she survives, she will be prosecuted. We've got all the evidence we need."

Travis bit down and shook his head. "Won't be the first time, you thought you found something."

Sawyer tilted on her axis. "You're taking shots at me, now?"

Travis seized up in defense, at first, but then he sighed. "No, I just..."

Sawyer watched him soften, which softened her too. "I'm sorry, it just seemed like you were defending her."

Travis cut his eyes and said, "I wasn't defending her. What did I say that makes you think I was defending her?"

Sawyer came to him and put one hand on his chest, and with the other hand she put a finger to his lips. "Shshsh... You've been through a lot, hon." She kissed him, but there was no spark, like kissing a statue. "I missed you," Sawyer said, and her ear, expecting an *I miss you too*, heard no such reciprocity.

Travis slipped away from her and headed back toward the living room. "Travis?"

He looked back, still wearing frustration.

"I'm leaving him." Sawyer's chin tipped up, as if she were neck deep in this daunting truth. "I've made up my mind."

Travis sipped from his cup and squinted with a hard swallow. "And what's that supposed to mean?" He seemed so un-celebratory, nonchalant even.

Sawyer's anger flashed a vision of her jump kicking Travis in the face, but she took a deep breath to calm herself. He's been through a lot, Sawyer reconciled. "What does it mean? Well..." Her palms turned up empty. "Maybe you should be alone, right now," she decided. Sawyer was leaving, but was yanked back by a sudden curiosity. "What's not making sense to me, though, is how you shot Sosa, yet you're all torn up about Chosen."

Travis threw his hands up. "That's low, Sawyer – and baseless. That's like me accusing you of calling Sosa to the studio – I mean, who else knew that Chosen would be there at the studio for the first time in who knows how long? I didn't tell anyone but you."

Sawyer placed fists on hips like a scolding mother. "Cool it with the shots, ok, because maybe it's the alcohol that's got you all crazy right now." There was a moment of silence, Sawyer stoic with her arms folded and Travis looking lost in his own living room. Sawyer asked, "One last thing, Travis. Tell me why you're the only cop Chosen was willing to talk to."

Travis finished the shot. "She needed my help."

"Needed your help."

"Yeah." Travis took a picture off the couch arm and presented it to Sawyer. "Chosen says someone was following her and watching her house. Look at that guy. He just has this look like this… this gritty, hitman type."

Sawyer pinched her chin and studied the photo. "Watching her house… Maybe he's one of us."

Travis's head shook no. "I've been asking around for the last few days."

"The last *few* days? So, you were speaking to Chosen about this before today and you didn't tell me?" Sawyer's face jut forward like a bird dog on alert.

"That's the rapport I was talking about earlier. She was afraid for her life. She called me asking for help."

"Of all people…" The fact washed over her that, again, Chosen met with the man Sawyer had eyes for. "She's after you now? First it was my ___" She'd held back the word husband, thinking it'd make her and Travis's relationship seem counterfeit. "Where did you and Chosen meet?"

Travis's face channel-surfed expressions: guilt, confusion, righteousness, but landed on humor, "Are you kidding me? You can't treat me as if I've cheated or something – when that's what *you're* doing, with me."

Sawyer remembered the empty kiss they shared a minute ago and had an epiphany. She pointed an accusatory finger. "You fucked her, didn't you!"

Travis went limp. "C'mon, now, Sawyer!"

"That's why you're so upset about Chosen being shot, instead of the man you did shoot; you're involved with her." She folded her arms and unfolded them, her foot tapped, her head twitched – some odd, persistent fury unloading into all these nervous mechanisms. No man of hers will ever be safe from Chosen, Sawyer thought. "Son of a bitch!"

"I didn't hit. It wasn't anything like that."

"Whether you did or not, you met with her in private and kept it from me!"

"Are you upset that I didn't *tell* you? Or are you upset that I didn't give you a chance to try to control the situation? What space do you give a man to operate under his own judgment?"

Sawyer's arms flopped to her sides like tired wings, but she realized: nothing's official between them, which is the only consideration upon which anything can be salvaged. "Let's start over, please. Do I need to walk out the door and come back in?" Her laugh seemed desperate. Sawyer took his hand and kissed his knuckles, kissed his neck and then his lips.

Travis backed away as if all of this was wrong. "I'm just messed up right now," was his excuse.

"Travis... Be messed up *with* me, then – not without. I'm here for you."

Travis was all twitches and fidgets, a spooked horse, like he wanted nothing to do with Sawyer, when just that afternoon, his heart jumped out of his chest when Sawyer explained that she didn't regret their near-sexual encounter.

The last time Sawyer faced rejection, it was before Darius, but the old ghost was familiar as day. She pressed her mouth to Travis's before he could say the words that would break her heart. She held his face there, prisoner to her kiss, until they broke away, out of breath. But no change in atmosphere.

"I can't." A tear dropped and Travis hid behind his forearm. Sawyer backed away from her ill-advised decision, realizing just how fragile a thing she and Travis had, but also how bedrock solid a thing she was willing to leave in order to be with him.

EYES WIDE SHUT

The mystery man watching Chosen's home drove away in his van as police descended upon the property like buzzards to a sunbaked carcass. This was Gil's doing. Although the video that incriminates Chosen could never be seen by a jury, it taught Gil that Cofield's suicide confession inadvertently claimed responsibility for a murder executed by Chosen. Knowing that only DNA evidence could reopen the double-murder, Gil used Duke's disappearance to charm Magistrate Margo Harvey out of a search warrant. Gil hoped to find traces of rabies, the inhaler, or even evidence relating to Duke.

As a team of forensics investigated Chosen's home, Sawyer deliberately violated her restraining order by going to the hospital where Chosen was kept, so she could deliver the message personally. To Sawyer, this was joy in a bottle; her only positive moment in recent memory. She kept her head down as she walked down the white halls of the hospital; her badge was hidden and she made no eye contact with staff.

She looked up when she heard a familiar voice saying nothing more than a simple *excuse me*. Sawyer's ears led her eyes, and she saw him. The sight of Travis cooked her blood. Before thinking, she called out, "Detective Jeremy Travis!" He turned; his eyes spooked. Sawyer walked him down with claws flexing at her sides, teeth clenched. "What are you doing here," she asked, but quickly added, "Came to see your lil girlfriend? You're not at Chosen's house for the big search?"

Sawyer was in his face. Travis swerved to avoid her, but she wouldn't let him escape her scorn. Travis asked, "What do you think they're going to find at her place? Duke's body? Huh... Don't hold your breath. She's not who you think she is."

Sawyer beheld a sight so despicable it was comical; she smiled teeth at it and floated a palm to it. "Look at you... defending her..."

"You're making something outta nothing, Sawyer. I'm not defending her." His voice pitched high. Nurses and doctors looked up from their clipboards, and an ailing patient rolling a catheter stand, stopped to observe the lovers' quarrel.

"Really, Travis, just how involved *are* you two, bro? You'd risk your career for her? Your freedom for her?"

With an almost playful disbelief, Travis asked, "What in the world are you talking about?"

"The gun, Travis," Sawyer said, wearily. "A witness from the studio said that Chosen handed you her revolver. You never mentioned it in your report, nor was the gun turned in as evidence–"

Travis's head was shaking. "Because there *was* no gun. Either the witness is lying about the gun, or *you're* lying about the witness."

Sawyer appraised him cheaply. "Mind games can't save you, Travis. By the description of that gun, you may well have, in your possession, the mini Colt Magnum 3-57 revolver that's registered to the murdered Benjamin Haulsey Jr."

He shrugged nonchalantly. "She never gave me no gun, so…"

"What is it about her?"

Travis remembered Chosen asking the same question about Sawyer. He replied, "You're crazy."

Sawyer's head shook wordlessly for two beats. "It's got to be more than having a body like a stripper to make a homicide detective fall for a murderer."

"Stop guessing, ok. You're way off."

"You lost it for me, all of a sudden. Now, you're here visiting Chosen. I'm *not* guessing; I'm believing your actions over your words."

Travis laughed in one shot. "Because I'm here doesn't mean I'm visiting her."

"Don't try that with me! What *else* are you doing here." Like a dart, Sawyer threw her pointer finger in Travis's chest. "And when I told you that I was leaving Darius, you frowned like you wished I hadn't done that. It's like the moment Chosen stepped in front of that bullet," Sawyer added, but in hearing herself say it, the meaning changed to something entirely new and insightful. "Oh my God!" Sawyer covered her mouth, her hand slipping away as she said, "It was *never* about me. You fall in love with the woman who saves your life. When Chosen stepped in front of your bullet, she broke my spell and put you under hers. Now you're risking your career by hiding a gun for her?" One revelation then led to another: Sawyer saved her own husband. Darius was the consummate bachelor, their relationship casual, until Sawyer sat him down for a heart to heart talk about his drinking, and then invited him to church where, to her surprise, he surrendered upon the altar. Darius asked for her hand in marriage just a month later.

"Hellooo… Sawyer…. Anybody there?" Travis was waving in front of her.

"I heard you, Travis, but you know what… Damn everything you've got to say. I'm giving you twenty-four-hours to bring that gun to the precinct, or I will arrest you myself."

Travis showed palms pressing the imaginary wall he put up in front of her logic. "Or maybe I should arrest you for contaminating evidence," he said, and backed away.

Sawyer watched him turn and walk, glad that their ties could sever so easily – glad that what they had, didn't have the opportunity to further complicate life as she knows it.

On to other things, Sawyer's head bobbled back to center

and she found herself staring down the hallway to the wing where Chosen was kept.

*

A couple days had made a world of difference. Chosen was still on liquids, wires coming out of everywhere, but she was sitting up in bed and talking. Trinece, seated bedside, pulled out Chosen's phone, read Travis's text and then said, "Travis said he can't make it."

Chosen swallowed hard and said, wearily, "Didn't he just say he was downstairs?" Chosen took a few breaths to catch up.

Trinece asked, "Should I call him?"

Chosen's head shook no. "This is something we can't talk about over the phone."

"Is it Duke? Does he know about Duke?"

Again, Chosen's head shook no.

Trinece asked, "Chosen, you say Travis is cool, right? Maybe Travis can help me get rid of Duke."

"He ain't *that* damn cool," Chosen said. Just then, Sawyer came in and sat down as if she were an invited guest. She pulled her police badge out of her blouse and let it hang outside on its necklace.

Trinece thumbed at Sawyer, and asked Chosen. "Is *she* cool?"

Chosen's head fell over to the other side of the pillow as she sighed, "*This* heifer…"

Sawyer asked, "What was Travis doing here?"

Trinece, answering for the ailing Chosen, said, "Travis was never here."

"Whatever." Sawyer crossed her legs and clasped her hands over a knee. "I guess I get to be the one to break the news to you, after all."

Chosen, though wearing a network of tubes from her wrists, she was still herself, smarting, even in a weakling's voice, "And *what*, bitch… Want a drum roll?"

"I now know why you killed Ben."

Trinece asked, "Who is Ben?"

"Leave us," Chosen ordered, and Trinece left.

Sawyer and Chosen stared each other down until Trinece closed the door behind her. Chosen starting off, "I remember you came to the club with that foolishness about Ben. That man died without nobody's help. You' the only one in that department who can't see that."

Sawyer crossed her legs and said, "What you don't know is that Ben was a Peeping Tom. He had his female tenants' houses rigged with cameras–"

"–Cameras!" Chosen showed a moment of fear, but quickly recovered.

"Cameras. The perv was trying to get a peek at some ass but saw you driving a knife through the bars of his racoon trap."

Chosen looked around the room, pretending to be confused. "What is this chic *talkin'* about!"

"Don't even try it, Chosen. I interviewed your neighbors who reported that city racoons were getting into the vinyl siding

306

and the insulation, so Ben put out traps. You must've woke one morning and struck gold when you found a rabid coon in the trap because you knew you had the skills to turn it into the perfect murder weapon, with your degrees in chemistry and biology, and a root lady as a foster mother. You, Yvetta, even worked as the assistant to the county coroner in Dade County for a year."

Chosen's head shook a tired no. "Good job, Sawyer. So, you got me with animal cruelty. For one: Cofield already confessed. Second: even medical examiners can't explain how Trap contracted rabies, so how do you expect that to stick?"

"The prosecutor will gladly explain to a judge and jury how the rabies was aerosolized in your pepper spray the same night you sprayed Trap and then told on yourself when you said he was already dead."

"Is that doctor coming back from the dead to recant his confession? Or do you plan on doing an autopsy on Trap's ashes? Hell, I can defend my*self* in court and expose your case as nothing more than retaliation against me for suing the police, and for upsetting the darling of the department by having my way with her husband." Chosen looked over at Sawyer and smiled like a loving aunt. "So, how *is* that happy home of yours that you like to brag so much about?"

Sawyer trembled with rage, a rage that she managed to somehow contain. "You know what? I feel sorry for you, actually. I know that you were raped by your uncle, as a young girl. No one should have to go through that. Even *you* didn't deserve to go through that. What that rape did to you, is it made you feel like you were never good enough, which is why you lay on a plastic surgeon's table hoping *he* could make you better – make you worthy. But if you never deal with your spirit, you will never see value in yourself, which is why Trap couldn't. If you knew your worth, you would never lay with a husband that wasn't yours."

Chosen thought about lifting her wired hand and ejecting a middle finger, but Sawyer's words, her empathy concerning her childhood rape, had affected Chosen. Chosen had been within an inch of her life and back, and since returning to consciousness she'd been weighing her sins, namely her sin against Sawyer's marriage. Chosen closed her eyes for a deep sigh and said, "Look, Sawyer, I just need to say this – and be done with it. Me and Darius did not have sex. I took some pictures while he was asleep. That's it. You were stalking me, interrogating me – talkin' all that shit, so I wanted to get back at you, like... You really don't understand the lengths I was willing to go to –"

"–As in, what? Trying to murder me like you did Trap and Ben? I wish your ass *would* try, so I could use self-defense as a license to beat your teeth down your throat."

Chosen was noticeably upset, how she pounded the bed with a fist and how the monitor sped up, its bouncing blue dot turning hyper, drawing electronic chicken scratch in its wake. "I'm not looking to go back and forth with you, Sawyer," Chosen fumed, while looking from the corner of her eye. "I'm not looking for forgiveness either, but all I'm trying to tell you is that I was wrong, ok?" Silence was heavy but brief, Chosen added, "*I* came-on to *him*... alright... But he wasn't having it. That man loves you – I mean, *really* loves you. One would think that after what happened, you'd be spending more time, now, with your husband, repairing your marriage – take some time off from work, have a period of rededication, but no... You have every woman's dream right at home, and where're you at right now? You're here in my hospital room violating the restraining order that I have on you. Girl, get yo *mind* right..."

Sawyer was still salty, but effectively disarmed. Another minute spent insulting Chosen would prove Sawyer's priorities to be misguided at best. Sawyer got up to leave, saying, "I hope you don't think that this little moment between you and me, is some right hand to fellowship. You're a murderer. And I won't stop coming for you until you're behind bars." On that note, Sawyer headed out but stopped and looked back from the doorway, adding, "I almost forgot the reason I came here: to inform you that you are now the prime suspect in Duke's disappearance. There's a crew under the order of a search warrant, turning your house upside down as we speak. Even if they don't find anything relating to Duke, maybe they'll come across that contaminated pepper spray bottle, or maybe, with their blacklights and swabs, they can pick up traces of rabies on that sequin dress you wore that night."

Chosen started breathing hard, her eyes wide with the shock of this news, and with a day-mare of growing old in a six-by-eight-foot concrete cell without even the chance to enjoy her millions. Chosen's blood pressure had risen to a dangerous level for her condition. Her body couldn't afford an anxiety attack. The EKG monitor started going haywire, Chosen's eyes rolled back. Sawyer left the room and walked down the hallway, seeing nurses scrambling toward Chosen's room.

MR. AND MRS. SAWYER

Darius, upon his own free will, was leaving; Aisha's arrival didn't slow his packing. He took armloads to his car and returned empty handed. A piece of Aisha died with each item Darius pulled from his closet. This is the man who, according to Chosen, 'didn't give an inch' to a woman who has the curves a video vixen; this is the man that is 'every woman's dream' right here at home. Sawyer sat on the bed with her hands in her lap and said, "Chosen told me that you two didn't have sex."

Darius, sidestepping her with shirts draped over his shoulder, responded, "*Now* you believe me?"

Sawyer waited for Darius's return trip and said, "She said she offered herself to you and you refused."

Darius held up a number one. "Trust is about the absence

of proof. You, now wanting to talk *after* you got proof doesn't make me feel any different."

"I saw *pictures*, Darius. How can you expect me to disbelieve my own eyes, just because you *said* you didn't do anything – and said it with the same mouth that lied about where you were that night."

"For as long as I've been loving you… for all the years that your doubts had been laid to rest, *that* should've accounted for something. But you react first and think second. Now, in my daughters' eyes, I'm an outcast, a fuck-up, sleeping in a kid's room, like them…" He raised a finger and grit his teeth, but he stopped himself from saying more.

"I didn't even want to discuss all this. Just stop packing. Go to your mom's and get the rest of your things. Come home."

Darius huffed at a comical truth revealed. "That's another thing about you. You think that once *you* stop being mad that *I* have to. No." His eyes were glassy; his lips buckled. "You use trust like a weapon. You withhold it just to keep a dark cloud over my head. You used it to keep me away from my first love, music, only because it suited you. You don't deserve my love."

"I can't even trust what you're saying to me right now, Darius, because you're drunk. I smell it on your breath. I see it in your eyes."

"I had a couple drinks."

"There *is* no couple drinks with you. You're not well."

"I'm good."

"You're *not* good – not without me, you're not." Aisha got up from the edge of the bed and closed the distance between them, her bosom against his body, her face angled up to his. "You've tried it alone before. You already know where this is going. Let me help you."

"So, you think you can save me?" Darius stood tall and peered down, feigning indifference.

As sure as he is a man, Aisha was just as sure that she needed to save him. Aisha was no longer confused by Trap proposing to Meegan within less than a month of knowing her. Trap didn't need to know Meegan, he only needed to identify that she possessed the trait that could remedy the part of him that would destroy the whole. It explains why Travis had fallen madly love with the women who literally saved his life – why Darius turned down riches and fame for a skinny chic named Aisha from Decatur, Georgia. It is not the women who need to be saved; it's the men. So, if saving Darius is what made him fall in love with her the first time, saving him would win his love again.

"Yes, actually. I will fill you with so much love there won't be room in you for that sickness." Aisha slipped her arms inside of his and held him tight, let him feel the security of her love. Aisha kissed her husband for as long as she could, often drawing back to breath, to let him breath, like a loving resuscitation. Their kiss communicated that their marriage would recover. They lay on the bed, emotionally spent, and they slept that night with clothing strewn all over the bedroom floor. They lay on their sides fully dressed, Aisha spooning her husband.

THE UP-ENDING

The mystery man who had been spying on Chosen appeared by her hospital bed in the middle of the night, his blue eyes aflame with the blue reflection of EKG readings. Chosen woke just in time to see the chloroform rag descend on her face. The struggle was brief and futile. Chosen faded down to the sight of this buzz-headed blonde (older up close) wincing as he pressed the rag over her mouth. While Chosen's consciousness faded down, she heard the voice of another, and saw a man who was so black, darkness camouflaged him, like an invisible man in a collared shirt, the sleeves rolled up his invisible forearms.

Later, Chosen awoke blinded behind a tight blindfold – deafened by a rock band guitar loop of electric growls and metallic shrieks. She was unable to remove the blindfold or the headphones because her wrists were bound to the arms of her fastmoving wheelchair. Robbed of two senses, Chosen could only taste the gauze and duct tape gag, and feel the humid night outside, shift to the indoors' dry air. She felt the wheelchair stop.

And sit.

She smelled the burn of cigarettes. With a deep inhale, she picked up a strain of urine in the air. She pleaded to have her life spared, her cries smothered by the gag.

The blindfold lifted like a veil. Facing Chosen were those flame blue eyes. He smiled as he removed Chosen's headphones and gag. His arms spread proudly. "Welcome... to the dungeon," he said, in his best movie-trailer voice.

"Who are you?" Chosen had asked calmly, knowing no scream could be heard here. There were no windows; they were in an underground basement with grey, concrete walls and pillars.

"Who am *I*? I'm the reason why the bloody police didn't find Duke tied up in your basement. We've got Duke. We've got someone on the inside who alerted us a day in advance that police was going to search your place, so we sent our crew in to scrub the place clean. We've got your refrigerator of potions too."

"Why help me? Or, better yet, what do you want in return? And what did you do with Duke?"

The man crouched in front of Chosen. He put a hand on her dressed wound and squeezed. Chosen squealed in pain while the man calmly took a draw of his cigarette and flicked the butt. "You got a lot of questions for someone who's tied up. You should be thanking me," he growled, as he squeezed Chosen's wound.

Chosen jerked in her chair, squirming in agony. "Okay, *okay!*"

"What *I* want to know is, how did you get the rabies into Kendall Miller? Got *teams* of forensic experts scratching their heads. And what the fuck did you do to Duke? We thought he was dead until the bloke started wiggling his toes."

Chosen looked away, unwilling to confess to any of the crimes.

He gripped Chosen's chin; her lips shroomed. Blue-eyes said to her, "Oh you *will* help us, or you're going down for Duke's disappearance, and Duke will be the star witness in his own felony kidnapping case."

Chosen jerked her head back and her chin slipped out of his grip. "If Duke's alive, you prove it, or I ain't sayin' shit!"

The man, still crouching, twisted back and yelled. "What the fuck are doing back there?"

His partner, the dark-fudge man in an unbuttoned Hawaiian shirt, backed out of a room, pulling something that hadn't yet cleared into the view of the hallway. "Can a guy take a leak, Hymae? Damn!"

Hymae (Blue-eyes) marched towards his partner, his arms out like welcoming a fight. "Great! Call my name out to the fucking world, will ya?"

The partner pulled out what looked like a man strapped to a gurney that was rotated vertically. The man on that gurney was Duke. They positioned him in front of a distressed Chosen.

Blue-eyes lit another cigarette, hands cupped at his mouth

with the lighter's flame inside. In one slick motion, he pulled the shiny lighter away, and whipped the lid closed. He took a long draw of the cigarette and then said, "We also know about your old landlord, Ben. You're an outrageously talented killer, Chosen. That's why we chose you."

The dark-skinned man in the Hawaiian shirt added, "We're the good guys, believe it or not." He had a European accent, though not British. "We're part of an organization that seeks to snuff out political and corporate corruption. W e have an assignment with your name on it."

Chosen was staring at Duke, who had some movement, his brows flexing, his eyes oscillating.

The fudge man kneeled before Chosen. With a hand on her cheek, he steered her attention to himself. "You have two options, Chosen: either you're with me, or…" He peeked back over his shoulder. "Or, we break your collar bones and feed you to Sarah, a 26 ft, 500lb Venezuelan anaconda."

Chosen's face clenched and her eyes squeezed out tears while she prayed to wake up from this nightmare. These strange men, possibly members of a terrorist organization, was forcing her to kill again when she wanted nothing more than to be done with killing. After T rap, Chosen thought she would live out her happily ever after, but h ad to kill B en to cover u p Trap's death. She had then poisoned Duke because he put a young lady through the same horror Chosen went through as a girl. Chosen had already taken two more lives than she wanted to, when she had a hand in Sosa's death. She also had this feeling that, although the fudge man was asking for just one job, that he'd later use Duke to leverage more jobs. The dark-skinned man was still kneeling before her, now cutting the ties on her wrists.

"My name is Dwayne. My partner and I realize that you have a very special talent," he said. "And you use it against people who deserve it, like our next target. The world needs to be rid of him before he puts them under his spell. He's running for the 2020 senate race, campaigning on jobs and green technology, but he's playing the fiddle for wealthy government contractors who run our prison systems; they're his biggest donors. In fact, without them, he wouldn't have a campaign at all. Prison reform has already come at the federal level, next it's coming to the state level, ay? Once he's in, he plans to submit this bill that proposes the early release of prisoners who received overly harsh sentences; sounds noble right?"

Chosen nodded. "Well, yeah. Guess *who* got all those harsh sentences? *Us!*" She pointed at herself and Dwayne, blacks. "I'd like to see them out bettering themselves instead of soaking up our tax dollars, which would be better served going into public education."

Dwayne and Hymae looked at each other and laughed. "Public education… that's just grooming for corporate slavery, but I won't go there." Dwayne rolled his eyes and said, "Anyway, this man's campaign donors want to bog down the process in so many unnecessary hurdles and legal red tape that they would need to increase their staff in order to facilitate the process, which would justify them demanding exorbitantly more government funding, good for them, but it's bad for us," Dwayne said, his *us* also excluding Hymae. "It was *us* who got the harshest sentences; also, us who would need to hire a lawyer to get us through the legal maze that their trying to impose with this bill. This is the underprivileged we're talking about. These people don't got no money to pay lawyers, but they'll do anything to get their loved one out of that zoo! No money, no credit, so banks will put liens on their homes. This could accelerate gentrification into warp speed –"

"– Gentri*cation?* Wayment... What a loan got to do with gentrification?"

Dwayne huffed. "You folks in Atlanta are so progressive, you forget that Atlanta is still the south. So, you don't think if these families fall on hard times that the banks won't force the sale of the homes to satisfy the debt? And guess who will be there ready and waiting: white developers buying the property dirt cheap at auction, turning black-owned property into white-owned rental investments."

Chosen frowned. "Why kill him; why not do what it takes to ensure that his opponent wins? Or try to talk to him."

"Because if we make our desires known, police will look at us for motive, in the event that we must *off* him. So, to keep it simple, we just off him straight-away. *Our* problem is, we can't get close to the bastard. That's why we need you. The people need you, Chosen. Do you accept?"

Chosen looked down at her hand in Dwayne's hand, and

made the choice that keeps her out of the mouth of a giant snake; Chosen answered, "I do."

Dwayne cut the straps from her ankles. She stood with them in her paper hospital robe and wrist tags. She followed them as they wheeled a trembling, blinking Duke back to a room-sized aquarium that was rank with urine. She thought there was a pile of muddy tires in the corner, but when Chosen saw the licking, forked tongue, she nearly fainted.

Hymae put a hand on Duke's chest and drew back a hatchet, measuring a blow to Duke's collarbone. Dwayne stayed beside Chosen, explaining, "Big as an anaconda is, a full-grown man is an awkward swallow, although they can swallow a young cow with no problem." Hymae hatchetted away at Duke's collar bones with little reaction from Duke who was still under the effects of Chosen's nerve tonic, but he could feel every bit of the pain. Duke's mouth opened wide, but he still didn't have the motor skills to scream. The giant snake grew restless. Dwayne kept on with his zoology lesson as if there wasn't a man-eating monster behind clear plexiglass, and a man being hatcheted in the chest. "The shoulders of a four-legged beast is situated in front; man's shoulders flanks him, and Sarah doesn't instinctively know to break him in the middle, so we have to help her out a little; break the collarbone and breast bone so he'd fold like a hot dog. Don't wanna give Sarah indigestion."

Chosen became squeamish, watching Duke's blood fly with each blow. "Why put him through this? I thought you were the good guys, but *this?*" A palm floated t oward t he travesty. "This is just cruel and sadistic."

Dwayne turned to look at her. "Can you think of a better way to get rid of a body? Or would you rather we bury him and have him found and exhumed; toss him in a river and have some fisherman find him at low tide? This way, after some weeks of digestion, he's totally liquified by stomach acids, and then caked out the back of end of this beast in the form of dung. Gone without a trace."

Hymae wheeled Duke out. Chosen truly feared the company of men she'd just joined. Chosen asked Dwayne, "How many people have you killed?"

"It's not how many you kill. It's *who* you kill. The higher up the chain, the more discreet the death needs to be. We don't want this man's death even looking accident. Do you have anything in your refrigerator or that pantry of yours that can make his death look like natural causes?"

"Perfectly healthy people don't just drop dead, Dwayne. It would help to get his medical records, to find a documented weakness, like a heart murmur, asthma, high blood pressure, sleep apnea. Give me something to work with. Can you do that?"

Dwayne sighed. "Do you know what that will cost us?"
"You're the one who needs this man's death to look like natural causes. By the way, what is this man's name?"

"Broussard," Dwayne answered. "Thaddeus Broussard."

It was the answer that Chosen feared. Thaddeus Broussard is Isabell's fiancé, Vic's future son in law; the man who will marry into Chosen's surrogate family. Working at Savoy was the happiest time in Chosen's life, playing daughter to Vick, sister to Jackson, daughter to Mrs. Gwen, and kin to all the aunts, uncles, and cousins and-them that she met over the years. These people are the reason Chosen planted roots in Atlanta. Chosen stared at her faint reflection in the plexiglass barrier, determined to keep her own life and the people in it that makes her life worth living.

Hymae appeared at the feeding door at the back of the large aquarium where he tossed Duke in, naked and fetal. Sarah wasted no time. Chosen was amazed at how a beast as thick as tree, could bend and whirl so quickly across the aquarium and wrap a grown man in its coils as fast as a hand wraps around a drinking glass. Under that immense, muscular pressure, Duke's bones snapped and popped like the sound of molars crunching ice cubes. Sarah squeezed and she squeezed, its tongue flickering every few seconds; she squeezed until she was sure that Duke was dead. It then brought its head around its own body, facing the top of Duke's head, dislocated its own jaw with a yawn, and began shimmying its mouth down over Duke's corpse, its neck stretching wider than the thickest part of its body, the plates of its scales separating at the bulge.

Hymae came around front and joined Chosen and Dwayne as they watched. "Poetic justice isn't it," Hymae said. "We did our homework on this Duke. His cock is what led him to assault women and now, ironically, he's being consumed by a beast that looks like a giant fucking cock."

TO BE CONTINUED

ABOUT THE
AUTHOR

Rod Palmer is from rural Charleston County, SC from a small Gullah Geechee community where storytelling is the life-blood of the culture. Rod honed his inherent storytelling ability at the University of South Carolina where he received his degree in English, writing concentration. His writing style translates the vigor and power of Gullah Geechee storytelling into contemporary fiction. Rod Palmer is a former self-published author of *A Pimp In The Pulpit, The Work-Husband Caper,* and the three-part series, *The Harvest: Follow the Heart.*

To stay in contact with Rod, please visit:

www.rodpalmertheauthor.com